CAUTIOUS HEART

CHERIS F. HODGES

Genesis Press, Inc.

Indigo Love Stories

An imprint of Genesis Press, Inc.
Publishing Company

Genesis Press, Inc.
P.O. Box 101
Columbus, MS 39703

ISBN-13: 978-1-58571-301-1
ISBN-10: 1-58571-301-5
Manufactured in the United States of America

First Edition 2004
Second Edition 2008

Visit us at www.genesis-press.com or call at 1-888-Indigo-1

PART I

CHAPTER ONE

If anything moved faster than Caprice Johnson in the dead of night, it was the Chicago wind. Her feet glided across the pavement, seemingly not touching the ground. Each step led her closer to her mission: catching Damien King in the act.

Caprice had danced this dance before, but this was the last time. Tired of the lies and half-truths Damien fed her like tapioca pudding, she was putting an end to it, tonight. Caprice was sick of him treating her like an idiot. She knew he was in his house with another woman again. She called him earlier and she knew that a woman's voice answered the phone. She wasn't going to fall for the oh-that-was-my-cousin-from-Champagne line again either.

He thinks I'm stupid, she thought as she pressed the doorbell. *Damien thinks I'm the biggest fool in the world. But I'm stopping this tonight.*

She leaned on the button, making the chime linger like an echo. Seconds ticked away before the yellow light flicked on, illuminating the dark porch. She didn't flinch, despite the bright light shining directly in her eyes. Damien opened the door wearing a pair of silk boxers and white sweat socks. The look on his face expressed shock and disbelief. She wasn't supposed to be there. She was supposed to be on a stakeout.

"Caprice?"

"Damien," she spat as she pushed past him to enter the house. She refused to look at his cocoa brown skin and dazzling gray eyes. His bare arms and chest reminded her of the many nights of passion they shared. Damien always held her tightly and pressed her against his sculpted chest as they fell asleep. His words of love and devotion now felt like lies to her.

He'll say anything to keep me hanging on to him like a fool. And I must be a fool because I've held on for so long. Anger flowed through her body like blood through her veins as she glared at him. She was just as mad at herself for not leaving him the first time he cheated. Caprice stole a glance at the engagement ring he had given her two weeks after she caught him with another woman. She thought things had changed and that Damien was ready to love only her. She couldn't have been more wrong.

"What are you doing here?" His voice had a nervous pitch to it.

She didn't answer him as she continued looking around the dimly lit living room. Caprice, a vice and narcotics detective, was gathering evidence for her latest bust—a cheating fiancé. Her gaze fell on the two crystal wine glasses sitting on the oak coffee table. One had lipstick around the rim. Caprice wanted to pick up the glass and smash it against Damien's head. She had bought those glasses for him because he finished the nine-foot wine rack in his basement. Damien was proud of his hand crafted wooden creation. It took him nine months to finish it, because he wasn't good with his hands, at least not when it came to work. Caprice paid top dollar for those glasses. The price of the Austrian lead-crystal glasses was the only thing that stopped her from using them as a lethal weapon. She walked over to the mantle and noticed the still-smoking candles. She shook her head, then walked over to the CD player in the corner of the room.

If Luther Vandross is in here, I'm going to kill him, she thought as she pressed the open button. Inside the stereo were two smooth jazz CDs and one of Luther Vandross's greatest hits collections. Mood-setting music. The kind Damien always played when they shared intimate candlelit dinners or erotic evenings of passion. It was clear that Damien didn't spend this evening alone. There was no covering it up, either. She had her evidence, and now she was going to indict him as a habitual cheater. Caprice whirled around and faced Damien.

"Caprice, let me explain."

"Explain what?" Angry flames flickered in her hazel eyes. "You lied again. I'm tired, and I give up, D. You should never have gotten involved with me if you wanted to whore around like a dog in heat."

"Caprice, it's not like that," he said as he stepped closer to her. "You know I got love for you."

"And who else, Damien? I'm wearing your engagement ring. Isn't that supposed to mean something?" She threw her left hand in his face. "Why did you even put this ring on my finger?"

He looked dumbfounded. But Damien was confident this argument would end like so many others. Caprice would storm out. Then, days later, he'd call her and all would be forgiven. This wasn't new. About a year ago, she caught him with one of the waitresses from his club. Caprice cussed, screamed, and eventually forgave him. Why would this time be any different?

"I'm sorry."

"Tell me something I don't already know. Your tired little apology isn't good enough, not anymore. I'm sick of forgiving you for doing the same thing. Goodbye, Damien." She tossed the oval shaped, three-karat diamond ring in his face.

"Caprice, we can work this out. She meant nothing to me. You're the one I love. You have to know that." She took one last contemptuous look at Damien before walking out the door. It was the end.

ONE YEAR LATER

Caprice stood on the corner of Trade and Tryon streets in uptown Charlotte. The shoulder-length blonde wig she wore was starting to itch her neck. She wondered if it was lice crawling on her neck and not the synthetic hairs of the wig causing her discomfort. She pulled at her ultra-tight leather mini-skirt. It stopped mid-thigh. Definitely not her normal style.

I hate doing this crap. You would think the only thing women cops can do is play prostitutes.

She waited for someone to approach her so she could bust him or her for solicitation. Playing the prostitute was just part of paying dues at a new department. She was one of the few women in the elite vice unit with the Charlotte-Mecklenburg Police Department. And since she was the newest, she was drafted to play the decoy in most of the stings.

"Caprice," her partner, Nathan Wallace, said into the radio. "Are you okay?"

"If you count itching from this wig, no. But I'm not in any danger."

"Got any johns yet?"

"No, nobody's biting yet."

"All right, well, I'm on your left, and Thom is on the right. Don't worry, someone will bite when they get a look at you."

"Okay," Caprice said, looking around hoping to catch someone in search of a hooker. The mayor made it seem as if Uptown had become as bad as a Las Vegas brothel. She'd been on the corner since sundown and it was starting to get cold.

And they call Chicago the Windy City, she thought as a frigid breeze cut into her exposed skin. *Why do we have to have these things in the fall?* she mused.

Finally, a tan Lexus drove up to the street corner. "Hey baby!" the driver yelled. "Come on over here."

Caprice sauntered over to the car with her hand on her hip. She puckered her lips. "How you doin', Daddy?"

"I'd be doing a lot better if I could get a date tonight." He licked his lips as he sized up Caprice. She raised her eyebrow at him. The oily-skinned man had a huge stomach that pressed against the steering wheel. There was no wonder why he was on the street paying for it.

"A date? You a cop?" she asked.

He laughed, revealing a gold tooth. "Hell, no. I'm a horny old man."

She smiled. "So, what do you want?"

"Just a blow job tonight. I got to go home to the wifey."

"That's all you want? You sho?"

"Yeah," he said as he reached into his pocket and pulled out his wallet. "Is twenty dollars enough?" Caprice nodded and took the bill from his hand. Thom and Nathan descended on the man's car like hungry vultures. "Sir, step out of the car. You're under arrest," Thom said. Nathan pretended to arrest Caprice. "Get your damned hands off me," she yelled. Nathan hid his smile as he cuffed his partner. "Come on, you want to add resisting arrest to your list of charges?"

"Whatever," she replied with attitude. Nathan walked Caprice over to an unmarked car.

"You play the scorned hooker well."

"Shut up and take these cuffs off."

"Wait. I got to make sure Thom has the suspect secured."

Caprice sighed and turned around to face Nathan. He smiled at her. "Leather looks good on you."

"Don't start. I hate these stings. You know, male detectives could be prostituted, too."

"Well, you don't get to show off that body often. I didn't even know you had legs like that."

"Please, this isn't what I call showing off a body. This is putting it all on display. I look like a two-dollar tramp."

"Even under all of that, you still have class. And a beautiful…"

"Don't say it!" Caprice cautioned. "Anyway, I heard through the grapevine that this may be our last sting together."

"Yeah, it's official, I'm moving to Internal Affairs next week."

"Congrats," she said. "I'm so proud of you. My partner is going to be an inspector."

"We have to go out and celebrate."

"Sure, I'm going to need a drink after this shift."

Nathan shook his head. "I was thinking something more than a beer and hot wings at a bar."

Caprice looked at her partner with a question in her eyes. "Are you asking me our on a date?"

"Am I that bad? Caprice, have dinner with me."

"I don't date."

"Come on, we won't be working together after tonight. I know how difficult it can be to date a partner, but since we won't be partners anymore, it won't be an issue."

"Are you listening? Hello. I don't date, period, point blank, the end. It has nothing to do with you being my partner."

"Why?"

"Take these cuffs off so I can get back to my job," she said in an attempt to change the subject.

"We will talk later, and I like Icehouse beer," he said as he uncuffed her. "You're buying, and I'm real thirsty."

"Okay, whatever," she said as she walked back to the corner, shaking her head. She didn't want to get into why she didn't date. That would mean reliving her relationship with Damien. Nathan and Damien, though both had a harem of women at their beck and call, weren't exactly cut from the same cloth. For the last year, Nathan juggled girl-friends like a circus clown but was always up-front about it. For Damien, on the other hand, lying was second nature—like breathing. He was fantastic at keeping his stories straight. Hell, he managed to fool Caprice, a woman who made a living at uncovering secrets.

Still, Nathan represented the possibility that love would betray her again. As much as she tried, she couldn't deny the stirring his milk chocolate skin, wavy black hair, and piercing ebony eyes caused in her. He was the kind of man most women would follow to the ends of the earth, but she couldn't allow herself to get caught up in Nathan's charms. That part of her life was behind her, and her career had to take priority.

"I guess you don't want this money," a man yelled from his car, interrupting her thoughts.

"Sorry, Daddy, I was blinded by your car," she said as she ran her hand across the fender of his 1978 lime green Cadillac. "The Caddy is my favorite car."

The man smiled. "I want you for the rest of the night. Here's fifty bucks. What can I get for that?"

"Hmm, let's just say I will rock your world."

"That sounds good to me." He salivated like a dog eyeing a juicy steak on a grill. Caprice smiled. She knew what was going to happen next. About five seconds passed before Thom and Nathan swooped in for the arrest.

Three hours later, Caprice, Thom, and Nathan were sitting in Champion's Bar at the downtown Marriott sipping beers and chomping on wings and potato skins. Caprice felt more comfortable in a pair of black slacks and a teal green oxford shirt.

"These stings are murder," she said after her second beer.

"You got a lot of johns tonight. I didn't realize people still had to pay for it," Thom said as he looked at his watch. "Damn, I got to go home to the wife before she accuses me of having an affair."

"I thought you were," Nathan joked.

Thom stood up and tossed a pretzel at his friend. "Come on, Mr. Internal Affairs, where's the evidence?"

Caprice shook her head and held her tongue. *Are there any faithful men left?* she thought as she watched Thom walk out the door.

"Caprice Johnson," Nathan said as he stared at her intently.

"What?" She took a slow sip of her beer. She knew where the conversation was heading, and she didn't want to go there. She was just glad Nathan didn't say anything while Thom was there. She knew people always assumed women cops slept with their male partners at some point in their careers. She had to fight those rumors in Chicago, and she didn't need that baggage in Charlotte.

"I hope you don't think I forgot about the little heart-to-heart we're supposed to have. Or the beer you owe me."

"I know you haven't forgotten, but you should. I don't want to talk about it." She set her beer bottle on the edge of the bar.

Nathan shook his head. "Do I have to treat you like a perp? I will ask the hard questions until I get the answers I want. I'm not above using force either," he joked.

"Why is this so important? Let it go."

"Because for the last year, you've listened to me talk about my woes with women, and you've given me some good advice. Who's messing with you? I'll lock him up. You should be treated right."

Caprice smiled and turned around on the bar stool to face the door. *How am I going to make him back off?* she thought.

"Avoiding the subject isn't going to make it go away."

"Nathan, I don't want to have this discussion," she whispered.

"Why?"

"Why don't you answer this question? Why are men never satisfied with one woman? You have three or four women that you string along like popcorn garland."

"Come on, Caprice, you know me. I don't string anyone along. I tell my friends I'm not looking for a relationship."

Caprice snorted. "That's a good story. Tell me another one."

"I'm looking for Ms. Right, and to tell the truth, I know the women I'm seeing aren't her. Not even close. But a brother hates to eat alone."

"Okay, Nathan." Caprice didn't believe a word he was saying. She knew there was no way he didn't make some promises to those women.

"Why don't you believe me?" Nathan asked.

"Because there's no such thing as a good, committed man. I know that for a fact."

Nathan groaned. "Don't tell me you are one of those fine, independent, bitter, woman—the type that doesn't need a man for anything."

"I'm going home." She stood up to leave.

Nathan grabbed her arm, and she sat down. "No, Caprice. Talk to me. We've been partners for a year, and you never talk about Chicago or yourself. I don't know anything about you."

"Yes, you do. You know I have your back on the street. What else is there?"

Nathan shook his head. "You're right about that."

"What are you looking at?" she asked when she noticed his intense gaze.

"Sorry. But until you answer my questions, I'm going to stare."

Caprice sighed then picked up her beer bottle and drained it. "All right, ask away."

"What made you leave Chicago and come to Charlotte?"

"I wanted a change. I was tired of the Midwest. And the winters there are horrible."

"That's a load of BS," he exclaimed. "Come on, Caprice, keep it real."

"What? Why do you think I left?"

"It has something to do with the reason you don't date. But that's just my theory. So what's his name?"

"Well, Einstein, I don't date because I don't like playing games. That's all men want to do these days, play games and collect panties. I see it in the squad room every day. Married men are cheating on their wives; single men are dating eighty women at one time. I refuse to be number two, and I damned sure won't be number three or four."

"Whoa, that was some monologue," he joked. "He really did a number on you, didn't he?"

"You wanted to know, so I told you. You shouldn't ask questions you don't want to know the answer to."

"So you hate men?" he inquired.

Caprice turned around and faced him. "Did I say that? If your next question is am I gay, I'm going to slap you."

"I'd never ask you that. Although…"

"I know. I've heard the rumors. I just don't understand why men think a woman has to be a lesbian because she doesn't want to sleep with him. There is nothing a woman can do for me, except hook up my hair."

"Well, men are ego-driven, and instead of us admitting that there's something wrong with us, we put it off on other people: that fine woman doesn't want me, oh she's gay, or something's wrong with her. Never mind that I just stepped to her like a jackass. Some men just don't understand the only thing you have to do to get a woman is be a gentleman."

Caprice chuckled. Maybe she was wrong about Nathan. *No,* she thought. *He's just saying what he thinks I want to hear. That's what they all do.* "You have a point."

"See, I know some brothers give sisters a reason to be bitter and angry, but all of us aren't that way. So, you can't hold what Mr. Chi-Town did against every other brother."

Caprice rolled her eyes. "And on that note, I'm going home. It's late, and I've eaten entirely too much."

"Come on, Detective, let me buy you dinner. You still have to help me celebrate my promotion." She studied his handsome face, and tried to harden her heart, but the word yes floated from her lips.

"Great. Since we're off tomorrow, let's go out then."

"I could have plans for my day off that don't include you."

"Well, now they do. I'll pick you up at seven. Wear that leather skirt."

"Shut up," she snapped as she stood up. Nathan looked at her and smiled.

I can't believe I said yes, she thought as she walked out the door.

CHAPTER TWO

When Caprice got home that night she was too wired to sleep. Nights like this made her miss her girlfriends in Chicago, especially Serena. Since she'd been in Charlotte, she didn't have a chance to make friends outside the police department. But one thing she learned about her fellow officers was the fact that they loved to gossip. Caprice valued her privacy, so she saved her deep dark secrets for Serena, or she kept them to herself.

Serena and Caprice were more like sisters than friends. When Caprice's father, Sgt. Thomas Johnson, was killed in the line of duty with the Chicago Police Department, Serena and her mother, Mary, were there to help Caprice and her mother, Eula, pick up the pieces.

In the weeks after Thomas's death, Mary was there to cook and clean for Caprice and Eula. Serena tried to take her friend's mind off her father's death by treating her to facials and styling her hair with her portable style child play set.

Caprice was only ten when her father was killed, but his influence over her life lived on. She wanted to continue his legacy as a police officer, even though her mother didn't want her only child putting her life at risk. As hard as Eula fought to push Caprice into another career, something safe like teaching, Caprice fought for her dream.

The two women fought constantly until Caprice entered the police academy. Eula threw her full support behind her. On the way to Caprice's graduation, Eula stopped at the florist to pick up some roses for her daughter. When she returned to her car, a run-away tractor-trailer rear-ended her, killing her instantly.

Caprice was walking across the stage, receiving her badge and silently berating her mother for missing the most important day of her life. Then Serena walked up to her with tears in her eyes. She told her about Eula's death. Caprice felt so small when she thought about her anger toward her mother. The happiest day of her life turned into the saddest.

With Serena's help, Caprice was able to mourn her mother as well as start living her dream. She had to make both her parents proud now. Caprice looked at the clock on her nightstand. It was only 10 p.m. in Chi-Town, so she decided to call her friend. "Hello."

"Serena."

"Caprice. Oh my Gawd! You sound like a Southerner. You're drawlin' and everything."

"Shut up. You know you're just one generation out of the South yourself."

"Okay, yeah, whatever. What's going on, Miss Policeman? I haven't talked to you in ages."

"Well, I can't sleep, so I decided to call you. How goes it in Chicago?"

"What's his name?" Serena asked.

"Why does this call have to be about a man?"

"Because, Capri, the only time you can't sleep is when you think your man's cheating or when you meet a man you like. You and Damien broke up, so I know it isn't about cheating. Again I ask, what is his name?"

"You think you know me, don't you?" Caprice had to laugh at how well Serena did know her.

"Who has been your best friend since forever? I do know you. So, are you going to get to the point or what?"

Caprice sighed. "He's my partner."

Serena gasped. "Oh, isn't that against the rules or something?" Caprice could imagine the look on her friend's face; her mouth was probably wide open, and her eyes were stretched to the size of silver dollars.

"Well, he's moving to another division. But he's everything that I said I'd never deal with again."

"Reminds you of Damien, huh?"

"Yes. Only he looks better."

"Details, please!"

"He's about six foot three. He has short wavy hair, and his eyes are black as coal and sparkle like the Hope Diamond. His skin looks like a Hershey bar. It has taken willpower beyond belief to keep me from jumping this man in the gym or while we're on a stakeout. Then tonight, he asked me out on a date."

"So, what's the problem? I can't remember the last time you've been excited about a man. Well, yes I can. But I won't go there."

"Nathan's cool, I guess," Caprice said, glossing over Serena's comment. "I won't say he's like Damien, but he's got lots of other women, and I'd rather keep myself out of harm's way."

"Girl, you need to step outside of that box and live a little. Maybe those women allow him to treat them like that. We know Detective Caprice Johnson won't have that again. A man is only going to do what a woman allows him to do."

"Whatever. So are you saying I allowed Damien to cheat on me?"

"First of all, Damien isn't a man. A real man wouldn't have asked you to marry him and then slept with every woman that happened to cross his path. And no, you didn't allow him to cheat on you. He just did it, because he was an asshole. Well, since you're already in a pissy mood, I might as well tell you." Serena sighed. Caprice could tell her friend was bracing herself for a bomb to go off.

"Tell me what?" Caprice asked.

"Damien's heading down south. Specifically, he's headed for Charlotte."

"What?"

"Yeah, he's going into business with some guys, and they're opening a jazz bar down there."

"Well, Charlotte's big enough for me to avoid him."

"He kinda got your phone number."

"How did that happen?" Caprice could feel sweat beading on her upper lip—something that always happened when she got irate.

"It just slipped out. Literally, your card slipped out of my planner while I was at his club, and he already had me cornered asking about you and your whereabouts. You know I wouldn't have given that jerk your number. But he has reflexes like a cat or something. Capri, I'm really sorry."

Caprice muttered a string of curses that were surely illegal in some states.

"Just don't talk to him. You do have caller ID, don't you? Avoid him."

Caprice rolled her eyes and slapped her hand against her forehead. "Why is he coming here? Why couldn't he open a jazz club in Atlanta?"

"Damien wants you back. He told me he's going to move heaven and earth to make you you his again."

"People in hell want ice water."

"Ouch."

"Look, I have to go. I got to clean my gun or something."

"Capri, you don't have to see him, and if he pisses you off, lock him up. What's the point of being a cop if you can't abuse your power?"

"Goodbye, Serena." Caprice hung up the phone and stared at the walls. Her mind drifted back to the warm March afternoon when she and Damien met. She had been with the Chicago Police Department for about two months. Her assignment was to patrol Garfield Park, one of the city's most popular spots for joggers and walkers. When Caprice got the assignment, pick-pocketers had made Garfield Park a thieves' paradise.

Damien was jogging on one of the paths when he collided with her. They both tumbled to the ground.

"Officer, are you okay?" he asked as he helped her to her feet.

"I'm fine."

"I didn't see you."

"That's okay."

"No, it's not. You have to let me make it up to you. I don't like bowling over pretty women and not making it up to them."

"That's not necessary." Caprice couldn't take her eyes off his bare chest. His dewy skin glistened with sweat. He seemed to know she was staring at him because he ran his hands across his sculpted chest, calling more attention to it.

"Hey, it's good to have friends in high places. Besides, you're the cutest cop I've ever seen."

"You say that as if you've been in trouble with the law before." She raised a suspicious eyebrow at him.

"No, no, you got me all wrong. I own a nightclub. I've had to call Chicago's Finest to get rid of riffraff from time to time."

"Oh, what's the name of the club?"

"Excitement."

"I've been there once, with my friend Serena."

"You have to come back, as my guest for dinner, tonight."

"I...I don't think so."

"Come on. It's the least I can do for knocking you over and getting your uniform dirty."

Caprice smiled. "How about a rain check?" she suggested.

"How am I going to get in touch with you?"

"Give me your number," she said.

"I know that trick. You're going to take my number and never call." She looked away from him because that was indeed her plan.

"I'll call."

He flashed a ten-thousand-watt smile at her, making her heart skip a beat. "I'd give you my number, but I don't have a pen or paper."

"In other words, I have to give you my number?" she said.

"Come on, Officer Johnson. I'm a nice guy."

"What's your name?"

"Damien King."

Caprice pulled out her notebook and wrote her cell phone number down. "I'll call you tonight, so we can meet for dinner," he replied when she handed him the slip of paper.

Before she could respond to him, she was called on the radio. "I got to go." Caprice sprinted off. *I should've kept on running,* she thought as she shook her head to rid herself of the memory. *Sorry Nathan, I won't be hurt again.*

Nathan flipped through the channels hoping to find something to take his mind off Caprice. Every day, Nathan fought to hide his feelings from her. The first day he saw her, Nathan was hooked.

The way she carried herself with the strength and self-confidence of a goddess. Once he got past the copper skin, mysterious hazel eyes, and short auburn hair, he found

Caprice to be an able, no-nonsense detective and an intelligent, well-rounded lady. While most men found themselves intimidated by such a woman, Nathan was intrigued. His yearning to know her on a deeper level was one of the things that influenced his move to the Internal Affairs Department. Their professional relationship had created a boundary that kept him from exploring the possibility of being her lover. Now that had changed. Nothing was going to stop Nathan from making Caprice his.

The phone rang, interrupting his thoughts.

"Yeah?"

"What's up, little brother?" Cordell Wallace asked.

"What do you want?" These calls always irritated him. Cordell never called unless there was some sort of problem that required Nathan's help.

"I can't call my family to say hello?"

"No, Cordell, you always want something. What is it this time?"

"I'm in trouble."

"What's new about that? Are you ever not in trouble?"

"Man, I was set up. Somebody put drugs in my car."

"Cordell, I'm not getting involved in your bullshit this time. Remember when I put a good word in for you because of that burglary charge? That blew right up in my face. I'm not sticking my neck out for you again."

"Look, bro, I swear I'm innocent. You know how busters hate on you when you try to better yourself."

"Cordell, goodbye."

"Wait, wait. Nathan, I need you. I can't go to jail."

"Then you should stop selling dope and get a real job. You're thirty-five years old. When are you going to grow up?" Nathan slammed the phone down.

Cordell was the total opposite of his super cop brother. Trouble seemed to follow him like a storm cloud everywhere he went. Cordell had been in and out of jail since he was seventeen. His parents tried to keep him out of trouble, and Nathan vowed that he would never cause his mother and father, Betty and Alex, the heartache Cordell did with his petty theft and drug charges.

No one knew why Cordell turned to crime. Betty and Alex tried to give their boys everything they wanted. But Cordell started hanging with thugs who spent their time stealing and selling drugs.

Nathan didn't want to be anything like his big brother. That's why he got into police work. He hoped his career would spark a change in his brother, but it didn't.

As Nathan started moving up the ranks at the police department, Cordell got deeper into crime. Nathan was glad his parents were long dead and didn't have to witness Cordell's antics. Despite the voices in his head telling him to let Cordell take his punishment, Nathan called the captain of the vice narcotics unit.

"Leland," Capt. Joseph Leland said when he answered the phone.

"What's up, Captain?"

"Detective Wallace, or is it okay to call you Inspector?"

"It's still detective. At least until Monday morning."

"What's going on?"

Nathan sighed. "I need to check on a case."

"Cordell Wallace?"

"Yeah. What is he charged with?"

"Possession with intent to sell and deliver cocaine."

"How much?"

"A half kilo."

"Damn. I can't believe him."

"Man, I can't believe you two are brothers. How many times have we busted him?"

"Too many to count," he replied with a frustrated sigh.

"There's nothing you can do about this."

"I know that. I just wanted to know what the charges were. I'm staying away from this."

"If you want me to, I'll talk to the DA about this case."

"No, maybe this is what Cordell needs to grow up. I told him this was a mess I wasn't going to attempt to clean up. If he gets a mandatory minimum sentence, it won't be enough."

"Spoken just like an IAD man. They made the right choice when they picked you for the job," Leland said with a laugh.

"All right, Captain, I'll see you around the station."

"Congrats about the promotion. Gonna miss you on the squad, though."

"Thanks." Nathan hung up the phone and tried to focus on the action movie the Superstation was broadcasting.

His mind flipped back to his brother. *A half a kilo of cocaine? Is he insane?* Nathan thought. He turned the TV off and decided to head to bed, but the phone rang again.

"Yeah?"

"Well hello, Nathan," a sultry female voice cooed.

"Who is this?"

"It's Lisa. I'm so upset you don't remember me."

"Sorry, it's been a long day."

"Need some company?"

Nathan thought about her offer. Lisa was an exciting woman, but he wasn't in the mood for company or Lisa's conversation. However, if Caprice called, he wouldn't dare turn her down. But there was no chance of that happening.

"Nah, I have an early day."

"Every time I call you, you blow me off. Why is that?"

"Look, Lisa, this thing isn't working out."

"This thing? What do you mean this thing?"

"Us, or however you want to describe it. I'm not ready for a relationship." *At least not with you.*

"Fine. Goodbye." She hung up the phone.

Nathan was ready to show Caprice that he wasn't the player she thought he was.

CHAPTER THREE

Caprice's plan was to catch up on some much-needed rest on her morning off. Things just didn't work that way. She kept tossing, turning, and thinking about Damien. *I know he's going to call,* she thought as she kicked out from underneath the quilt. She didn't want to talk to him at all, but Damien's the type of person who doesn't take *no* for an answer, just like Nathan. *Why do I always meet men like that? Can I just meet someone who knows when to leave me the hell alone?*

Caprice frowned and sat up in the bed. The red numbers on the alarm clock read 7:30 a.m. Unable to sleep, she sat up in the bed.

As she got out of bed, the phone rang. She wondered who had the gall to call her this early in the morning. *This better be an emergency, and I'm not going in to work today.*

"Hello?"

"Caprice, it's Damien."

She slammed the phone down; then it rang again.

"Caprice, don't be that way," he said when she answered.

"You have some nerve calling me."

"I wanted to call the day you walked out on me."

"Damien, I don't have time for this. You're tired, and this game you're playing now is tired, too."

"Look, I'm in Charlotte, and I want to see you tonight."

"So you call me early in the damn morning? I'm trying to rest."

"I figured you were getting ready to go in to work. I remembered when you were in the Windy City how you would roll out of bed like a zombie. But when you put that blue uniform on, you were ready for action. That's one of the many things I love about you. You've always been a go-getter. Nothing stops you from doing what you want to do."

"What's the purpose of this trip down memory lane?" she asked with a sigh.

I've been thinking about you a lot, Capri. We had a lot of good times together. I want that back."

"Don't call me that," she snapped, referring to her childhood nickname. She used to like to hear Damien call her Capri. But this morning it was grating on her nerves like nails against a blackboard or feedback from a microphone in the speakers at church. "And I don't want to hear your lies this morning. Goodbye, Damien."

"Come on, give me a chance," he pleaded.

"I've given you more chances than you deserve. There's nothing you need to say to me or anything I want to hear from you besides goodbye!" She slammed the phone down, nearly breaking it in half.

She dropped her head in her hands as she sat on the side of the bed. Her morning was turning out to be a disaster, and she hadn't even taken her shower yet.

Caprice was about to step in the shower when the phone rang again. She rolled her eyes thinking it was Damien again. "Look, jackass, I'm not having drinks or anything else with you. You can just go to hell!"

"Damn, partner, I'm sorry," Nathan said. "I know it's early, but don't bite my head off."

"Nathan, I didn't know it was you. I thought you were someone else."

"I heard. I was just calling to see if you wanted to go to the gym this morning."

"I wasn't planning on it, but that sounds like a good idea. I need to release some tension."

"Cool, I'll see you in about twenty minutes."

"Wait, I just got out of the bed. I need a little more than that."

Nathan laughed. "All right, just meet me at the gym."

Caprice hung up the phone and brushed her teeth. She pulled her gym bag out of the closet and changed into her gray spandex CMPD shorts and a matching T-shirt. She looked at her reflection in the mirror. *Maybe Damien won't recognize me if he sees me,* she thought.

She had changed, but not dramatically. Her eyes didn't have the hope that was there when she fell in love with Damien. He would always complement her on her truthful eyes. He called them hazel soul windows. She glanced at her watch; it was time to go.

Nathan stood in the police gym, working with free weights but watching the door. *Where's that woman?* he thought as he did a second set of arm curls. He was starting to feel the burn in his bulging biceps. He set the weight down. Caprice walked in. Nathan's breath caught in his chest when he caught a glimpse of her in her tight shorts and T-shirt. Her hips and thighs were toned and defined. She had a body that wouldn't quit. She was muscular, but still soft in all the places a woman should be. Nathan's gaze fell to her 38C breasts. He salivated at the thought of seeing her without a bra and taking one of the peaks into his mouth. *Lawd have mercy,* he thought as she walked over to him. She glided across the floor with a dancer's grace. Her face was as clear as a cloudless summer day. *I wonder how she looks first thing in the morning?*

"I know, I know, I'm late," she said, misreading the look in his eyes. "It took me a little longer to get myself together this morning."

"It's all right."

"Show me to the weights, because I have energy to burn."

"You did warm up, didn't you?"

"Yes, I did, Mr. Universe."

Nathan chuckled at her joke. "I'm going to miss your smart-ass mouth when I'm in IAD."

"Aw, you're not getting sentimental on me, are you?" Caprice punched him playfully on the shoulder.

He smiled and ignored the question. He'd had sentimental feelings for her for so long. "Come on, Wonder

Woman, let's work out. You haven't forgotten about dinner tonight, have you?"

"Ah, about that."

"You aren't canceling on me. You made a date, and I'm going to arrest you if you break it."

"Talk about an abuse of power. Come on, Nathan, we shouldn't do this. It just wouldn't be right for us to go out and—"

"Caprice, I'm asking you to go to dinner with me, not marry me." *Not yet, anyway,* he thought.

She looked at him as if she was considering his offer. She nodded. "All right. Fine, I'll go."

"Wow, I'm so honored," he mocked. "Is spending time with me that bad? Do I smell?"

"Shut up," she said, popping him on the shoulder with her towel. "And sometimes you do smell."

"So who was the jackass that called you this morning?" he asked nonchalantly.

Caprice sighed. "Someone that I didn't want to talk to, and I don't want to talk about it."

Nathan threw his hands up. "I'm just a spotter."

"A nosey spotter," she muttered.

"You call it nosey; I call it concern. If someone is messing with you, I told you…"

"You'll lock him up," she said as she picked up the seventy-pound barbell.

After their workout, Caprice and Nathan headed to Starbuck's for some iced cappuccinos. "I don't know why you like these things," Nathan said as they took a seat at a table near the window.

"They're good," she replied. "Live a little. It's better than that mango fango crap you brought me last week."

"Now you know that mango coffee was off the hook. But hey, I'm picking the place for dinner and you're just going to have to deal with it, Johnson."

Caprice shook her head and smiled slightly. "I really wonder about you sometimes," she said. "You just don't take no for an answer. I'm sure there are so many other women in Charlotte who would love to hang out with you. Why not pester one of them for a dinner date?"

"Don't pretend you're not one of them," he said as he grabbed her hand. Caprice tensed at his touch, then relaxed. She was surprised that she felt so comfortable with him holding her hand. Nathan's gaze seemed to penetrate her soul. She looked away from him and discreetly slid her hand from Nathan's grasp. "Caprice, you know you want to go out to dinner with me as much as I want to go out with you," he said.

"Whatever," she replied. But she had to admit, even if it was only to herself, that she was looking forward to their date. Of course, she wasn't going to tell Nathan that.

"So, are you going to tell me about that phone call this morning?" he probed.

"No."

"I'll leave it alone, then. But if you want to talk, you know I'm here for you."

"Thank you," she said as she sipped her drink. Caprice turned toward the door and saw Damien walk in. Nathan followed her gaze, then he looked at the scowl on Caprice's face. He wondered if this was the asshole who called her this morning. She didn't seem too happy to see whoever this guy was. He looked at the gray-eyed black man making his way to their table. Another glance at Caprice's color-drained face told him that man was the reason her heart was as frigid as a Chicago winter.

"Caprice, hello," he said.

"Hello."

Nathan sized up Damien. *Who is this clown?* he thought.

"You look awesome; I see you're still working out," Damien said, noting her gym clothes.

"What do you want?" she snapped.

"I just wanted to say hello."

"Well, you said it, now be on your way."

Damien turned to Nathan. "Oh, am I interrupting something?" He smirked at Nathan as if to let him know Caprice was still his woman. Nathan watched Caprice leap up from the table, gripping Damien's arm like a vice and leading him outside.

Once Caprice got Damien away from Nathan, she lit into him. "Why are you here?" she demanded.

"I came for the coffee. Seeing you was an added bonus. Am I getting you in trouble with your new man? You know, you can do so much better than him."

"Stay out of my way, Damien. I told you in Chicago that it was over, and I meant it. You don't need to worry about what I do or who I do it with."

"Oh, I'm not worried at all, and I know things aren't over between us. How many times have we ended it and gotten back together? Maybe you should inform Mr. Musclehead of that."

"Maybe you should kiss my ass," Caprice said.

Damien winked at her. "I'd be glad to." Caprice stomped away from him and sat down at the table with Nathan.

"What was that all about?"

"Nothing." She picked up her cup and quickly slurped down the rest of her cappuccino. "I have to go."

"Caprice, wait," he called out as she tore out of the coffee shop. Nathan walked outside and ran into Damien.

"Excuse me," Damien said.

"Do I know you?" Nathan asked.

"No, but let me inform you about something. Caprice and I go way back. We have a long history, and we will get back together. So whatever you think you have, enjoy it now, because it won't last."

"Who the hell are you?" Nathan demanded.

"Your worst nightmare," Damien said as he walked away. Nathan stood on the sidewalk with a bewildered look on his face. After a few seconds, he got into his car and headed home. He tried to ignore the mystery man's comments and focus on his date with Caprice, but he wasn't thrilled about the way she left Starbuck's. He hoped after their dinner date she'd see him in a different light. *That woman is an enigma,* he thought as he pulled into the driveway.

Nathan looked up and saw Lisa waiting in his front yard. This was the last thing he needed. Nathan was hoping Lisa was out of his life for good. She walked over to his car and waited for him to get out. To any other man, Lisa would be considered a brick house. She had an hourglass figure, long black hair that blew in the wind, and light brown eyes that sparkled in the sun. Nathan fell for her charms temporarily, but she wasn't the kind of woman he saw a future with. His future was with Caprice.

"What do you want?" he asked, trying hard not to be rude.

"We need to talk," she said with a sigh.

"About what?"

"I'm pregnant."

Nathan's eyes nearly popped out of his head. *How, when, what's she talking about? Did she just say she was pregnant?* His frazzled brain held his tongue hostage.

"Are you going to say something?" Lisa asked.

Nathan shook his head, trying to clear it enough to form a complete sentence. "What am I supposed to say? How long have you known?"

"I just found out this week. I know the timing is off, since you dumped me and everything."

"Lisa, I didn't dump you because we didn't have a serious relationship."

"I know that."

"How far along are you?"

"I don't know. I haven't been to the doctor. I took a home pregnancy test."

"Don't you think you should go to the doctor and confirm this?"

"And when the doctor says I'm pregnant, what are we going to do?"

Nathan sighed. He didn't know what to say, and he didn't want to say what most men said when a woman dropped this news on them. "We'll cross that bridge when we get to it." He took several deep breaths, trying to calm the quick pace of his heartbeat. This couldn't have happened at a worse time.

"I'm glad you're being understanding about this," she said.

"Do you want to come in and have some water or something?"

"No, I'd better go. I'm on my lunch break."

"Lisa, we're going to have to get blood tests."

"I should've known you were going to take it there. You don't believe I'm carrying your child?"

"Lisa, it's not about what I believe. Hell, you don't even know for sure you're pregnant. We only had sex once."

"And? It only takes one time, Nathan. Did you sleep through that lesson in high school biology?"

"What am I supposed to think?"

"You know what, I'll handle this myself." Lisa stomped off and got into her car. Nathan sighed. *This is just what I need,* he thought as he unlocked the front door.

Nathan thought about the night he and Lisa shared. Caprice and Nathan had been involved in a shootout at an apartment complex on the east side of town. Caprice was almost hit when one of the men they were chasing for traf-

ficking cocaine opened fire on them. That night was the
first time Nathan had never been involved in a shootout,
and he was too wired to sleep. Lisa just happened to call at
the right time. She came over with a bottle of Grey Goose
and a sympathetic ear. By the time the bottle was empty,
they were naked on the sofa. The next morning, he knew it
was a mistake. He just didn't know how big of a problem it
was going to be.

Damn, he thought as he poured himself a glass of water.
He sat on the sofa. Nathan wanted to be a father, but he
also wanted to be married and have his child with his wife.
The last thing he wanted was to have a "baby's mother."

He didn't love Lisa, and he didn't want to have this kind
of bond with her. But if this was his child, he would take
full responsibility for it. But he knew Caprice would be lost
to him forever if this was his child.

CHAPTER FOUR

Caprice looked at the clock. She had two hours before her dinner date with Nathan. *I could tell him I'm not feeling well,* she thought as she stood in the middle of her walk-in closet looking for a suitable outfit. But she knew Nathan wouldn't let her get away with that. He'd probably come to her place to make sure she was sick. Caprice just kept thinking that someone was going to get hurt if this relationship changed, and it was going to be her. The phone rang, breaking into her thoughts.

"Hello?"

"Are you getting ready for your date?" Serena asked.

"What are you, a psychic or something?"

"Yes. I want to be sure you aren't going to flake out and call him with a lame excuse. 'Oh, my stomach hurts; I have to stay home and rub it.' "

Caprice sighed. "Serena, I don't want to do this. I mean, why should Nathan and I mess with the great friendship we have by trying to date each other?"

"Girl, stop tripping. You need to go on this date."

"Why?"

"Because it's high time for you to get over the whole Damien thing. It's been a year, Caprice."

"I know this, but we were together for three years. I loved him with everything in me. It takes time to get over that kind of pain."

"You won't let yourself get over it. You keep pulling away from every man who wants to get to know you. Caprice, you can't keep punishing yourself because Damien was an asshole who broke your heart. Just because he did it, it doesn't mean Nathan will."

"I hear what you're saying, but it's hard to open up and trust another man completely again."

"Do you think you're the only woman who's been hurt by the man she loved? Remember Torrey Michaels?"

"Yes, I do. I remember what he did to you."

"I was hurting when he told me, on the eve of my wedding no less, that he got his ex pregnant. I was devastated, but I dumped him and moved on. You have to move on, Caprice. If you wallow in self-pity, Damien wins."

She sighed again. "I hear you."

"But are you listening to me?"

"Okay, fine. What should I wear to dinner?" Caprice was ready to change the subject. Serena could be quite preachy about love.

"Anything that doesn't look like the uniform you wear to work. A nice skin will work."

Caprice looked at the black pantsuit she had in her hand. "I guess you're right. But I don't want to look too…"

"Feminine?" Serena broke out in laughter.

"Ha ha, heffa. Maybe you should take your jokes to amateur hour at the Apollo. I can look feminine in pants. I do it every day."

"And he sees you in pants every day. Come on, live a little. I expect a full report at the end of the night."

"Sure, why not?" she replied sarcastically.

"Call me, or I'll assume you're spending the night with him. That might not be such a bad idea, though. You sound like you need some, bad."

Caprice laughed.

"Shut up! Anyway, I have to go so I can get dressed."

"Remember, no pantsuits!" Caprice hung up and walked back into the closet. She pulled out a baby blue halter dress. The dress stopped at her knees and flowed like a tropical breeze. Well, she thought as she held the dress against her body, it wasn't her every day look. She reached down and grabbed the matching blue pumps she'd only worn twice. The weather was perfect for the dress even though it was the middle of autumn. North Carolina weather was fickle. The fall flip-flopped between spring and summer with days when the temperature struggled to get out of the 50s and other days when the temperature was a balmy seventy degrees. Caprice loved it. She hardly ever had to wear her heavy winter gear that was a staple in Chicago.

She walked into the bathroom, applied a light dusting of foundation and a layer of plum lipstick. Caprice sprayed her hair with water, causing it to curl up. She teased it with her fingers then stepped into her dress.

Here goes, she thought as she picked up the phone and called Nathan.

"Hello," he said.

"Nathan, are we still on for dinner?"

"You're not getting out of it, Detective."

"I didn't think so. Do you want to meet at the restaurant?"

"Sure." Nathan's voice sounded flat, as if he was forcing himself to be cheerful.

"What's wrong?" Caprice asked.

"Why do you think something's wrong?"

"You sound strange."

"Nothing's wrong," he said with a sigh. Nathan shouldn't have tried to hide anything from Caprice. They could read each other like books.

"Oh, I'm convinced now. Maybe we should have dinner another night."

"I really need to talk," he said. "Do you think we can go somewhere quiet and private?"

"Why don't I just come over there and we have dinner delivered? Your house is quiet and private."

"All right," he said.

Caprice hung up; grabbed her purse, jacket, and keys; then dashed out the door. *I wonder what's wrong with Nathan?* she thought as she drove to his house.

Nathan was still dressed in his gym clothes when Caprice arrived. She looked at him with questions in her eyes. He looked at her shapely legs peaking from underneath her dress.

"What happened?" she asked when she walked in.

"Come in and sit down."

"Nate, what's going on?" Caprice sat on the sofa and took her jacket off. Nathan paced back and forth in front of her. He glanced at her dress and turned away quickly. He had to focus on the problem at hand.

"Do you remember me telling you about a woman named Lisa?"

"Two-steps-away-from-stalking Lisa? The one who kept calling you and showing up at your place with food all the time."

"Yeah."

"What did she do now? Did she slash your tires, smash your windshield?"

"She's supposed to be pregnant."

"With your child?"

Nathan nodded.

"Wow," Caprice said. She exhaled loudly.

"I can't believe I'm in this situation."

"I can't either, especially when you said you weren't serious with any of your friends."

"It happened once…" She waved her hand in the air, cutting him off.

"You don't have to explain yourself to me. When are you going to find out if it's your child?"

"When we get blood tests. She had an attitude because I asked her for one."

"That's strange."

"What?"

"Her copping an attitude because you want to make sure it's your child."

"I know. I'm not sure what to do."

"There really isn't anything you can do until you know whether you're the father." Nathan sat down on the edge of the sofa. Caprice stroked his back. "I'm sorry," she said.

He turned around and grabbed Caprice's hand. "You look really nice, better than nice."

She smiled nervously. "Thanks. I feel silly now, though. I got all dressed up for no reason."

"You shouldn't. We can still go out if you want to."

"No, no. You don't seem like you're in the mood. We can just order a pizza and talk."

"I'm not really hungry," he said as he stood up and started pacing again.

Caprice walked over to Nathan and touched his shoulder. "Don't get down on yourself about this. It'll all blow over soon enough."

"I guess I'm proving your theory about men, huh? Here I am about to have a nervous breakdown because this woman may be having my child." Caprice didn't say anything. She just let Nathan talk. "I want children, but not with a woman I don't love and not at this point in my life."

"Maybe you should've thought about that before you slept with her," she said harshly.

"Where did that come from?"

"Sorry, I'm not trying to make you feel worse."

Nathan nodded. "I guess you've heard this sort of thing before."

She dropped her head. "I think I'd better go."

Nathan grabbed her arm. "Don't, please."

"I need to. Call me if you want to talk," Caprice said.

Nathan watched as she dashed out the door.

CHAPTER FIVE

The alarm clock sounded and Caprice groaned as she looked at the time. It was 4:30 a.m. Roll call was at 6 a.m. She hated working day shift. Caprice wasn't a morning person. This morning was particularly bad, because she spent the night thinking about Nathan and Damien. She couldn't get over the bomb Nathan dropped on her last night. Caprice closed her eyes. *If they would be more selective about who they lay down with, things like this wouldn't happen,* she thought.

Nathan felt bad enough without her passing judgment on him. But at that moment, he reminded her of Damien. There was a pregnancy scare once when they were together. One of his waitresses claimed she was having his child and was threatening to tell Caprice everything. So Damien came clean first. That was the first woman Caprice found out about. After that, a flood of affairs burst forward until she just couldn't take it anymore.

If Lisa were carrying his child, any notion she had about being with him was as good as dead.

And Damien—she couldn't get his silky smooth Barry White voice out of her head. He made her knees weak just saying hello. Seeing him in the coffee shop didn't just bring back bad memories either. It made her remember being hopelessly in love with him. It made her remember nights of endless passion and mornings of intense pleasure. *I can't do this, and I won't,* she thought. Instead of hitting the snooze button, Caprice pulled herself out of bed and headed into the bathroom to shower. The water shot out of the nozzle cold and fast, making her shiver until the water heater kicked in.

Why did Damien call me? Hasn't he hurt me enough? I'm not going to let him do this to me again. Sure everything will be good at first then, just like the last time, some other woman will catch your eye, and you'll just have to have her. I wonder if you even know what self-control is? she thought as she wrapped herself in a plush towel.

She grabbed a gray suit from the closet and spread it across the bed. The best thing about being a detective was being able to wear civilian clothes. She hated the uniform almost as much as she hated thinking about Damien. But he invaded her thoughts as she dressed. She remembered cold Chicago mornings when he'd heat things up by stepping in the shower with her. She closed her eyes and fought the images of Damien's muscular body stepping into the steamy shower, sweat and beads of water glistening over his body. Caprice rocked back and forth, getting lost in the memory. She knew Damien hadn't changed, and only a fool would let him back into her life and heart. She wasn't going to be that fool. Caprice dressed and dashed out the door.

When she walked into the squad room, the other vice detectives stood up and clapped. Caprice scrunched up her face and shrugged her shoulders. "What's this all about?"

Captain Leland walked over to Caprice and shook her hand. "You broke a record yesterday. Thirty johns in one night."

She rolled her eyes. "Okay, whatever."

"Must have been the blonde wig," Thom said in between chomping on a glazed Krispy Kreme doughnut and sipping coffee.

"Shut up."

"All right, all right, let's get down to business," Leland said.

The five detectives got quiet and serious. It was time to work. The officers in the vice unit were a unique and elite group. Everyone was dedicated to getting drugs off the streets, and they had each other's backs, because what they did was too dangerous to play politics. Caprice valued and respected that. Personal feelings didn't belong in the squad room. It was their mantra.

Caprice pulled out her notebook, ready to take notes on the day's case. She looked to her left at the empty seat where Nathan used to sit. She was relieved he wasn't there, because she didn't want to have to talk about the scene in his living room last night. But she was a little saddened to lose her partner. *They're probably going to team me with some rookie,* she thought angrily. Budget cuts would probably make the already small unit smaller. No new hires or promotions would be made this year.

"Last night patrol got some information about a shipment of cocaine that some players from New York are supposed to be bringing to Donovan Harris. Johnson, brief us on Harris's operation," Leland said.

Caprice stood up and walked to the front of the squad room. "Harris is set up in Hidden Valley in two old apartments. He's rarely there, but it's where he checks big shipments. Until last week, we couldn't trace those deliveries to anyone. Luckily for us, we've gotten solid information that those are Harris's drugs. We have to be careful when we go in there. There are eyes and clockers all over that neighborhood. If we time everything just right, we can catch him red-handed. The best way to get in is to set up at a gas station on Sugar Creek. Harris's weakness is that he doesn't trust anyone. He checks all of his shipments at those apartments."

"Barren," Leland said, pointing at Thom, "you and Johnson are going to Hidden Valley and sit on the shipment. Williams and Rogers, I need you two and a couple of marked units in the area, but out of sight. I want everybody to go home tonight."

Everyone nodded. "All right, let's get this guy this time," he said as the detectives filed out the door. Thom smiled at Caprice when they made it to the motor pool to get an unmarked Chevy. "I've never had a female partner before."

"There's a first time for everything."

"I guess this feels funny without Nathan. He wanted to nail Donovan's ass to the wall."

"We can't worry about Nathan right now. Word on the street is Cordell's involved with Donovan, one of his lieutenants no less. The drugs he got busted for the other night came from Donovan's stash. And I hear that Donovan's lawyer bailed him out of jail."

"This can't be good for Nathan's career."

"Nathan never did anything improper when it came to his brother," she said defensively.

"Sorry. I see we're a little touchy about the ex-partner."

"You don't see a damned thing, and I'm driving," she said as the got into the car.

"Yes, ma'am," he replied in mock salute.

Nathan walked into his new office. For the first time in his career, he didn't have to share a desk in a crowded squad room. He was the youngest officer in IAD. At twenty-eight, he was moving quickly up in the ranks.

"Inspector," Major David Chaney said when he walked into Nathan's office. Nathan stood up and shook hands with his commanding officer. "Good morning, sir."

"I understand your brother was arrested last night. Is that going to be a problem for you?"

"No, it's not. Cordell's a grown man who can't follow the rules."

"Yeah, but he's still your brother."

"An accident of nature. I don't have anything to do with my brother's crimes."

"Let's keep it that way," Chaney said. "Welcome to IAD." He dropped a stack of files on Nathan's desk.

"Thanks." He began flipping though the papers, not knowing what he should be looking for.

"You're in the big leagues now, youngster."

Nathan ignored the comment. He knew the stakes were higher, but he was ready.

"So, what's my first case?" he asked. Nathan was ready to get rolling.

"Officer Michael Smith. We have five reports of excessive force on him."

"Okay."

"You need to go out on patrol with him and observe how he does his job. I talked to his L.T. about the investigation. You'll have patrol's full cooperation."

"When is Smith on duty again?"

"Tomorrow."

"What do I do today?"

"Investigate. Have fun," Chaney said as he walked away from Nathan's desk.

Nathan took a deep breath and opened the file. Michael Smith was a patrol officer with a family and it was up to Nathan to determine if he was fit to keep his job. *Should I be doing this?* he thought. *This might not be the best start for me.* Then Nathan came across a report filed by a fourteen-year-old's mother. "Broken jaw, cracked ribs," he whispered. "This is ridiculous! He doesn't deserve a slot on this force if this is how he handles himself."

Nathan stood up and headed out to his car. He wanted to see what this boy and his mother had to say about what happened that night. The report of abuse reminded him why he took the promotion in the first place.

Caprice watched the door of Harris's apartment through a pair of binoculars. "Any movement?" Thom asked.

"Nope. Is everyone in place?"

"Yeah."

"I hope Harris comes. I can't wait to see him go down."

"You and me both. We've been after him for years. How did you get an informant to talk to you?"

"He thought I was cute." Thom laughed.

"And you wonder why you play the prostitute."

"Don't start," she cautioned.

"All right, all right."

"There he is! And he's not alone. Damn, that's Cordell with him."

"Thom picked up the radio. "Everyone, hold your positions. We have an eyeball on Harris, and he's not alone. Use extreme caution and don't make any moves until I give the signal. We need a clean bust."

"They're inside," Caprice said.

"Move, move!"

Caprice and Thom hopped out of the car and ran to the apartment with their guns drawn. The door was cracked and Harris was standing over a suitcase filled with white powder. *Got him!* she thought as Thom kicked the door wide open.

"Freeze! Police!" he yelled.

Harris and Cordell turned around.

"Put your hands up!" Caprice commanded.

"Shit!" Harris exclaimed.

Cordell turned and tried to run out the side door, but three officers blocked his path. He threw his hands up and surrendered. "I didn't know what was going on," he said.

"Tell it to the judge," one of the officers said as he cuffed Cordell.

Caprice looked at him as the officer carted him out. *Nathan's going to be crushed,* she thought.

Harris looked at Caprice. "You should let me go," he whispered.

"Shut up. You're going to jail."

"I can buy and sell your ass four times over. Do you think I'm going to stay in jail for more than a few hours? Little girl, you have fucked with the wrong person this time."

"Get this scum out of here!" Caprice yelled to a uniformed officer. As much as she hated to admit it, she knew Harris wouldn't have a problem posting bail. But they had him dead to rights this time. Not even Johnny Cochran could get him out of this one.

"Don't let him get to you, this is a clean bust," Thom said. "They all make the same threats. I guess there is a drug dealer handbook that gives them catch slogans to toss around once they get busted."

Caprice laughed, but she had a queasy feeling in her gut. "Well, we don't need to give him any wiggle room. Get the OA on the phone. I want a warrant before we touch anything."

Thom nodded and pulled out his cell phone. Caprice walked outside and watched the squad cars leave with Harris and Cordell. *Why do I have the feeling that this case is going to be bigger than anything I've ever dealt with?* she thought when Harris winked at her.

Nathan knocked on the door of Maurice Boxer's mother's apartment. A tall brown-skinned woman with a cigarette between her fingers answered the door. "What do you want?" Her face looked like a piece of weathered leather. Her eyes were dark and hostile. Her salt-and-pepper hair was pulled back in a tight bun that gave her a harried schoolteacher look. She held her tattered white terry cloth robe together with her free hand.

"I'm Inspector Wallace from the Charlotte-Mecklenburg Police Department."

"I ain't got nothing to say to you unless you're going tell me you bastards are paying for my son's doctor bills." She blew a puff of smoke in Nathan's face. He fanned it away and fought back a cough.

"I want to talk to you about that night."

"Why? So y'all can cover up the fact that a racist cop beat my fourteen-year-old? Talk to my lawyer." Mrs. Boxer dropped the cigarette on the concrete and angrily stomped it out.

"I'm trying to get to the truth. I know you have every right not to trust me or any other police officer, but it's my job to weed out people like Smith. The department has launched an internal investigation into this incident."

"Whatever," she said with a snort. "This is like having the greedy fox guard the chicken coop."

Nathan nodded. "I read the file about your son and his arrest. What he was charged with didn't warrant that kind of abuse."

Mrs. Boxer raised an eyebrow. "So you're not here to tell me that my son got what he deserved?"

"No one, your son included, deserves to be beaten because he was driving without a license. Your son was treated worse than an animal. Our department doesn't operate like that. This isn't Los Angeles."

"Come in," she said, stepping aside. She led Nathan over to a tattered black leather sofa. He looked around the small apartment. Everything was in its place. Even the papers and magazines on the table were neatly stacked.

"Tell me what happened that night."

Mrs. Boxer turned to him and sighed. "I should have been driving, but I had a little too much to drink at my sister's house. I gave Maurice the keys. He was speeding, and I told him to slow down. Before he did, we got pulled over. He left his permit here at the house, and he wanted to explain that to the officer.

"So Maurice got out of the car to talk to the cop. I told him to sit down and wait, but he's hardheaded like his father. The next thing I know, I heard shouting, and then I looked and saw that man punching my son like he was Lennox Lewis or something. Maurice is six foot two, 150 pounds. He didn't stand a chance against that big ol' man. I got out of the car and another cop grabbed me and held me back. I had to watch my son get beaten. When that cop who was hitting Maurice saw the other one, he started saying my son threatened him. Threatened him with what?

I know he didn't have a weapon or anything. The only thing Maurice did wrong was getting out of the car. That's it. All these cops kept saying he was justified, because he thought his life was threatened."

Nathan took notes as she talked. When he was with the vice unit, he hated seeing Smith at a crime scene. He knew he had a bad attitude. Nathan just didn't know how violent Smith was. He closed his notebook.

"So, what's going to happen now?" she asked.

"There's going to be a hearing. He could be suspended or lose his job."

"Really? That kind of man doesn't need a badge."

"I agree," Nathan replied. "Are you willing to testify at the hearing, you and Maurice?"

"Yes. I'll be there with bells on. I want that man gone."

Nathan handed her his card. "Call me if you need anything."

She shook Nathan's hand as he stood up. "Thank you, Inspector. Out of all the police officers I've talked to, you're the first one to listen to me. I hope you're different, and I didn't waste my time and breath talking to you."

Nathan nodded then headed out the door. *Smith has got to go*, he thought as he got into his car.

Before he got back to the station, Nathan's cell phone rang. "Wallace."

"Man, it's me, Cordell."

"What is it now?"

"I just got arrested again."

"Who set you up this time?" Nathan asked sarcastically.

"I was at a friend's house, and the cops bust in like he was Osama bin Laden or something."

"There's nothing I can do for you. You made this mess. Get out of it the best way you can. Call a bail bondsman. Stop calling me when you get in trouble."

"Oh, so it's like that?"

"Just like that."

"Whatever, man. I see you're just like the rest of these cops. All you want to do is lock a brother up."

"If you would stay out of trouble, you wouldn't end up in jail. I just wish I'd been the one slapping the cuffs on you."

The other end went dead. Nathan shook his head and hung it low. He didn't know what to think about his brother. *I don't have time for this,* he thought as he turned into the parking lot of the police department.

CHAPTER SIX

Caprice sat at her desk typing Harris's arrest report. She wanted to make sure all Ts were crossed and all Is dotted. There was no way he was going to get off on a technicality or some other legal maneuver. As long as she was leading the investigation, everything about this case was going to be above reproach.

"Are you going to lunch?" Thom asked when he walked by her desk.

"As soon as I finish this report."

"Nathan always called you a workaholic. I see he wasn't lying."

"I'm just trying to make sure this worm doesn't slide his way out of these charges."

"I hear you."

Caprice looked up from her typing. "I really feel for Nathan."

"I know. His brother's a liability to his career."

"He got out of vice at the right time. Could you imagine what some reporter would do with this story if the connection between Nathan and Cordell was made?"

"They'd swear there was a cover-up. You want me to bring you some food back?"

"I'm going to grab something later," she said.

"All right, don't let me come back and find you sitting there."

Caprice smiled and waved Thom away. "You're too young to be a mother hen, Thom." After she finished the report, Caprice called the district attorney.

"David Thompson."

"Mr. Thompson, this is Detective Johnson."

"Detective, I hear congratulations are in order. You collared Harris today. This has been a long time coming."

"Yes, and I want to go over charges with you."

"All right, meet me at 2 p.m. in my office. I want to throw the book at him."

"Okay. I can fax the report over to you now if you want."

"Detective, I'm impressed. An arrest and report in the same day. They don't make too many like you."

"I want him off the street as much as you do," she said.

"Fax it over and we'll talk about it this afternoon."

Caprice hung up the phone then printed out the report. She looked up and saw Nathan walking into the squad room as if he was on a mission. "Caprice, can I talk to you for a second?" he asked.

"Sure." She hoped this wasn't about last night. He sat in the chair beside her desk.

"I understand you guys busted my idiot brother today."

She nodded. "Him and Donovan Harris."

"Make sure the charges stick," Nathan said.

"You know I will. I'm meeting with the DA about the case this afternoon."

Nathan smiled. "I'm sorry about last night. I know I killed the moment with my drama. Let me make it up to you with lunch."

"Great. Just let me fax this report."

As Nathan watched her walk over to the fax machine, her phone rang.

"Detective Johnson's desk."

"Is Caprice around?" a male voice asked.

"No, can I take a message."

"This is Damien King. She can reach me at 704-555-4355. She'll know what it's about."

"Is this about a case, because I'm her partner," Nathan lied.

"No, it's personal." Then he hung up. Nathan looked at the message he wrote down.

"Are you ready?" she asked when she returned to her desk.

"Yeah. You have a message. Some guy named Damien King called a few minutes ago."

Caprice's face blanched. "What did he say?" Her voice was shaky.

"He said it was personal, and you need to call him." Nathan handed her the slip of paper. "Who is this guy, and why are you so shaken up about it? You just faced down one of the baddest drug dealers on the East Coast. Damien King can't be that much worse."

"He's my ex-fiancé," she said with an exasperated sigh. "Remember the jerk who came over to our table at Starbuck's the other day? That was him, Mr. Wrong in all his glory. I was hoping when I left Chicago I'd never see him again. But here he is, springing up like an ugly weed on new grass."

"Oh." He decided not to tell her about the little confrontation they had on the sidewalk after she left.

"And I don't want to talk to him, see him, or hear from him again. I wish he would permanently disappear."

"Those are some harsh words," Nathan said as they headed out to the parking lot.

"Yeah, well, you don't know the hell and heartache that man put me through. He lies as easily as he breathes. There was always another woman. He made a fool of me."

"You know, this is the first time you've ever opened up about something outside of work. And for the record, he's the fool, because he let you slip away."

"Whatever," she said as they headed outside. "So, where are you taking me for lunch, Inspector?"

"Let's go to the Happy Face Café."

"Your treat, right?"

"Of course." Nathan opened the car door for Caprice and watched her slide in the passenger seat.

"How has your day been so far?" she asked him as he started the car.

"Interesting. Of course, I can't talk about it. You know the rules."

"I know. Hell, as long as you aren't investigating me, I really don't care who's in the bubble."

Nathan laughed. "Who would complain about you, Super Cop?"

"I have a bad feeling about this Harris case," Caprice admitted.

"Why?"

"I don't know. He threatened me, in an underhanded way, when he was arrested."

Nathan clenched his jaw. "What did he say?" He had an overwhelming urge to protect Caprice, even though he knew she could hold her own against anyone.

"Typical stuff, you messed with the wrong person. It's what every dealer says, but we know Harris has a full network on the streets. He could make something happen if he wanted to."

"Well, I wouldn't worry about it. Knowing you, you caught him with his hand in the dope jar. He's going away for a long time."

"I'm not worried. I just said I had a bad feeling," she said.

Nathan pulled into the parking lot of the café. "Well, if you have any problems, you let me know."

"What are you going to do?"

"I still have your back, remember that. You're always going to be my partner."

"Okay," she said with a smile. "That's good to know."

They got out of the car and walked into the restaurant. "Have you talked to Lisa?" Caprice asked.

"No, not since she dropped the bomb on me."

"Don't you think you need to find her and talk to her? Damn, Nathan, she could be carrying your child."

"Caprice, I know all that. I just don't know what to do. I've never been in this predicament before." Caprice looked at him but kept silent. She wanted to comment on why he was in this predicament, but she didn't. "What?" he asked, noticing her gaze.

"I guess she was a one-night stand, huh?"

"Come on, Caprice, you know I'm not that kind of guy."

"Really?" She raised her eyebrow.

Nathan sighed. "I was that night. Are you going to hold that against me?"

"It doesn't matter what I think."

"Yes it does, Detective. I see those looks you give me. You can't judge me because of what Damien King did."

"Excuse me?" she snapped. Caprice was starting to regret telling him anything about her former lover.

"Come on, I was a detective. He's your ex-fiancé, you don't date, and he's calling you at work. He's the reason you won't give me a chance to be with you."

Caprice rolled her eyes. "Do we really have to go there? I mean, look at your own sins, Nathan." He threw his hands up. "Okay, if you don't want to talk about it, we don't have to."

"Good, because I don't," she said as she sat down at the table. "I said too much at the station."

"One day, you're going to want to talk about it."

"Yeah, when hell freezes over."

"I heard Satan's wearing a parka these days."

"You're so funny," she said sarcastically.

"Let's just order and talk about something else."

Caprice smiled and opened the menu. "You know what?" she said snapping the menu shut. "Damien has some nerve popping back into my life after what he put me through. If he thinks he can just come into town and pick up where we left off, he needs to forget it."

Knowing he was treading on deadly ground, Nathan quietly asked Caprice to explain why she and Damien broke up in the first place. "I went to his house and he was just finishing up with one of his many extracurricular activities. I gave him his ring back and moved to Charlotte."

"He cheated on you? What a fool."

Caprice rolled her eyes.

"Are you over it?" he asked.

"Been over it."

Nathan rolled his eyes. "Yeah, sure."

Her right eyebrow shot up. "What's that for?"

"If you were truly over him, you would be dating and having fun. You wouldn't look for a reason to distrust every man who wants to buy you dinner. Because of him, you think everybody is full of it until they prove you wrong."

"You're wrong, Sigmund. I don't date because I don't have time for the stress and drama that goes along with it. What's so hard to understand about that?"

Nathan looked at her and smiled.

"What are you looking at?" she asked.

"Nothing."

Caprice shot him a questioning look, but she decided to keep silent.

"Are you going to call him?" Nathan asked nonchalantly. His heart was beating in overdrive. *If you do talk to him, will you take him back?* he thought.

"You just can't let it go, can you?"

Nathan threw his hands up. "It's let go. But usually when a woman has this much hate for a man, they get back together." And leave a good man out in the cold, he added silently.

"There's no way, Damien King and I would ever get back together. I'd kill him or myself before falling for his crap again."

"If you say so," he said with a laugh.

Caprice rolled her eyes and waved for the waiter.

"Anyway, Nathan, you have your own drama to worry about."

He nodded and sipped on a glass of water. "That's true."

After Nathan and Caprice ordered lunch, they sat in silence.

CHAPTER SEVEN

Donovan Harris wrapped his hands around the cold steel bars of the holding cell. "Yo, officer! I need to make my phone call now."

"Pipe down, Harris," the guard replied.

"I know my rights. But that's okay, you're giving me grounds for an appeal."

The officer sucked his teeth, then walked over to the cell and opened it. "All right," he said as he cuffed Harris. "Make your call at this desk right here." Harris sat down and picked up the phone. He cradled the receiver between his shoulder and ear as he dialed.

"Ethan, it's me. I'm in jail. Yeah, that's what I said. I need you to check on something." Donovan's voice dropped to a whisper. "Get my arrest report, find out the name of the officer who arrested me, then get some dirt on her. Yeah, it's a her. I got to go. Make it quick and get here like yesterday."

The officer looked at Harris as he dropped the phone. "Call the shots now, Harris, because soon you're going to be in Central Prison. You're going down this time."

Harris smirked before the officer pushed him back into the holding cell.

About thirty minutes later, Ethan Washington walked into Harris's cell. Washington was one of the sleaziest defense attorneys in Charlotte. His client list included gang bangers, drug lords, and corporate raiders. Disbarment always loomed in the distance for him because he was usually in on the crimes. Ethan laundered money, helped dispose of murder weapons, and used his knowledge of the law to find the most outrageous loopholes to save the guilty from punishment.

"How did the police finally catch you?" he asked once the guard left them alone.

"There's a leak in my organization. How long will it take you to get me out of here?"

"Were you actually caught with all these drugs?" Ethan asked as he flipped though the three-page police report.

"That's not the point. I need to get out of here. And I need to get out now."

"This won't be easy. I'll have to see the case against you. Maybe there are some angles we can work."

"There better be, or I might have to tell someone about some of your sins. I'm not going down alone," Donovan hissed.

"It won't even come to that," Ethan said nervously.

Harris folded his arms across his chest and rolled his eyes at Ethan. "It better not."

"Who was the arresting officer?"

"Some bitch."

"Do you know her name, Donovan?"

"Nope. The last thing I was doing when she was putting cuffs on me was asking for a name and badge number," he replied sarcastically.

"Have you ever seen this officer before? Maybe we can prove there's a vendetta against you or something. It worked last year."

"Nah, I haven't seen her before."

"We'll figure something out."

"Look, I don't care how you do it, but you better get me out of here."

"All right. Let me get to work. When's your arraignment?"

"I don't know. I've only been in here two hours."

"All right, I'm going to find all of that out. I'll be in court when you get there."

Harris nodded as Ethan called for the guard to open the door.

Damien sat in the lobby of the Adam's Mark Hotel waiting for his potential investor. *This guy needs to hurry up,* he thought as he looked at the directions to Caprice's house on his laptop. *Gotta love the Internet.* Damien typed Caprice's number in a reverse directory. Her address and a map to her house were available to him with a few keystrokes.

"Mr. King," Charles Robinson said as he walked over to him.

"Mr. Robinson." The two men shook hands and walked into the hotel's bar. "Sorry I'm late. I got held up at some other meetings. So do you have the paperwork for the club?"

"I have them right here." Damien opened his briefcase and handed the financial projections to Charles.

He read over the figures and exhaled a long and slow breath. "This seems like a lot of money."

Damien sensed his apprehension. "I know Charlotte isn't Chicago, but I think this club will work here. The people I've talked to say they're tired of the same old hip-hop clubs. They're looking for something different. That's what I'm offering."

"Youngblood, for some reason, I think you can pull this off. I'm going to invest," he said as he pulled out his checkbook.

Damien grinned as he watched Charles write the check. *This is great. Now that business is taken care of, I can go see Caprice and take care of that, too.* Charles handed the check to Damien.

"I'll have my lawyer get the contracts to you by the end of the day," Damien said.

"All right." The two men stood up and shook hands again.

"It's going to be a pleasure doing business with you," Damien said.

"Yes, it is. I feel like we're going to make money hand over fist," Charles said.

When Charles left, Damien pulled out his cell phone and called Caprice's office.

"Detective Johnson."

"I'm glad you answered this time. Your partner is rather nosey."

"Damien, I don't have time for this," she snapped.

"Then let's talk over dinner tonight."

"I don't think so. Look, I'm working, and I'm hanging up on you again. Please don't call me back."

"Caprice, come on. After all the years we had together, you can't have at least one drink with me? I want to share my good news with you."

"Unless you're telling me you're going back to Chicago, there isn't any good news for you to share with me."

"Is it like that? Caprice, be honest. You want to see me as much as I want to see you."

"I don't want to see you at all, Damien! I was there for you so many times and you lied to me, cheated on me…I don't have time for this."

The dial tone sounded in Damien's ear. He looked at his phone before pressing the end button. *Who is she trying to fool? Caprice knows we do this dance all the time. She loves me, and we will be back together,* he thought as he stood up and walked out of the hotel.

Caprice left the district attorney's office feeling confident about the case against Harris. But in the back of her mind, Damien still lurked. *Why is this man still calling me? Can't he take a hint? I haven't talked to him in a year-and-a-half. What does he want from me?* She slid in the car and drove back to the station. Her shift was almost over. *I've got to change my phone number,* she thought as she pulled into the parking lot.

When she walked into the squad room, Nathan was sitting at her desk. "You don't have enough to do in your own division?" she asked.

"Ha ha, I'm off. I just wanted to see if you wanted to go have a drink."

"Everybody wants to get me drunk tonight," she mumbled.

"What was that?"

"Nothing. I'm really tired. I'm just going to go home and go straight to bed."

"Are you sure?"

"Yes. It's been a long day. I just want to put it behind me."

"All right," he said standing up. Nathan turned around and looked at Caprice. "Is everything okay with you?"

"Nathan, I'm fine."

"I didn't ask you how you looked. Are you still worried about Harris's threat?"

"No," she said rolling her eyes at him. "Let me sign off and you can walk me to my car."

"Then we can go have a drink, and I'm not taking no for an answer," he said as he walked to the door of the squad room.

Caprice groaned as she watched Nathan. Like Damien, she thought, he has no idea when to back off. Caprice walked over to Nathan and squeezed his cheek. "You're too much sometimes."

"I just want you to know," he said in a whisper, "I'm going to woo you."

Caprice stopped still and looked at him. She opened her mouth to say something, but Nathan put his finger to her lips. "There's nothing you can do to stop it either."

"Nathan, this isn't going to work."

"Because you won't even give it a chance. If this is about Damien King, forget him. I'm not that guy."

"I never said you were. Look, we shouldn't have this conversation here," she said looking around the squad room to make sure no one was eavesdropping.

"You're right. Let's get out of here."

The duo headed out to the parking lot.

Caprice hid her eyes from Nathan. She didn't want him to know that she wanted to melt in his arms. She couldn't afford to do that. What about his situation with Lisa? She might be carrying his child. She glanced at Nathan and his eyes seemed to cut through her soul. She prayed he couldn't see the desire growing inside of her. *I can't do this,* she thought as she looked at him. "Nathan, this isn't smart. We shouldn't try to date each other. Look at what you may be facing with Lisa."

Nathan grabbed Caprice's hand. "You're all that matters to me. Lisa doesn't even know if she's really pregnant. And if she is, I'll deal with it."

"But I don't want to deal with it. I care for you. But not in that way. Don't want to risk my heart again. And until you know what's what with Lisa, I'm not going to—"

Unable to resist the temptation of her lips, Nathan leaned in and kissed Caprice with a fiery passion. She tried to fight it, but within seconds she was dizzy with desire. Time stood still in the parking lot. It didn't matter that someone could see them, or that she was afraid to trust in love again. Caprice wrapped her arms around Nathan and received his kiss. She savored the sweetness of his tongue as it probed the depths of her mouth seemingly searching for her soul. But in an instant, Caprice was back in the real world and she pulled away from him. She didn't say a word as she dashed to her car and sped off. Nathan stood in the parking lot, watching Caprice drive away with a satisfied smile on his face.

Caprice walked into her house and tried to rid herself of the memory of Nathan's kiss. She was shaken to the core, because she liked it so much. *Pull yourself together,* she thought. *This is not supposed to happen.* She took a deep breath then walked over to her answering machine. When she pressed play, Damien's voice pierced the silence in her kitchen.

"I know you're probably at home listening to this message. Caprice, I miss you, and I want to talk. All we have to do is talk. I know I have a lot to atone for. Give me a chance."

She hit the erase button. The next message started playing. It was Damien again. Caprice didn't let it play for longer than a second before she erased it. *This is going to stop,* she thought as she pulled the piece of paper with

Damien's number on it from her pocket. She picked up the phone and dialed his number.

"Damien King."

"Stop leaving me messages."

"Caprice, I was wondering when you were going to call," he said.

"You're really working on my last nerve, do you know that?"

"All I want is to see you. Is that too much to ask?"

"Why do you want to see me?"

"Because I still love you. I love you with all my heart and soul."

"Damien, do you know what love is? Love is being faithful, which you never were."

"Baby, I know I hurt you, and I was wrong for doing some of the things I did."

"Some? That's a joke, right? Damien, I loved you with everything I had in me. All you ever did was lie to me over and over again. I didn't deserve it then, and I don't now. I'm not letting you back into my life, because you feel the need to be here."

"I want to show you that I've changed. Why do you think I came here? I could've opened a club anywhere. Charlotte isn't known for its nightlife. This last year has been hell without you."

"Yeah, well life was hell with you!"

"Just let me see you one time, and if you feel the same way after we have drinks, I'll leave you alone." *I must be the stupidest woman in the world,* Caprice thought as she agreed to meet him for a drink. "Let's meet at the Adam's Mark in an hour. If you're not there, then you'll never see me again."

"I'll be in the bar in an hour watching the door."

Caprice hung up the phone. She didn't want to admit it, but she wanted to see Damien. Maybe if she had closure with him, she could move on with Nathan. Or was this going to send her back down Heartbreak Lane?

CHAPTER EIGHT

Nathan picked up the phone and dialed Caprice's number. He hung up before the phone rang. *Why am I doing this to myself?* he thought. *Caprice needs to make the next move. And that isn't going to happen until she faces her demons.* His phone rang. He hoped it was Caprice calling him back because his number showed up on her caller ID. "Hello."

"Nathan, it's Lisa."

"I've been meaning to call you," he said with a sigh. "We need to talk."

"I see that you haven't. But that's neither here nor there." They both fell silent. Minutes ticked away without either of them saying a word.

"Why did you call, Lisa?" he asked, breaking the uncomfortable silence between them.

She sighed heavily. "To make a confession."

"What? What's this all about? I really don't have time for games, Lisa."

"I feel like such a fool," she began. "Nathan, I really care about you and I wanted to be with you, but I know that this isn't the way to do it."

"Can you please get to the point?"

"I'm not pregnant. I never was. I made up that story hoping it would bring us closer." Nathan's mouth dropped open.

"That's beyond sick, Lisa. Why would you do such a thing?"

"I told you, I wanted to be with you. I knew the truth would come out, but…"

"Lisa, this was a stupid stunt. You played a game with my life and made yourself look like a fool."

"I'm sorry." She began to cry. "I just know you're the man I wanted to love. I knew, in time, you'd grow to love me, too."

"You need help, and I hope you get it," Nathan snapped.

"Can we at least be friends?"

"No, friends are people you can trust."

"Please, Nathan."

"Goodbye, Lisa." He hung up the phone and shook his head. *Unbelievable! What the hell is wrong with that woman?* he thought as he walked in the kitchen to grab a beer.

A light bulb went off in his head. Now he had a clear shot at Caprice. There was no baby and no baggage. The only thing that was going to stop him from being with Caprice would be her.

Caprice walked into the Adam's Mark and spotted Damien as he walked toward her. She inhaled sharply. God, he still looks good, she thought. She drank in his image, the way his ivory Armani suit hugged his toned body, his wavy hair, his gray eyes, and his big manicured hands. Those hands used to caress her body and make her feel like a real woman. She remembered grabbing his hands in the throes of passion. She sighed and turned away from him.

"Caprice, you look wonderful," he said as he attempted to hug her. She stepped back. His cologne was intoxicating, like a fine French liqueur.

"Too bad you don't," she mumbled. *He has to know I'm lying,* she thought. Her heart was beating ten thousand times a minute. "I don't have all night. Let's get this over with." Caprice tried to use the forceful voice that rattled drug suspects.

Damien smiled. Caprice rolled her eyes. "Well, let's go in the bar," he said.

She walked two steps in front of Damien and the two found a pair of seats at the bar. "You have five minutes," she said turning to him.

"Come on, Caprice. I thought you were giving me a chance."

"Damien, say whatever you have to say. I'm not here to revive the past."

"Let's have a drink and a toast first," he said as he waved for the bartender. "I got the money for the club, so I'm here to stay."

"Is that it?" Caprice grabbed her purse and was poised to hop off the barstool.

"Just one more thing. I love you."

"Empty words, Damien."

"I know I hurt you."

"That you did, over and over again."

"Will you stop interrupting me, please?" he said with a flash of annoyance in his voice.

Caprice folded her arms across her chest and arched her right eyebrow. Anger flickered like flames in her eyes. Damien ignored her evil look and continued talking.

"I came to Charlotte because I want to make up for all of the pain and heartache I caused you. Caprice, I was weak, childish, and ignorant." She snorted, but held her tongue. *He has some damned nerve,* she thought. *He still thinks I'm a fool and believes everything he says.* "Please tell me that I'm not wasting my time. Do you still love me as much as I love you?" he asked. Caprice glared at him angrily. Did he think it would be that easy to worm his way back into her life?

"Damien, it took me a long time to realize that all the love in the world won't make us happy together. You have no self-control. No matter how much you say you love me, the fact remains that you're a piece of garbage. Matter of fact, you're lower than garbage. You broke my heart so many times I don't think I'll ever be the same. I hate you, Damien King. I hate what you did to me over and over again. How many lies did you tell me? How many times did you bring other women into our bed? You made a fool of me, and I'm tired of being a fool for you."

"We've worked our problems out before. We can do it again. Caprice, I know you love me. You can't deny that."

Caprice laughed. "Our problem was your wayward dick! Have you changed that? Do you have a special lock on it now?"

Damien shook his head. "I see this isn't going the way I hoped it would."

"What did you think was going to happen? Did you think a few sweet and tender words would have me falling all over you? Did you think you could smile, apologize, and all would be forgiven? You need to think again."

"Caprice, I need you in my life."

"You had me in your life, and you threw me away. You can't have me when you want me. It doesn't work that way." Caprice stood up.

Damien grabbed her arm. "Please, don't leave me again. I'm sorry."

With her free hand, she grabbed a half-empty bottle of beer and tossed its contents in Damien's face. "Go to hell!" she shouted vehemently. Caprice stormed out of the bar.

"She just left here. She was with some guy. They argued and she tossed a beer in his face. Yes, he's still sitting at the bar. Sure, I think I can swing that. I want cash. Oh, I get results, Ethan." The woman snapped her cell phone shut and stood up. She was a towering six feet tall. Her shoulder-length auburn hair was pulled behind her ears, revealing an oval-shaped face with cold black eyes. She was dressed in a turquoise spandex dress that left little to the imagination. She walked with a bounce that caused her breasts and hips to jiggle. She walked over to Damien as he wiped his face with the bar towel.

"Hardly the place for a shower," she said in a throaty whisper.

"Excuse me?"

"You're all wet."

"Yeah," Damien said as he tossed the towel on the bar. "All wet."

"What a shame," she said with a sly smile. "I'm Sabrina." She extended her well-manicured hand to him.

"Damien," he replied as he shook her hand.

"I noticed you when you walked in."

"Really?"

"Was that your wife?"

Damien laughed. "No."

"Where is your wife?"

"Are you flirting with me?"

"I must not be doing a good job if you have to ask."

Damien smiled again. "You're doing a great job. Can I buy you a drink?"

"Only if we can have it in your room." She licked her lips and grabbed Damien's knee. "I'm so attracted to you."

Damien's ego didn't let him see the red flags about this woman. How did she know he had a room at the hotel? He was too blind to see the evil gleam in her eyes. He ordered a two-hundred-dollar bottle of champagne and escorted Sabrina to his room.

Caprice drove around aimlessly, her path muddled. First she drove down the residential streets. Then she made her way uptown. She passed the skyscrapers, not paying any attention to the silver, shimmering lights. She headed south, barely noticing traffic signals. Luckily, all the lights were green. Caprice drove by Nathan's house and started to stop. Maybe he could help her understand what was going on. *No,* she thought. *Nathan will just tell me to get over it. And I don't want to hear that right now.* She sped up. Caprice turned toward Interstate 77 and drove until she ended up in Rock Hill, South Carolina. Caprice stopped at the first Waffle House she saw off the interstate.

She walked into the half-empty restaurant and sat at the formica bar. Its sticky surface didn't bother her tonight, nor did the smell of the bleach water used to clean the dishes.

"What can I get for you, sugah?" an older waitress asked.

"Black coffee." Her voice was barely above a whisper.

"Rough night?"

"You could say that."

"You too pretty to be sittin' in here frownin' like dat."

Caprice wanted to smile at the old woman, but she couldn't.

"I'll leave you be," she said, noting the deep scowl on Caprice's face.

She nodded and took the coffee mug from the woman. She sipped the hot liquid. She dropped five dollars on the counter to cover her coffee and a tip for the waitress. Caprice headed back to Charlotte after three cups of coffee. As she drove home, her mind was still focused on Damien and the conversation they had at the bar. *I need to forget about that idiot. He isn't worth this, and I have to go to work in the morning.*

When she walked into her house, Caprice expected her answering machine to be filled with messages from Damien, but it wasn't. She smiled. *Maybe I got through to him after all,* she thought as she took her clothes off and fell into bed. *Things are starting to look up.*

Sabrina looked at Damien as he drifted off to sleep. Does he really think he did something? she thought as he snored loudly. She slid out of the bed and dressed quickly. She looked around the room, making sure she didn't leave anything that could be traced back to her. Sabrina grabbed a towel from the bathroom and wiped down everything she touched. Then she grabbed the phone from the nightstand and pulled it into the bathroom.

"This is Caprice Johnson. I need a wake up call at 3 a.m.," she said. "Thank you."

She hung up the phone, careful to wipe it and the nightstand of her fingerprints and walked over to the bed. Sabrina reached into her purse and pulled out Caprice's business card, then dropped it between the nightstand and the bed. Damien stirred slightly in the bed. Sabrina reached into her purse and pulled out the police-issued Beretta that Donovan had delivered to her.

Damien coughed and sat up in the bed. "Sabrina, where are you?" he asked. She stepped out of the shadows and stood at the foot of the bed. "Say goodbye," Sabrina said as she adjusted the silencer on the gun.

"What…what is this all about?"

"It's about you dying," she said before unloading the clip into his chest. Damien gasped one time before falling dead. Blood poured from his chest and stained the crisp white bed sheets. Sabrina wiped her prints from the gun with the edge of the blanket and then threw it beside Damien's corpse. *Now,* she thought, *I have to get into this detective's house and get her gun.* She opened the sliding glass door and jumped off the second-floor balcony, landing on her feet like a cat. A cool wind blew as she ran to her car. When she got to her car, she called Ethan Washington.

"Washington."

"All right, Ethan, I killed that guy. Who did you say he was again?"

"The detective's ex-fiancé. Ron said she's been home for about an hour, and he thinks she's sleeping. He said her gun's in a desk drawer in the den. The den is on the east side of the house. He opened a window for you."

"I can't believe I'm breaking into a cop's house. Are you sure this plan is going to work?"

"Look, I'm just following Donovan's orders. As long as you don't get caught, everything should work out. This will discredit the detective and keep her from testifying against Donovan."

"All right, give me her address."

"Sabrina, you know if you're caught, you're on your own."

"Trust me, I won't get caught. Why do you think Donovan pays me the big bucks?" Ethan gave her directions to Caprice's house, then she sped out of the parking lot.

CHAPTER NINE

Lydia, the second-floor housekeeper, walked past Room 235 about six times before she decided to check and see if someone was still inside. The do-not-disturb sign hung on the doorknob, but she was ready to finish this floor and go on break. She knocked on the door twice before opening it with her pass key.

"Hello, sir," she whispered when she noticed a figure in the bed. "Sir, do you want your room cleaned today?"

When she didn't get a response, Lydia walked closer to the bed. She looked down at the floor and saw the drying blood. Frantic, she turned the lamp on and screamed. Two of the other housekeepers ran into the room. "Call the manager and the police," she screamed.

Other guests opened their doors trying to find out what all of the commotion was about. Most of them peeked out from behind the doors then went back inside when they saw the housekeepers running down the hall. The guests never dreamed there was a dead man a few doors away from them. That's until the uniformed police officers came upstairs.

Murmurs of "what's going on" rippled through the hallways as the officers began putting yellow tape over the door. Detective Kevin Harrington walked into the room, pushing the tape back. "What do we have here?" Harrington asked.

"The maid found this guy shot to death this morning," a uniformed officer said.

"Is the M.E. here?"

The officer shook his head no.

Harrington exhaled loudly.

"Anything strange in the room?" The officer grinned, but shook his head. "I did find Detective Johnson's card near the nightstand."

"Really?" Harrington frowned and the wheels inside his head started spinning. "Does this look like a bad drug deal?"

The officer shook his head. "There's no evidence of drugs in here."

"Was there any ID on the stiff?" he asked the officer.

"A Chicago driver's license. Damien King."

"Get Detective Johnson over here. I want to see if she knows why this guy had her card." Another uniformed officer ran over to Harrington. "Looks like we have the murder weapon, and it's one of ours."

"What do you mean?"

The officer held up the plastic evidence bag. "This is a standard-issue Beretta."

"Let me see that," Harrington said as he took the bag from the officer. "I'll be damned. Get Johnson here now!"

Nathan followed Michael Smith into the Adam's Mark Hotel. "What was the call again?" Nathan asked.

Smith sighed and rolled his eyes. "Homicide."

Nathan nodded. He had been on patrol with Smith since 6 a.m. This was the first actual call they had taken, and it was nearly 10 a.m. Smith was on his Ps and Qs but inside Nathan knew he was steamed.

You just better not say it, buddy, Nathan thought as their eyes locked. "Any idea who the victim is up there?" Nathan asked as they walked over to the elevator.

"Some tourist, I think."

"You don't like this, do you?"

"Having some IAD insider second-guess my every move, oh I love it" Smith replied.

"What did you think was going to happen when you kept beating the shit out of suspects?"

"When's the last time you walked a beat? These animals spit in my face, curse me, and threaten me. I have to defend myself."

"Then you must be a sorry-ass officer if you have to defend yourself against a fourteen-year-old."

Smith rolled his eyes at Nathan. "So, that's what this is all about? He shouldn't have gotten out of the car."

"And you shouldn't have hit him! Is this how you deal with all your problems?"

"I'm good at my job. But I'll be damned if I'm going to let one of these nig—"

"You need to watch your fucking mouth!" Nathan was fuming.

"Damn, IAD's here already? Can we get a medical examiner here?" Harrington bellowed when he saw Nathan enter the hotel room.

"Why would IAD be needed on the scene of a homicide?" Nathan asked.

"A police officer might be involved," he replied.

"Who's the dead guy?" Nathan asked, shifting his attention to this case and away from Smith. This was the first time in years there had been a police shooting. Wait a minute, he said a police officer might be involved, he thought.

"Some guy from Chicago named Damien King," Harrington said, looking down at his note.

For a second, Nathan stopped breathing. Damien King? Caprice's ex-fiancé? Harrington did say that a police officer might be involved. She did say she hated him. She said she wanted to kill him. *No no, she wouldn't,* he thought. *He could've pissed somebody off, and they could've killed him. He did have one of these infuriating personalities.*

"What's that look?" Harrington asked him.

"Why do you think a cop had anything to do with this?"

Smith walked into the room and started talking to the other officers. Harrington inhaled sharply and looked at Nathan. He knew Nathan and Caprice were extremely close, but the truth is the truth. "It might be Detective Johnson."

"What?"

"I found her card at the scene, and the weapon used was a Beretta, just like this one," he said parting his hip. "And she's originally from Chicago, right?"

"But she wouldn't risk her career like this."

"I'm just going where the evidence takes me. Right now, I need to talk to Johnson. Maybe it's best for you to leave this crime scene."

"I'm just here to observe Officer Smith," Nathan replied. It would've taken a pack of wild horses, dogs, and boars to move him from that hotel. He had to see if there was anything linking Caprice to this murder.

Caprice ransacked her den looking for her gun. *This is weird,* she thought as she dumped the contents of her desk drawer on the floor. *I know I put my gun in this drawer last night.*

Her phone rang. "What?" she said snatching the phone off the hook.

"Detective Johnson, this is Officer Carter."

"What is it?"

"We need you at a crime scene."

"I really can't come right now," she said. "What's the problem?"

"There was a shooting at the Adam's Mark…"

"I'm not in major crimes. Why are you calling me?" she asked, interrupting him. Caprice continued to look for her gun as she juggled the phone between her ear and shoulder.

"Detective, you need to come here and answer some questions."

"Why do you need me? Is it one of my informants?"

"The victim had one of your cards in his room."

Caprice furrowed her brows. She didn't know anyone who could afford a room there. The only other person she knew staying at the Adam's Mark was Damien. *But Damien didn't have my card,* she thought. "Fine, I'll be there as soon as I can."

"Capt. Leland said get here now."

Shit! Caprice thought. "Fine," she said then hung up the phone. She grabbed her jacket and empty gun holster then headed to the hotel.

When Caprice got there, she saw two news trucks, five marked police cars, and a couple of detectives' vehicles parked in the front. She was taken aback by the number of people at the scene.

"Detective," Officer Carter called when he spotted her as she walked in.

"This looks big."

He shrugged his shoulders. "Follow me."

Caprice walked behind him. "Carter, what's going on?"

"You need to talk to your captain," he said flatly.

"Is this a drug deal gone bad?"

Carter didn't answer. He pressed the up button on the elevator.

"Are you at least going to tell me the particulars about this case?" she demanded as they stepped on the elevator. "I have other things to do."

"I was told to let you speak to your captain. I can't tell you anything."

"What in the hell is going on?"

"Leland can answer your questions."

The doors opened and they stepped off the elevator. Leland met Caprice before she took two steps toward the crime scene. "We need to talk," he said through tight lips.

"What's going on?" She knotted her brows as she looked at him.

"I need to see your gun."

"I—I don't have it. I couldn't find it this morning when I was getting ready for my shift. I was planning on reporting it as soon as I got to the station."

"Do you know Damien King?"

"Yes."

"How?"

"We know each other from Chicago."

"You knew each other. King's dead."

"What?" Caprice's bottom lip quivered.

"Shot ten times."

Caprice inhaled sharply. "He's dead?"

"Yeah. Do you have any idea why he would have one of your cards? When was the last time you saw him?"

"He didn't. At least I didn't give him one. Urn, I saw him last night in the bar."

"What was your relationship with him?"

"It was a personal relationship," she said, not wanting to answer the question. She knew what Leland was doing. He was trying to see if she had a motive. That answer wouldn't fly, and she knew it when she looked at the frown on his face.

Leland shook his head. "Johnson, I need specifics and now."

"He's my ex-fiancé. We broke up before I moved here."

"Were you two on speaking terms? Why was he in Charlotte?"

"He told me he was opening a jazz club, and no, we weren't on good terms."

"Why did you see him last night?"

"Am I a suspect?"

"Where's your gun, Detective?"

"I don't know," she said frantically. "But I didn't use it to kill anybody."

"What time did you get home last night?"

"After midnight. I went to Rock Hill."

"Why?"

Caprice closed her eyes and ran her hand across her forehead. "I needed to clear my head, so I started driving. I stopped at the Waffle House and got some coffee."

"And you were alone?"

"Yes. Captain Leland, you have to know I don't have anything to do with this."

"Captain," Harrington said when he stepped off the elevator. "I need to talk to you."

The two men walked down the hall and spoke in a quiet whisper. This can't be happening, Caprice thought as she watched the men talk. She couldn't hear what they were saying, but the conversation looked intense.

"Caprice," Nathan said as he walked up behind her.

She turned around and looked at him. "Nathan, what's going on here?"

He shook his head. "Caprice, he was shot with a police-issue gun."

"Why? Why would anyone want to shoot Damien?"

"Who else knew him in Charlotte besides you?"

Caprice stepped back from Nathan. "Is this an official questioning?"

"No," he replied. "I'm trying to help you."

"Sure." She rolled her eyes and folded her arms across her chest.

"Caprice, come on, you know I have your back."

"All I know is that you're IAD now."

Nathan grabbed her arm. "I would never sell you out. I know you didn't do this."

Caprice searched his eyes. Was he telling the truth? Did he believe her? Could she trust him? His eyes told her that she could. "What am I going to do?" she whispered. "Somebody is out to get me, and they're doing a good job. They think I did it." She motioned towards Leland and Harrington.

"Who?"

"I don't know. All I know is, I didn't kill Damien."

Captain Leland walked over to Caprice and Nathan. "Detective, I need your shield," he said somberly.

"What?" Caprice said. Never had she been in trouble on her job. Caprice was good at what she did and she didn't make any mistakes. There was no way in hell she could just hand her shield over. It meant everything to her.

"You're on administrative leave until this investigation is concluded."

Caprice gasped. "This is bullshit," she exclaimed.

"Detective, watch your mouth," Leland said.

Caprice threw her badge at him and stormed out of the hotel.

Nathan turned to Leland. "This doesn't look good for her, does it?" he asked.

Leland shook his head. "Her gun's missing. The guy was shot with a police-issue weapon and he was her ex-fiancé. What do you think?"

Nathan masked his shock by walking away. He didn't know Caprice's gun was missing. *Why did she keep that from me?* Was there a chance that she did it?

CHAPTER TEN

Donovan sat in the courtroom dressed in an orange Mecklenburg County Jail jumpsuit. He was pissed because he had to spend the night in jail. *Why do I pay Ethan?* he thought as he brooded in the corner. *He should've gotten me out yesterday.*

Assistant District Attorney Carole Young began calling cases. Ethan walked in and waved to Donovan. *I wonder if everything worked out last night? That detective should be feeling the pinch,* Donovan thought. He smiled when the ADA called his name.

"Your honor, we request that the defendant be held without bond," Carole said. "Donovan Harris is a known drug dealer who has the means and connections to flee prosecution."

"Your honor," Ethan interrupted. "I'm going to object to the characterization of my client. Mr. Harris has never been convicted of any drug-related offense. I subscribe to the U.S. Constitution, innocent until proven guilty."

"Mr. Washington, save the grandstanding; there isn't a jury in sight," the judge warned.

Carole rolled her eyes. "Your honor," she continued, "Charlotte-Mecklenburg Police have been investigating Mr. Harris for nearly three years. Convicted or not, we have solid information that Harris is indeed a drug dealer and could flee our jurisdiction if he's allowed to post bail."

"Ms. Young," the judge said. "I can't make judgments based on unproven allegations. The motion is denied, and bond is set in the amount of $10,000."

"Your honor, my client's ready to post bond," Ethan said.

"Pay the clerk," he said then banged his gavel and called for the next case.

Ethan walked behind Carole. "Better luck next time, counselor," he said snidely.

"Bite me, you sleazy worm," she replied before returning to the state's table. Less than an hour later, Donovan and Ethan were sitting at a corner table in Starbuck's sipping mocha lattes.

"So, did it go down?" Donovan asked.

Ethan nodded. "Without a hitch. Your connection in Chicago came through. He said the detective left the city after she broke up with that guy. He came here to open a jazz club. Sabrina said they were together in the bar last night and had an argument."

"I couldn't have scripted it better myself." Donovan grinned like a Cheshire cat. "Detective Johnson's going to be so caught up in defending herself, she isn't going to look credible to any jury. The DA would be a fool to call her as a witness."

"I hope the bitch gets convicted," Donovan spat.

"If Sabrina is as good as she says, Detective Johnson could be looking at a prison term."

Donovan smiled and took a sip of his coffee. "That's what I'm talking about," he said with a satisfied nod.

Caprice sat in her car and tried to wrap her mind around what was happening to her. Who would want to kill Damien and why? *Wait,* she thought as she squeezed the steering wheel, *this isn't about Damien. Someone's out to get me.* Her hands shook as she felt hot tears of anger forming in her eyes. She knew this was Donovan's handiwork.

Caprice remembered his threat. How could she prove it? She had seen enough murder investigations to know that she looked good as the perpetrator. She had the motive and the means. If she had been the lead on this case, she would have thought she was the killer as well.

Caprice started the car and drove home. Within a day, her problems shifted from worrying about Damien calling her to being accused of his murder. She pulled into her driveway, looking around for a reporter or a cameraman. She knew the media would descend on the story like vultures. *Damn,* Caprice thought. *What am I going to do?*

Nathan sat at his desk trying to type his report on Officer Smith, but his mind was filled with questions about Caprice. He pushed his chair back from the computer and ran his hands across his face. Nathan leaned his head back and closed his eyes. *I know she wouldn't, couldn't do this. There's no*

way in hell she'd kill someone and leave all of that evidence behind, he thought.

Then he remembered how venomously she spoke about Damien King. Maybe in the heat of passion, it didn't matter that she was a cop. *Damn it Caprice! I have to know you didn't do this.*

"Inspector," Major Chaney said, "it seems as if all the people in your life are causing you nothing but trouble."

"Meaning?"

"Detective Johnson is a suspect in a homicide."

"And?"

"I know the bond between partners. You two are close. She's probably like family to you."

"Major, I'm going to be honest; I have a hard time believing Caprice did this."

"That's why I don't want you anywhere near this case. Your objectivity is shot to hell. We can't afford to have even a semblance of impropriety."

"Okay," he lied. Nathan knew he was going to get involved in this case. He had to. There was no way he'd watch the woman he loved go down for a crime she couldn't have committed. One way or another, he was going to find out the truth. But could he handle the truth if Caprice was the killer?

"I mean it. If I hear about you doing anything concerning this case, looking at a report or asking Harrington about the direction of this case or anything, you will be suspended or out on the unemployment line."

Nathan nodded. "I understand."

"And it would be best if you stayed away from Detective Johnson."

"Major, Caprice and I are friends."

"I know, but we can't have any involvement with her because this division is going to have to investigate the shooting as well. There can't be any questions about our cred- ibility." Nathan started to say something in defense of Caprice and their friendship, but he held his tongue.

Chaney looked at him, seemingly reading Nathan's mind. "Make sure whatever you do off the clock doesn't cost you your job," he warned.

"Yes, sir," Nathan replied.

"How's the Smith report coming?"

"I think I need a little more time with him before I can file a complete report."

Chaney nodded. "All right, just remember what I said about Detective Johnson." When Nathan was alone, he thought about how he was going to find out information about Caprice's case without anyone knowing it.

His phone rang. "Wallace," he said.

"Nathan, it's Kevin."

"I can't talk to you."

"I know, but I also know you want to. So, let's have a drink tonight."

"How do I know this isn't a set-up?" Nathan asked.

"Because I have too much respect for you to do that. Nathan, I don't want you to risk your career over this. It looks like she may have done it."

"I'll talk to you tonight," he said. Nathan didn't believe a word Kevin was saying about Caprice killing Damien.

"All right."

Nathan hung up. Questions buzzed through his mind like hummingbirds. What if she was set up? But by whom? How would someone know about her past with Damien? Nathan turned away from the computer and looked out the window.

Sabrina walked into the police station dressed in a Federal Express uniform.

"Can I help you?" the receptionist asked.

"I have a delivery for Detective Caprice Johnson."

"I'll take it."

Sabrina shook her head. "This has to go directly to her. It's classified information."

The receptionist looked at her and sucked her teeth. "That's not our policy here. When are you people going to learn? I have to sign it in and open it before it goes upstairs."

This isn't going according to plan, Sabrina thought as she turned away from the receptionist. "Well, I have to check with my boss to see if it's okay." Sabrina walked out of the police station. Her plan was to get into the evidence room and switch the guns. She got back into her car and headed over to Donovan's house. *You know what, he doesn't pay me enough for this shit,* she thought. *I'm done with this. If I get caught in the evidence room, I'm toast, and I know Donovan won't bail me out.*

When she got to Donovan's home, Ethan was there. She shook her head when she saw his Lexus parked in the driveway. Somebody's slumming again, she thought as she walked up to the front door and rang the bell.

"It's about time you got here," Donovan said when he opened the door. "Did you get in the evidence room?"

"This isn't a movie. It's not like I can just walk in there and switch the guns."

"You'd better find a way."

"No," she hissed. "This is too risky. I'm not sticking my neck out for you anymore."

Donovan got in Sabrina's face and glared at her. "Did you say 'no' to me?"

"Yeah, I did."

Ethan stood up and walked over to them in an effort to calm the situation. "Donovan, we don't need to go that far. The fact that a police gun was used and Detective Johnson's gun is missing gives the DA enough to charge her."

Donovan nodded and stepped away from Sabrina. "Give me the gun," he ordered. She handed him the box. He ripped it open and held the gun in his right hand. "Is it loaded?"

Sabrina turned her back to Donovan and headed for the door. "What do you think?" she asked with annoyance in her voice. He pulled the trigger, shooting Sabrina once in the back. She fell to her knees.

"What did you do?" Ethan shrieked.

"No one tells me 'no.' Besides, she's outlived her usefulness. Remember that, everyone is expendable, even you. So, you'd better make sure I don't spend another day in jail."

"Is that a threat?"

Donovan shrugged him off. Then he looked at Sabrina's body. "Is she dead?"

Ethan glanced at her. She didn't seem to be breathing. "I think so."

"Take care of that. I'm going to dump this gun." Donovan tucked the weapon in his waistband and headed out the door.

Ethan kneeled over Sabrina and felt for a pulse. "She's gone," he whispered as he dropped her arm. Ethan dragged her body down to the basement, leaving a scarlet trail behind him. Once he got to the basement, he wrapped her body in a blue tarp. *Someone else will have to dispose of her body, because I've done enough of Donovan Harris's blood work. He's out of control,* Ethan thought as he watched Sabrina's body twitch.

Donovan drove the speed limit for the first time in his life. He didn't want to give a cop any excuse to pull him over. He had to get rid of the gun. He drove north on Interstate 77 heading toward Lake Cornelius. He exited then drove over to a boat ramp. He parked his car and stepped out. For a warm, mid-autumn afternoon, the lake was empty. Donovan smiled as he pulled the gun out of his waistband. He tossed it in the water, where it quickly sank. *Now,* Donovan thought, *We'll see what kind of case they have against me.* He whistled softly as he walked to his car.

Kevin and Nathan sat at a corner table in Champion's Sports Bar. Kevin lit a cigarette and waited for the waitress to take their orders.

"So, what's up?" Nathan asked. "Why do you think Caprice did this?"

"Because that's where the evidence is taking me. With her gun missing, it doesn't look good."

"What if she's being set up?"

Kevin looked at Nathan with an expression of disbelief. "By whom? Mind you, if someone is setting her up, they would have to know her from Chicago."

"Maybe it's someone she's arrested before? It doesn't take much these days to find out a person's life history."

"The only person I can think of who would have the balls to do this is Donovan Harris. But he was in jail last night, so that rules him out."

"All he had to do was make a phone call. You know how deep his network runs."

"Do you really think he would have made that phone call from the police station? All suspect calls are monitored," Kevin said.

"Have you checked into it?"

"You're grasping at straws, man," Kevin said. "I know it's hard to believe that a fellow officer and your former partner would do this, but facts are facts. That man was her ex and he probably did something bad to piss her off and she snapped."

"Have charges been filed?"

Kevin shook his head. "They should be in the morning."

"You know, this is going to ruin her career."

"I know, but we have to treat this like any other case. A man is dead."

"That's easy for you to say," Nathan mumbled.

The waitress came to the table and sat a platter of steaming hot wings and clams in front of the two men. Nathan barely touched what was usually his favorite food, but Kevin chomped down the wings and clams. Nathan wanted to say something to spark Kevin to look for some other evidence that would clear Caprice, but no words formed in his head.

"I got to get out of here and finish up the report. I'll slip a copy to you," Kevin said as he wiped grease and red-hot sauce from his lips.

"Thanks, Kev," Nathan said as he stood up. "Wait, how do you know that gun is Caprice's when there weren't any prints on it?"

Kevin scowled at Nathan. "We have motive. We have opportunity. She was there. Eyewitnesses can attest to your classic crime of passion."

"Circumstantial evidence."

"I know you believe in her because she was your partner, but Nathan, if this was any other case, you'd be saying 'great collar'. Maybe the less you know the better." Kevin stormed out of the restaurant.

Nathan pulled out his cell phone and called Caprice.

"Hello?"

"Caprice, it's Nathan."

"Hi."

"You okay?"

"My career's on the line, I'm suspended, and I'm a suspect in a murder. How do you think I'm doing?"

"All right, it was a stupid question. Do you need anything? Have you had dinner?"

"You know what I need? I need the proof that I didn't do this. Nathan, are you really going to help me?"

"Yes. Caprice, I believe you. I know you didn't kill Damien."

"Then you have to help me find my gun. Someone must have broken into my house last night and stolen it."

"I'm coming over there so we can talk and look for evidence of a break-in."

"Nathan, you can't do that. What about your career?" she said.

"It doesn't matter," he said. "I'll be right there."

"All right," she sighed.

Nathan sped over to Caprice's house, where she was sitting on the porch waiting for him. He could tell from the look in her eyes that she was scared. Nathan walked up to her and pulled her into his arms. "Everything is going to be all right. We're going to clear your name."

"I wish I could believe that," she said as she melted in his embrace. She needed to be reassured and comforted. Nathan rubbed her back. He squeezed her tightly and gently brushed his lips across her neck.

She pulled away from him as if a bee had stung her. "Don't do that," she whispered.

"I'm sorry." Nathan grabbed her chin and looked deep into her eyes. "Caprice, I have to ask you this. Did you kill Damien?"

"No. Nathan, I didn't."

"I had to ask."

She nodded. "I have to find my gun."

"The case against you is circumstantial at best," Nathan said. "I talked to Kevin before I came over here. They're hanging everything on the fact that your gun's missing."

Caprice trudged over to the edge of the porch. "Look, right here, a footprint in my flower bed."

"A man's footprint."

"That window leads into the study where I keep my gun at night."

Nathan leaned over and studied the windowpane. "Is this removable?" he asked.

"Yeah, I think so." Nathan jumped off the porch and looked at the window. He pulled a handkerchief from his pocket and yanked at the pane. It came off easily. "I'm going to take this to the lab and have it analyzed."

"How are you going to do that without getting in trouble?" she asked. "I know you've been forbidden to get involved in this case."

"Some people owe me favors."

Caprice looked at Nathan. "I don't want you risking your career for me."

Nathan set the pane on the porch. "I told you I had your back. Keep looking for your gun, okay. I'll be back tonight."

"Be careful," she cautioned as Nathan headed to his car.

CHAPTER ELEVEN

The shrill ringing of the phone broke the tense silence in Caprice's house, startling her. She had gotten used to the quiet. It gave her time to reflect on her life. What would she do if she wasn't a police officer? Law enforcement had been her dream since she was a seven-year-old growing up in Chicago. She was glad her father didn't have to see her career being flushed down the toilet. He would be so disappointed. But Caprice didn't do anything; he would believe in her. She needed someone to believe in her. Was it Nathan? Was he really on her side? Caprice picked up the phone, hoping it was Nathan with some good news or someone calling to say "April Fool."

"Hello?"

"Is this Detective Caprice Johnson?" a female voice asked.

"Yes. Who is this?"

"This is Sharon Lewis. I'm a reporter with the *Charlotte Observer*. I'm calling about a shooting at the Adam's Mark Hotel. I have sources at the police department that say you're the prime suspect in the shooting."

"Excuse me?"

"Are you a suspect in the shooting of Damien King?"

"No comment." Caprice slammed the phone down. She dropped her head in her hands and cried. The phone rang again. "Hello?"

"Caprice Johnson?"

"No!"

"Detective, we're doing this story with or without your comment. You might as well tell your side." She slammed the phone down again.

The doorbell rang. Caprice opened the door and flash-bulbs momentarily blinded her. "Detective Johnson, have you been charged in the Adam's Mark shooting?" a reporter asked.

"Detective Johnson, how did you know Damien King?" another one asked.

"Get off my property. Leave me alone!" she screamed. "Leave me alone!"

"Detective Johnson, did you shoot him?"

"Get off my property before I call the pol…" She couldn't bring herself to complete the threat. Caprice slammed the door then flung herself on the sofa. The door-bell rang again. She snatched the curtain back and saw Nathan standing on the doorstep.

"I'm glad it's you," she said when she opened the door.

"What's wrong?"

"A bunch of reporters were camped out on my porch and calling me nonstop. This is only the beginning. Nathan, I don't know how much more of this I can take."

He pulled her into his arms and squeezed her tightly, and she clung to him as if he were her life preserver. "Come on, let's sit down." Nathan led her to the sofa. She leaned back, and he put his arm around her.

"Did you get anything from the windowpane?"

He shook his head. "They haven't found anything yet."

"No proof my gun was stolen," she whispered as Nathan stroked her cheek.

"Caprice, don't worry; there's no way this case is going to stick. Kevin's a good detective, but there are more holes in this than Swiss cheese. The lab is going to continue to test the windowpane."

"I still think I need a lawyer. This thing isn't just going to go away because of wishful thinking."

"Have you called the PBA?"

"No, I don't know what to do. I've never been in any kind of trouble before." She buried her head in Nathan's chest and wept. His heart broke into a million pieces. But being this close to her aroused him. He tried to fight it, but he couldn't. He ran his hand down her back.

Caprice looked up at him with tears in her eyes. Nathan couldn't read the smoky look in her eyes. It was a strange mixture of sadness, fear, and a flicker of desire. Their lips were drawn together like magnets. She was searching for comfort in his kiss, and he was eager to provide it. He received her urgent kiss, accepted her roaming tongue. She pressed her body against his, crashing her pelvis into his. Heat enveloped them as they ripped each other's clothes off. Nathan pushed Caprice back into the sofa and grasped at her bra, freeing her perfectly shaped breasts. She wrapped her legs around his waist, drawing him into her. She needed this closeness. She needed to escape the tumult her life had become. Nathan suckled at her breasts, gently biting her nipples, as she loosened his belt buckle and unzipped his jeans. Nathan kicked out of his pants, and then he looked up at Caprice.

"Are you sure you want to do this?" he whispered. He was afraid she'd change her mind. Nathan knew he wasn't going to be able to turn back. He had wanted her for too long. His desire was too strong.

She answered him with a hard, penetrating kiss. Her tongue erased any questions he had about not making love to her. Nathan returned her passionate kiss with one just as heated. He plunged his tongue into her mouth, staking his claim. Breathless, they separated and looked deep into each other's eyes. Caprice urged him on pulling him closer to her waiting body. She needed him inside her.

"Do you have protection?" he asked.

"In the bathroom," she replied hoarsely.

Nathan ran down the hall to the bathroom. He opened the medicine cabinet and found an unopened box of condoms. He paused for a brief second. *Should we be doing this?* he thought. *Maybe this isn't the right time.* Nathan closed his eyes and opened the box. His desire for Caprice was guiding him now. When he walked into the living room, she was curled up in a ball on the sofa. He stared at her brown skin. She looked like a wounded doe, lying there crying out for help. He walked over to her and ran his finger down the small of her back.

"Caprice, are you all right?" He pulled her into his arms. She buried her head in his bare chest. Nathan felt her hot tears falling on his skin. "It's going to be fine," he cooed.

Caprice shook her head. "I need you," she moaned. "I need you."

Nathan wrapped his arms around her and pulled her close to him. His muscles twitched. His throbbing penis grew against her thighs. Nathan ripped the condom wrapper open and rolled it down his erect shaft.

Caprice pulled him on top of her. "I need you, I need you," she repeated.

Nathan pressed into her waiting body. She clutched his back and dug her nails into him. Nathan didn't feel any pain, just her need. He dove deeper into her pool of femininity. Her moans mixed with sobs as they grinded against one another. They tumbled from the sofa in a ball, hitting the floor, but not separating from each other. Caprice moved her hands up and down his back, pressing him closer and closer to her, as though she was trying to lose herself in him. Nathan moaned as she squeezed her legs around him and tightened herself against his most sensitive muscle.

"Oh, Caprice," he called out as he felt his climax over take him.

She said nothing; she just continued to ride him like a champion steed. Sweat covered their bodies. The heat in the room was almost unbearable. Nathan felt as if he was going to explode. Finally, he and Caprice collapsed in each other's arms. They fell asleep on the floor. He clung to her and she to him.

It was about 3 a.m. when Caprice woke up. She looked down at Nathan. *What have I done?* she thought. *What in the world have I done?* She inched out of Nathan's arms and went into the bathroom. She felt as if her life was spinning out of control. Having sex with Nathan was a vivid illustration of that.

Caprice made her way to the bathroom, turned the shower on, and stepped inside. She let the steamy water beat down on her. She could hear Nathan moving around in the living room and prayed he wouldn't follow her.

Seconds later, Nathan was knocking on the door. "Caprice, is everything okay?" He walked into the bathroom and watched her through the shower curtain.

"Yeah, I...I just wanted to take a shower."

"Are you sure that's it? Do we need to talk about what happened?"

Caprice turned the water off. "C...can you hand me a towel?"

Nathan, who had put his boxers on, handed her a towel from the rack above the toilet. She wrapped up in the towel before pulling the shower curtain back. "I'm going to get dressed," she said.

"Do you want to talk about this?" he asked again, sensing tension in the room.

"There's nothing to talk about, really."

"I think there is."

"Can I at least put some clothes on?"

"Caprice, I've seen you naked."

"We made a mistake," she blurted out. "I lost control, and I let something happen that should never have happened." Nathan stepped closer to her, and she took a step back.

"This wasn't a mistake."

"Then what was it? Nathan, honestly, I don't need this. I need to focus on clearing my name."

"I told you I was going to help you."

Caprice pushed past him. "You should leave."

"No," Nathan replied. "Not until we talk this out."

"What do you want? Round two? I told you this was a mistake! It won't happen again."

Nathan sighed. "Caprice, you should know me better than that. I'm here because I know you need help, and that's what I intend to do."

Caprice walked into her bedroom, and Nathan followed her. She sat on the bed and looked up at him. "I'm sorry. Everything is just so crazy right now."

"It's all right," he said.

"I just don't want you to think that…"

He waved his hands. "We don't have to discuss it anymore. I'm going to take off"

"You don't have to leave. It's late. I want you to stay."

"I don't want you to feel uncomfortable," he said. "I think my being here makes things a little awkward."

Caprice smiled weakly. "It doesn't get more awkward than this."

Nathan sat down beside her. "I'm going to go take a shower and crash on the sofa."

"I'll put a pillow and blanket out there for you," she said.

Early the next morning, Detective Harrington sat at his desk sipping a cup of watery coffee. *Nathan's right about this case, some of this stuff just doesn't add up,* he thought as he read over his copy again. *I need to find out if that was Caprice's gun.* He picked up the phone and called the supply room.

"Granger."

"This is Detective Harrington. I need to get some information from you."

"What do you need?"

"Have any officers reported losing weapons?"

"What kind of weapons? People lose pepper spray and asps everyday."

"I'm talking service pistols."

"About three months ago, Officer Eric Hunt reported that his gun was stolen during a robbery investigation."

"What's that database where the officers log in their serial numbers? How can I access that?"

Granger sighed. "You know that you can't. I have a list of the serial numbers."

"I need to see that list as soon as possible."

"That is a big request. We have over 2,000 officers on the force."

"Do you think you can send it to me by the end of the day?"

"How about first thing tomorrow?"

"I need this for a murder investigation, so the sooner the better."

"Is this about that detective?"

"You got it."

"I've always liked her."

"Well, how about you getting off this phone and getting that list together?"

"Fine," Granger said then he hung up the phone.

Nathan, you'd better be right about Caprice, Kevin thought as he tossed his half empty coffee cup in the trash can. Captain Leland walked over to Kevin's desk. "Detective," he said.

Kevin stood up. "What can I do for you, Captain?"

"I need to know where this case against Detective Johnson is headed."

Kevin sighed. "I'm checking into her story about the gun. That might not have been her gun used in the shooting. But she did argue with him that night. I'm going to do some checking with some folks in Chicago to see what kind of relationship Johnson and Damien King had."

"If it wasn't her gun, then who killed him?"

"I don't know if it wasn't her gun yet."

"Find out, because I need her back on my team."

"Captain, I wouldn't get my hopes up if I were you."

"I don't like the sound of that."

"This isn't an investigation just to clear Detective Johnson. I'm looking for a killer." Captain Leland nodded and walked away from Kevin's desk. Kevin sat down and looked at the report one more time.

CHAPTER TWELVE

Caprice unplugged the phone and shut off the television. After Nathan left her house, she decided she needed to avoid him, too. Last night complicated everything, she thought as she flipped through an old copy of *Ebony* magazine. She hadn't been with anyone since her breakup with Damien. Being with Nathan felt so good.

It had been over a year since a man touched Caprice in that way. She hadn't felt that kind of electric passion, and it scared her. She was afraid she was going to want to be with Nathan again and again. The last thing she needed or could handle was that kind of distraction in the middle of everything else she had going on in her life. Caprice stood up and paced back and forth, trying to rid herself of the memory of Nathan's kiss.

The phone rang, temporarily giving her something else to think about. She saw the department's number on the caller identification.

"Hello," she said.

"Caprice, it's Captain Leland."

"I'm going to be arrested, aren't I?" she asked.

He sighed. "Yes. The DA filed charges this morning. Two officers are on the way to your house to bring you in."

"I guess I need a lawyer."

"You do. If you want, I'll call a PBA representative for you."

"How much time do I have before they get here?"

"They're en route now. Detective, you know I really hate this."

"Captain, I didn't kill Damien."

"Good luck to you," he said before hanging up.

He doesn't believe me, she thought as the dial tone sounded in her ear. She hung up the phone, and then there was a knock at her door. Outside the window were two uniformed officers. Caprice knew the officers: Allen had been on the force for two years, and McMillian was a thirty-year veteran. She closed her eyes and opened the door.

"Detec...Caprice Johnson?" Officer McMillian said.

"Yes."

"You need to come with us. We have a warrant for your arrest."

She nodded. "You have the right to remain silent, anything..."

"I know the spiel," she said. "Let's just get this over with."

"Place your hands behind your back," McMillian said. Caprice did as she was told.

"Do we have to cuff her?" Officer Allen asked. The first officer nodded.

"Will you lock my door, please?" Caprice asked.

McMillian nodded and Allen led Caprice to his car. He placed her in the back of the squad car and handed her a jacket. "The media has been camping out at the department and the jail. You might want to cover your face."

"Why, so I can look guilty?"

He shrugged his shoulders, then closed the door. The back of a squad car was new territory for Caprice. She never realized how cramped and uncomfortable the space was. Her knees ached as they bumped against the backseat. The cuffs pinched her skin every time she moved her hands. She willed herself not to move. Caprice tried to fight the tears welling in her eyes, but it was futile. They flowed down her cheeks and onto her shirt. One of the officers turned around and looked at her. *How am I going to get out of this?* she thought. *How am I going to prove my innocence?*

When the officers got to the police department, swarms of reporters were waiting for them. "Get back; get back," the officer yelled as he opened the rear door. He helped Caprice out of the car. Flashbulbs went off, and she threw her hands up to shield her eyes.

"Detective Johnson, any statement?" a reporter called out.

"Leave her alone," one of the officers said as he rushed Caprice inside.

"Thanks," she said once they were safely inside the police department.

"I think you're getting a bum deal," he said in a near whisper.

Nathan watched Caprice being led into the interrogation room. Seeing her in handcuffs tortured him. This is too much, he thought as he turned away. He walked back to his office and called Nina Gilliam, a PBA attorney.

"This is Nina."

"Nina, it's Nathan Wallace."

"What's wrong?"

"I have a friend who needs your help."

"What's going on?"

"She's been charged with first-degree murder."

"Is this the detective who was on the news this morning?"

"Yes."

"I was wondering when she was going to call someone. I asked around to see if she had representation."

"Well, they just brought her in. Do you think you can get over here pronto?"

"Yeah, I'll be right there."

"Thanks," Nathan said then hung up the phone. He looked up and saw Officer Smith standing beside his desk. "What can I do for you?"

"I need to know what your report's going to say."

"What?"

"Are you going to recommend I get the ax?"

"I haven't finished the report yet."

"This is bullshit." Smith banged his fist on Nathan's desk.

"You need to get away from my desk."

"I need to know if you're going to take my job away from me!"

Nathan stood up. "Will you get away from my desk? I have work to do."

Smith sighed. "Can you recommend something like counseling? I have a family. I can't lose my job. I'll do anything."

"Did you think about that before you smacked around a fourteen-year-old? Now, please, get the hell away from my desk."

Smith stormed off, and Nathan sat down. He had almost forgotten that Smith had a family, but what about Maurice Boxer and his family? Nathan stood up and walked into Major Chaney's office.

"Inspector?" he said when he looked up.

"Major, I want to talk to you about Officer Smith."

"Go ahead."

"What he did was horrible, but he has a family. Maybe he was just having a bad day."

"I know we're human, but as a police officer, we can't take a bad day out on someone we pull over for a traffic violation. What do you recommend?"

"He needs a hearing. I don't think I should make this decision alone. Maybe we should tap the Citizen's Review Board for a recommendation before we make a final decision."

Chaney smiled. "Good choice. Every day, I see I made the right decision bringing you on board."

"Thanks," Nathan said. "I'm going to lunch."

"You know they arrested Detective Johnson today."

"I heard," he said nonchalantly.

"I'm going to head the investigation into the King shooting," Chaney announced.

"Okay," Nathan turned to leave the office. He was already trying to formulate a plan to help Caprice without Chaney knowing.

"My prior warning still stands. You need to stay away from this case and Detective Johnson if you value your career as much as I think you do."

Nathan nodded and walked out of Chaney's office. *This is more than a case to me,* he thought as he walked out to his car. Nathan drove to the McDonald's Cafeteria on Beanies Ford Road for lunch. He wanted to get away from the precinct for as long as he could. When he walked in the restaurant, he saw Lisa sitting at a corner table. Damn, he thought. She waved to him. Nathan sighed and waved back, and Lisa came over to his table.

"Nathan, I heard about your partner on the news. This is unbelievable. It sounds like a plot for a Hollywood movie. Did she really do it?"

"I don't want to talk about this with you," Nathan said.

"I always thought there was something going on with you and her. I never said anything because…"

"You know what Lisa, I don't want to talk to you about Caprice or anything else. So why don't you take yourself back to your table and finish your lunch."

"You're in love with her, aren't you? I should've known. She's what kept you away from me. All that talk about you two being just friends was a load of crap." Nathan turned his back to her. Lisa grabbed his shoulder. "It's true, isn't it?

You've been in love with her all this time. What was I? A distraction?"

"No, Lisa, you kept me away from you. Your lies, your smothering, it was you, not Caprice."

"I hope she goes to jail for what she did. That's right, you probably think she's innocent. I guess she'll have to kill you before you believe she's a murderer, huh?"

Nathan clenched his jaw and glared at her. "Caprice didn't do this. She would never hurt anyone."

"Spoken like a true fool in love. I don't know why I wasted my time with you. I'm much too good for you."

"Yeah, this from a woman who lied about being pregnant to trap me."

Lisa turned on her heels and walked out of the restaurant. He fought back the expletive he wanted to yell at her. Nathan no longer had an appetite.

Donovan and Ethan walked into the courtroom for Donovan's probable cause hearing.

"This case should be dismissed today," Ethan whispered.

"It better be."

"Come on, have a little patience," Ethan said.

"I didn't get where I am today by being patient. I'm losing millions. The cops are watching my every move. It's like living in a damned fish bowl."

"And do you think this case is raising my stature? I'm an accessory in a murder, remember?" Ethan kept his voice low. The last thing he needed was to have a nosey bailiff overhear this conversation. Then he'd be sitting behind bars.

"At least you're not a victim," Donovan hissed. "If you fuck up this case, I can easily change that."

Carole walked up to Ethan and Donovan. "Excuse me," she said. "I'm going to ask that this hearing be continued."

"Why is that?" Ethan asked smugly. "I thought you had a strong case. A continuance is a sign of weakness."

"I'm not in the mood for this. You know one of the detectives who made the arrest has been arrested herself."

"That sounds like grounds for a dismissal to me," Ethan said.

"I don't think so. There was more than one officer involved. Face the facts, Mr. Washington, your client is finally going to pay for his crimes."

Ethan smiled. "Then the state is going to turn around and prosecute one of its own."

"Don't worry about that, it doesn't concern you or your client."

"Let's go," Donovan said.

Carole rolled her eyes and stomped over to the state's table.

"All rise," the bailiff said.

Donovan looked over to Carole and smiled. "I'm getting out of here and the next time you're in court, that bitch will be sitting at the defense table, not me."

"Be seated," the judge said as he called court to order. "Ms. Young, call your first case."

"Your honor, the state requests a continuance in the Donovan Harris case."

"Your honor," Ethan said. "We object."

"Why is the state asking for a continuance?" the judge inquired.

"One of the arresting officers isn't available to offer her testimony."

"When will the officer be available?" the judge asked.

"Ten to twenty years," Ethan said under his breath.

Carole glared at him. "One of the detectives involved in this case has been arrested on unrelated charges. The other detective is on vacation."

"I don't see a problem with granting the state a continuance," the judge said. "However, I will have a problem with granting more than one. Let's make sure you're ready to proceed in three weeks. Next case."

"Your honor, if it pleases the court, I would like to renew my objection to Mr. Harris's bail. I have new evidence," Carole said.

"Your honor, if the state can present evidence, then we can continue with the hearing. If not, what's the point of the continuance?" Ethan asked.

"I agree," the judge replied. "Ms. Young, you're skating on thin ice and wearing out my patience. Move on to your next case."

Ethan and Donovan stood up and walked our of the courtroom. Everything was going according to their plan. If things continued going this way Donovan wouldn't spend a day in jail.

CHAPTER THIRTEEN

Caprice had been in interrogation rooms before but never as a suspect. She sat in the cold metal chair and looked at Kevin Harrington. She had always respected him as a homicide detective. But slowly, she was losing any respect she had for him. Why couldn't he see she was innocent? What fool would leave a business card at a crime scene? she thought.

"Come on, Caprice, just tell me what happened." He leaned across the table and looked directly into her eyes.

Caprice knew that trick. He was trying to intimidate her. She did it all the time with drug dealers and other suspects. It usually worked on a guilty person.

Caprice met Kevin's stare with an icy one of her own. "I told you what happened. I saw Damien that night, we argued, and I left. I don't know what happened after that. Whoever killed him is still out there."

"I don't believe you. Come on, Caprice, tell me the truth, and things will be easier for you."

"Since you know so damn much, tell me what happened," she snapped.

Kevin smiled and leaned back in the seat. "Damien, your ex-fiancé, said something that pissed you off. You argued with him in the bar and in his room. He must have said something pretty harsh to make you lose it. You shot him, then dropped your gun before dashing out of the room."

"Have you ever thought about writing fiction? That story would be a bestseller."

"Caprice, if it was a crime of passion, the DA may go easier on you. But you're going to have to give me something to work with."

"Maybe it was a crime of passion. Only it wasn't my passion or my crime. I didn't shoot Damien. I never went to his room."

"Okay, how did your card get there?"

"Do you know how many of my cards are floating around this city?"

"That's not an answer."

The door to the interrogation room flung open, and Nina walked in. "Detective, don't say another word," she ordered.

"Nina?" Kevin said.

"I'm representing Detective Johnson, and this interrogation's over. Kevin, how could you even question her without an attorney present? Are we just skimming over the Constitution these days, Detective?"

Caprice looked at the woman. *Who called her?* she thought.

"Nina, I'm just doing my job. Save the dramatics for the court room or a news crew," he said.

She raised her right eyebrow. "Now, I'm here to do my job. I'd like to speak to my client alone."

"She's all yours," he said as he walked out of the room.

Nina turned to Caprice and extended her hand. "Nina Gilliam."

"I know who you are," she replied as she shook the famed attorney's hand. People either loved or hated Nina Gilliam. She was brash and in-your-face. And she rarely lost a case or backed away from controversy. Right now, Caprice didn't know what to think about her. She was just glad to have Nina in her corner.

"A friend of yours called me and told me you needed help. I just went through the evidence they have against you. This case is purely circumstantial."

"There should be no case whatsoever. I didn't shoot Damien. I was never in his room."

"Well, we have a bail hearing in a few hours. I'm going to push for your release."

"Great," she said. "But I'm going to have to go into lockup, right?"

"Unfortunately, yes. But I promise you won't spend the night in jail."

Caprice took little consolation in Nina's words. She dropped her head in her hands. "I need to know what happened that night," Nina said quietly.

"I met Damien for a drink. He was talking about how he wanted to get back together. We argued, I tossed a beer in his face, and I left."

"Where did you go after you left?"

"To Rock Hill."

"Why is that?"

"I needed to clear my head, so I just drove. I stopped at a Waffle House and had a few cups of coffee."

"Then?"

"I went home."

"Okay. The only thing they have placing you in the room is your business card. Now, we need to find your gun."

"Have they even checked the records to see if that gun's mine?"

"I'll have to look into that."

"Who called you and told you that I needed an attorney?" Caprice asked.

"Inspector Wallace."

Caprice's breath caught in her chest. *He was serious about helping me,* she thought. "Thank him for me. I'm sure his supervisor told him not to have any contact with me," Caprice said.

Nina smiled. "We have a good chance of getting you out of here."

She wasn't very hopeful. Caprice nodded. "I'll wait and see."

Nina patted her shoulder. "I know this is hard for you. But at least you have two people in your corner who believe in you." Caprice smiled weakly. She needed more than people in her corner, she needed to get out of jail and prove to everyone that she didn't kill her ex.

Nathan couldn't push Lisa's words out of his head. He did love Caprice. But he'd probably never have her in his life the way he wanted. *She won't open up to me,* he thought.

*But if Lisa can see that I love her, then Caprice can see it too.
She must think I'm the biggest fool. Once this case is over, I'm
moving on. She'll have to find another idiot.*

He walked into the precinct with a scowl on his face.
Even though he was trying to harden his heart toward
Caprice, he thought about the wounded looked in her eyes
last night. She needs someone; he just wished she would see
he was the one.

Nathan sat at his desk and scanned the Smith report.
He couldn't focus on his work. Every five seconds he was
thinking about kissing Caprice, the sweetness of her
tongue, and the softness of her lips. He inadvertently licked
his lips as he fantasized about her. The phone rang, interrupting his thoughts.

"Wallace."

"Nate, it's Cordell."

"What now?"

"Just wanted to let you know the case against me was
dismissed," he said happily.

"What?"

"Yeah, one of those cops who set me up got caught up
in some shit, but I'm sure you know that already."

"You've been given another chance. Don't blow it this
time."

"I'm going to try to do right, but it's hard out here."

"That's bullshit."

"I bet you've given that damn cop more support than
you've ever given me. We're brothers, we're blood, and you
treat me like a common hood."

"Cordell, you are a common hood. I got work to do, and you're keeping me from it. If you're really serious about turning your life around, you'll do it. And you won't have to announce it."

"I wish you'd support me. All you do is ridicule and judge me."

"What do you mean support? The only time you call me is when you're in trouble. How do you expect me to support you? You're so full of it."

"I don't need this shit." Cordell hung up the phone. Nathan shook his head and returned to his work. *Chaney was right; the people in my life are causing me nothing but trouble.*

By the time his shift was over, Nathan was bone tired. But he couldn't and wouldn't rest until he knew what was going on with Caprice. *How did her hearing go? Is she still in jail? Maybe I should just drive over there and check on her,* he thought as he got into his car. *No, if she did get out on bail she probably doesn't want to see me.*

Despite his misgivings, Nathan drove to Caprice's house. He parked his car a half block away and waited. About thirty minutes later, Nina dropped her off. He observed Caprice as she walked in the house. Even from a distance, her pain was evident. Her clothes were wrinkled, and her hair was out of place. He fought the urge to run to her. He wanted to hold her tightly and tell her everything would work out and she would be cleared. She stood on the porch and watched Nina drive off.

Caprice looked down the street and waved at Nathan. "Did you think I wouldn't see you?" she called out.

He got out of the car and walked slowly. "I should've known," he said with a tense laugh.

"Thanks for calling Nina for me."

"How much was your bond?"

"A hundred thousand."

Nathan whistled. "That's a lot."

"Some people seem to think I'm a murderer." Caprice unlocked the front door then looked at Nathan.

A tense silence hung over them like storm clouds.

"Do you need anything?" Nathan asked.

"No. I think everything's under control now."

"Are you sure?"

Caprice shook her head. "I don't know what I need or what's going to happen next. I was in court, and it was like everything good I've ever done didn't mean anything. How many times have I worked with David Thompson? How many times have I been a witness in Judge Byrd's court-room?"

"I know," Nathan said. He wanted to reach out to her and hug her, but he didn't know how she would react. "I think I'm going inside and take a shower to get the jail stench off me," she said after another uncomfortable silence. She turned toward the front door.

"Do you want to have dinner tonight?"

"Nathan, I don't think that's a good idea."

"Come on, you have to eat. I know you didn't eat in lockup."

Caprice frowned. "All right," she said. "But I don't want to go out anywhere. Every time I move, I think a reporter or a camera man is going to jump out of the shadows."

"I'll call something in and go pick it up." Nathan's cell phone rang. "Aw, I need to get that." He pulled the phone out of his pants pocket. "Wallace."

"Nathan, it's Jamie down in the lab."

"What's up?"

"I ran another analysis of that windowpane you brought in."

"And?"

"Why would Ron Torres be at Detective Johnson's house?"

"What?"

"I found his thumbprint on the glass."

"That's very interesting."

"Yeah, considering who Torres works for."

"I'll ask her about it," Nathan said.

"All right. Should I pass this information on to Kevin?"

"Not yet. Keep a copy of the report on file, though."

"All right," Jamie said.

"J, I really appreciate this. This is the kind of break we've been waiting for."

"No problem." Nathan hung up the phone and turned to Caprice, who was looking at him with questions in her eyes.

"What was that all about?" she asked.

"Remember the windowpane?"

"Yeah, you said the lab didn't find anything on it?"

"It seems as if Ron Torres paid you a visit. Jamie found his thumbprint on it."

"That son-of-a…"

"We have a lead."

"I've got to talk to this guy. He probably knows where my gun is and who killed Damien."

"Slow down, little red Corvette. Do you really think he'll tell you anything?" Nathan asked. "He knows you're suspended, and he knows you don't have your weapon."

"I may not have my service weapon, but I have something to protect myself with."

"Caprice, questioning Torres is dangerous. It could jeopardize your case. Let me talk to him."

"What else do I have to lose, Nathan? I'm going to find him."

"A lot more than you think. Caprice, these people could kill you."

"I know that, but this is a chance I have to take. I don't have any other choice."

Nathan looked at Caprice and shook his head. "You aren't going to let me handle this, are you?"

"Nathan, it's my life and my career that's on the line here. I have a bigger stake in this than you do! Besides, what about your career?"

"Caprice, why don't you admit that you need some help?"

"I can take care of myself," she snapped. "I don't need you standing over me like I'm a fragile piece of bone china."

"Usually, I'd back down and let you handle things your way, but not this time. When are you going to let someone else help you? I love you, and I don't want to see you hurt."

"What?" she asked, visibly shocked.

"I mean, I care about you, and I don't want to—"

"Nathan, maybe it would be best if you let me handle this alone. Things are really complicated between us right now. I knew last night was a mistake. You don't love me. You just want to protect me. I'm not a child."

"You need protection," Nathan said as he pulled her into his arms. "And I do love you. I've loved you for so long, I don't know what it's like not to love you." He tightened his hold as she tried to wiggle out of his embrace. "Caprice, listen to me. I'm willing to go out on a limb for you. Anything you need, I will do it."

"I don't need you to be my knight in shining armor!" she exclaimed as she pushed him in the chest.

"I'm just trying to be here for you!"

She pushed him away and turned to walk in the house. Nathan followed her.

"This isn't over," he said. "And I'm not going to let you push me away. You always think you have to do everything alone. That drives me crazy about you."

Caprice turned around and looked at him. "I don't depend on people because people die on you or disappoint you. The one man I gave my heart to hurt me in the worst way. I thought I could trust Damien and give him my all. He looked like the right one, and at first he was. He was sweet, kind, and supportive. Anything I did, he was there for me. Anything I wanted, he got it for me. I built my world around Damien. He was everything I thought I needed or ever wanted.

"But then he started cheating. That hurt me so badly that I had to get away from him and everything he meant to me. So I ran away. I came here with a chip on my shoulder. And you, you have to be so nice and so sweet. Nathan, I wish I could love you, and I wish I could open my heart to you and trust you with my life, but I just can't. History has a way of repeating itself with me."

"Caprice," Nathan said as he stepped closer to her. He opened his arms to her. "What do I have to do to prove I'm not like the other men who've been in your life? I'm Nathan, not Damien or any other jerk who hurt you in the past."

She shook her head. "It's not you, Nathan. I just…"

He silenced her with a kiss. Caprice responded, even though she didn't want to. She melted in his arms like an ice cube on a sidewalk in the middle of July.

Nathan stepped back from Caprice and looked at her. He thought he saw the faint glimmer of trust in her eyes. "I'm sorry," he said.

"What are we doing?" she asked.

"Falling in love."

"I can't afford to do that right now. I have to focus on this case. Everything that I've worked for is on the line. I could lose it all."

"I know."

"Do you really?"

"Caprice, I'm not trying to stop you from clearing your name."

"You just want to help."

"I have to. You can't do this alone, it's too dangerous."

"But how do I know you aren't going to have to give up on helping me when it becomes a hazard to your career?"

"Because I'm not going to stop until the truth comes out. You're not a killer, I'm going to make sure everyone knows that."

"And what happens when we're both unemployed cops?"

"Then we start a private investigation firm. We've always been great partners," Nathan said with a smile.

"About the other night, I…"

"Shh," he said as he stroked her hair. "The next time we make love, it will be all about us and not everything going on around us."

"You sound pretty confident there'll be a next time."

"I'd bet my life on it." Caprice smirked.

"Let's go find Torres," she said as she pulled back from him.

"I think you'd better get your other gun. This could get a little messy," he said.

CHAPTER FOURTEEN

Caprice and Nathan sat outside of Ron Torres's apartment.

"He has to come home sometime," Caprice said.

"I think we should get some backup," Nathan said. He was feeling wary about going to question Torres. There was no telling what kind of weapons he might have inside his home.

"Yeah, so both of us can get fired. I know you were forbidden to have anything to do with this case."

"So what if I was?" he said.

"Nathan, you need to think about how much you're willing to risk for me."

"Shh, there's Torres," he said. They ducked in the car so he wouldn't see them. He walked into a ground-level apartment.

"Looks like he's alone," Caprice said as she looked at him through a set of binoculars.

"What are we going to do now? You make the call."

"Let's go knock on his door."

Nathan nodded, and they got out of the car. Caprice almost ran to the door. Nathan had to quicken his pace to keep up with her. She banged on the door.

"Who in the hell is it?" Torres said before he opening the door. "Oh shit!"

He tried to close the door, but Caprice wedged her foot between it and the frame, preventing him from shutting her out. "Ronnie, we need to talk, baby." She forced her way in.

"Why are you here?" he asked. He looked up and saw Nathan standing by the door.

"You need to tell me what the hell you were doing at my house," Caprice said.

Torres laughed nervously. "I was never at your house. Lady, you're loco."

"Then why were your fingerprints there?" Nathan asked.

"What is this, an interrogation?"

"It's going to be an ass-kicking if you don't answer the question," Caprice said.

Nathan looked at her. This was the Caprice he was accustomed to seeing. She was forceful, assertive and in control. The way she handled Torres reminded him of their days on the streets together.

"Look," Torres said. "I don't know nothing about nothing."

"You'd better talk or I'm going to let her kick your ass," Nathan said.

Caprice smiled at Torres then sat on the sofa beside him and patted him on the shoulder. "I know you weren't working alone," she said. "You're not that smart."

"Go to hell, lady," he said.

Caprice grabbed him by the collar. "Where's my gun, and who hired you to steal it?"

"I didn't steal nothing, and no one hired me to do anything. Let me go!"

Nathan tapped her on the shoulder. "Let him go."

"You aren't even a real cop right now, lady," Torres shouted as Caprice released his collar.

"But I am," Nathan said. "I have enough evidence to link you to a murder and a robbery. I can arrest you right now. The question is, do you want to go down alone, or do you want to bring someone with you?"

Torres sighed, as if pondering what Nathan said. He would go back to jail for a long time with another arrest. He had several armed robbery convictions on his record. "All right," he said. "But if I talk, I need a deal and some real assurances. What's it called, witness protection or something? I can't be seen at the police station, either."

"This is my life we're talking about. I need to know, right now, who's setting me up," Caprice demanded. She kicked the coffee table over, sending papers, magazines, and an ashtray flying across the room.

Torres jumped up and shook his head. "If I tell you anything, then my life is over."

She closed her eyes. "Donovan Harris is behind this, isn't he?" Caprice stopped herself from grabbing Torres again.

"I didn't say that," he replied nervously.

"Come on, Torres, we know you work for him," Nathan said.

"I don't work for nobody."

"Just stop lying," Caprice shouted. "We know you work for Harris. One more lie, and they'll be digging my fist out of your throat."

"Where is the gun?" Nathan inquired.

"I never took the gun; all I did was jimmy the window open. I never touched no gun!"

"How did you know where the gun was?" Caprice asked.

"A little bird told me."

Caprice glared at him. "I don't have time to play games with you."

"I watched you for a couple of days. You should've switched up your routine or something. Isn't that what cops tell people to do all the time?"

"Getting off the subject, Torres!" she exclaimed.

"So, who killed Damien King?" Nathan asked.

"Who?" Torres asked. "I don't know what you're talking about."

Nathan pulled out his handcuffs. "Stand up and turn around," he said.

"You really gonna arrest me?" His eyes stretched to the size of silver dollars.

"Yes. You're under arrest for the murder of Damien King. You have the right to remain silent, anything you say can and will be used against you…"

"Wait wait. If I tell you what I know, what can you do for me?"

"Reduce the charges to breaking and entering, but that all depends on what you have to say."

"Can you guarantee my safety?"

Caprice snorted. "Yes. What do you know?"

"Donovan Harris wanted to get you off his back. He told me to follow you and find out where you kept your gun. That's all I did, and that's all I know. I don't know if someone was killed or what it had to do with you."

"Is that all you know?" Nathan asked.

"That's it."

"Put it in writing," Caprice said.

"Not until I know I won't be charged with murder!" Torres said.

"You're not going to be charged," Nathan said. "What else do you know?"

"That's all," he said, relaxing a little. Torres sighed happily.

"Where is Donovan?" Caprice asked. Her question caught Nathan off guard. Is she going to go after him? he thought.

Torres sat on the edge of the sofa far away from Caprice. "I guess he's in his house. I don't talk directly to Donovan. His lawyer gets in touch with me."

"Ethan Washington?" Caprice said.

Torres nodded. "He sends me my money, and I don't ask questions."

"Have you been paid for this job?" Caprice asked.

"What? You want my money now?"

"Answer the question," Nathan ordered, even though he didn't know what Caprice was going to do with the information.

"I'm supposed to get paid soon. I'm still waiting on a call from Washington."

Caprice walked up to Torres and got in his face. "Call him now and do exactly what I say."

"This isn't in the deal! They'll know if the police is here," he snapped. "Ethan's not stupid."

"I'm smarter and angrier," she said.

"And," Nathan chimed in, "I can still charge you with murder."

Torres mumbled a string of profanities as he picked the cordless phone up from the floor. Nathan looked at Caprice. "What are you doing?" he whispered.

"I told you I was going to get Harris and I meant it."

"Caprice, you're going too far," Nathan warned. "You're out of control. We can't do this kind of operation without backup."

Torres watched them as they talked in a hushed tone. Caprice turned around and glared at him. "Have you dialed the number yet?" She walked away from Nathan, ignoring his reservations about her plan to use Torres as bait.

"Y'all gonna get me killed," Torres said as he dialed the phone number.

"Do you want me to make the call?" Caprice asked.

"What?"

"Stop stalling and dial the phone before I break your finger. Set up a meeting with him, and make sure it happens tonight."

Nathan sighed as he watched Caprice strong-arm Torres. He knew the only thing he could do was go along with her, because she wasn't going to listen to him. *Damn, why does she have to be so hardheaded?* he thought as he watched her. *I swear, I'm not going to let anything happen to her.*

"Do you have another phone?" Nathan asked.

"What?" Torres said.

"You must really think I'm stupid. You're still a lowlife criminal, and I don't trust you, so I want to hear everything you say," Nathan replied. Torres shook his head and pointed toward the kitchen. Nathan walked in the small kitchen and picked up the receiver that hung on the wall.

"Ethan, it's Ron."

"I've been meaning to call you about your money, but our boss is on a power trip."

"Well, I need my money, y'know. I have plans with a sweet senorita, and I can't take her to Miami if I'm broke," he said.

"Miami, eh? That sounds like a lot of fun."

"Well y'know, when you mess with the police, it's good to lay low for a while."

Ethan cleared his throat. "I'll get the cash to you in a day or so."

Caprice shook her head. "Tell him you need it tonight," she mouthed.

"Yo, dukes, I need my paper tonight," he repeated. "I've been patient, but I can't wait no more."

"Have the police contacted you?"

"No. Why you ask that?"

"Because you're talking like a man who wants to get away because the cops are on his tail," Ethan said.

"Man, it's only a matter of time before they get all of us. Me, you, and Donovan."

"That's not going to happen, not as long as you and other people stay calm and quiet."

"I'm both, but I want to get away for a while. I can't do that without what you owe me. So you either pay me or…"

"Are you threatening me?"

"Not at all," Torres said.

"Wrap it up," Caprice ordered. "Tell him to meet you tonight."

"Look, meet me tonight with my money at Revolutionary Park."

"I don't think so."

Torres looked at Caprice and shrugged his shoulders. "Do something," she said.

"Either you meet me or I'm going to the cops. I'll tell them everything I know about Donovan, this murder, and all of your sins, Ethan. I'll get a sweet deal and walk. You'll end up in an orange jumpsuit," he threatened.

"If you go to the police, you've just signed your death warrant," Ethan warned. "Donovan won't hesitate to have you exterminated like a pesky insect."

"I want my money. I took a big risk for y'all," Torres said.

Ethan mumbled under his breath. "I'll meet you at the park in an hour." Then he hung up the phone.

Torres turned to Caprice. "Satisfied?"

"Let's go," Caprice said.

"Oh, hell no, I'm not going," he whimpered like a wounded puppy.

"You say that as if you have a choice."

Torres turned to Nathan, pleading silently for help. Nathan shrugged his shoulders. "I can't do anything with her when she's like this," he replied. He didn't want to go to the park either, but he knew if he didn't take her, Caprice would go alone.

"I should've never opened my door," Torres said as Nathan and Caprice led him outside.

They piled into Nathan's car in silence. Torres looked around the parking lot to be sure he wasn't being watched. "I just want you to know this is crazy," Nathan whispered as he and Caprice slid in the front seat. "We haven't even asked him if he wants a lawyer. Anything we gain tonight will be tossed out of court. Caprice, use your head about this."

"I told you I was going to do whatever I had to do to clear my name."

"What if this is a setup, Caprice? You could get yourself killed out here. How do we know they weren't talking in some kind of code?"

She sighed. "What's worse than this nightmare? My life is practically over. Someone has to pay for this."

"And you think we can trust Torres?"

"What choice do we have?" she whispered.

Nathan glanced at Torres in the rear view mirror. He looked as nervous as Nathan felt. He gnawed at his fingernails as he stared out the window. "I don't like this," Nathan said angrily.

"It's not your life that's in turmoil either," Caprice replied. "You said you were going to help me, but if you want to back out, I understand."

"Oh no, somebody has to make sure you don't end up dead."

Caprice smirked at him and stroked the back of his hand. "Nathan, all I'm going to do is see what I can squeeze out of this lawyer. Nothing bad is going to happen."

Nathan turned into the park's entrance. There were no other cars around. Half the street lamps were burned out, and a line of tall pine trees along the perimeter of the parking lot created huge shadows that gave the park an ominous look. Nathan shuttered inwardly. *This smells like a setup,* he thought.

Caprice turned to Nathan. "What time is it?"

"Nine."

"Are you ready, Torres?" Caprice asked.

"You think I'm getting out of this car? Lady, you are insane. This is the end of the line for me. If they see me with you, I'm dead."

"Fine," she said. "What does Ethan drive?"

"A car," he said sarcastically.

"Look, if you want to stay out of jail and alive, you'll stop being a wise ass and answer the question!" she roared.

"A burgundy Lexus," he mumbled.

"Looks like he just pulled in," Nathan said. "He's alone."

"Let's go, Torres," Caprice said as she opened the door.

"No. You wanted me to get him here. I've done that. You're on your own now," he replied, trembling.

Before Nathan could grab Caprice to stop her, she was out of the car, walking along the tree line hiding in plain sight. *Does she want to die?* he thought as he watched her walk two feet from the front of the Lexus. He knew she shouldn't have gotten out of the car. Neither of them should have been in the park to begin with. Reckless.

Caprice stood there and waited for the driver to get out. The door opened and Donovan, not Ethan, stepped out of the car. Caprice walked up to him. "Well well," she said.

"What the hell are you doing here?"

"Waiting for you."

"Don't you have enough problems without adding dying to the list?"

"Why are you doing this to me?" she asked.

"Doing what? I don't even know what you're talking about."

"You're too smart to try and play dumb. You know damn well what I'm talking about. You set me up."

Donovan pulled his jacket back and brandished a nine-millimeter handgun. "You're really boring me, and I hate to be bored," he said as he pointed the gun at her.

"What are you going to do? Shoot me?" Caprice laughed. "I just want you to know there is a high-powered rifle aimed at your head. Make a move for the trigger, and we'll see who goes down first."

Donovan turned his head away from her, looking for snipers. Caprice lunged at him, knocking him to the ground. He hit his head on the pavement then dropped the gun. It fired, lighting the darkness with a quick burst of orange. Caprice fell backward into a patch of grass.

Nathan heard the shot and radioed for help. He knew he was going to be in serious trouble, but he didn't care. All he could think about was Caprice's safety. He jumped out of the car and ran to her side. "Caprice, are youokay?"

Her eyes fluttered open as Nathan checked her for a gunshot wound. "I'm fine," she said sitting up. "Where is Harris?" Sirens pierced the silence, and blue lights flashed in the distance.

"Nathan," Caprice said. "You have to get out of here."

"I'm the one who called the police," he said as he checked Donovan for a pulse.

"Is he alive?" Caprice asked.

"Yeah, but he's out cold." Nathan looked up and saw Major Chaney's car pull into the park.

"Nathan," Caprice said, "am I really worth all this trouble?"

He smiled weakly at her then stood up when he saw his superior officer walking toward him.

"Inspector, what in hell is going on out here?" Chaney demanded. "I told you that your off-the-clock activities could cost you your job."

"Major," Caprice began. "It's not his fault."

"I don't want to hear from you right now. Inspector, until this investigation is over, you're suspended."

"Fine, but there's a suspect in the back of my car you should talk to," Nathan said.

Caprice looked at him and frowned. "You can't let this happen. You can't risk your career for me!"

Nathan smiled. "Too late. I already did."

CHAPTER FIFTEEN

Caprice and Nathan sat outside of Chaney's office. They felt like naughty children who were called to the principal's office. Caprice looked down at her watch. It was after midnight. She and Nathan had been sitting there for about three hours or so. It was only a matter of time before the other shoe dropped right on our heads, she mused as she toyed with the sleeve of her jacket.

"How long have Leland and Chaney been in there?" Caprice asked.

"Long enough to fire both of us," Nathan replied. "We might have to start that private investigation firm after all."

"Why did you radio for help? I had everything under control." She smacked him on the arm and rolled her eyes.

"Geez Caprice, I heard a gunshot and saw you on the ground. I thought you were hit. Forgive me for caring."

"Nathan, just let me take the heat on this. I'm already in trouble. You don't need to go down with me."

"No."

"Come on, Nate, your career is—"

Chaney and Leland walked out of the office and glared at Nathan and Caprice. "I'm disappointed in both of you," Leland said. "Johnson, what the hell were you thinking? You're suspended. You can't question anyone. You could've gotten Ron Torres killed."

"Captain, he broke into my house. He knows who stole my gun."

"That's not what he says," Chaney said. "At this point, I'm inclined to take his word for it. Do you know how many of this man's rights you two violated? Was his attorney present when you questioned him? We'll be lucky if he doesn't sue the whole damn department."

Caprice dropped her head in her hands. *This isn't happening,* she thought. *They still don't believe me.* "What? Do you think I beat that information out of him?" she said. Nathan shot her a "calm down" look.

"Major," Nathan said. "The lab has a report that places Torres at Detective Johnson's house."

"How do you know that?" he inquired.

Nathan cleared his throat. "I had the lab run an analysis on her windowpane, and I got the results earlier today. That's why we went to see Torres."

Chaney shook his head. "I ordered you to stay away from this case," he bellowed.

"I know, but…"

"You defied a direct order. I can't and won't have that. You're out of this division!"

"Major Chaney, this isn't Inspector Wallace's fault. I talked him into helping me because the investigating officer wouldn't listen to me," Caprice pleaded.

"That's no excuse," Chaney said. "And fingerprints on a windowpane don't prove anything." Nathan pulled a microcassette recorder from his jacket pocket and pressed play. Torres's voice confessing breaking into Caprice's house filled the room.

"Does this prove anything?" Nathan asked.

"It's a start," Leland said.

"But," Chaney interjected, "did you mirandize him before he made this confession? This won't hold up in court, and any defense attorney worth their salt will say this confession was made under duress. How did Donovan Harris end up in a coma?"

"Harris tried to shoot me, so I defended myself," Caprice replied.

Chaney folded his arms across his chest and looked at her. "Detective, we're not in the business of vigilante justice," Chaney said. "You had no authority to conduct any inquiry in this case."

Caprice stood up and glared at Chaney. "This isn't a case; it's my life." Nathan grabbed Caprice's shoulder, in an attempt to calm her down. She pushed his hand away. Caprice couldn't understand why Chaney wanted her to be the bad guy. Was he trying to prove that she killed Damien, even though the evidence was beginning to show otherwise?

"You still had no right to go out and use your authority as an officer to get any information about King's murder."

"Major, if I didn't do it, then who else would? All the department's worried about is what the press says. I'm fighting for my life and my career here. But this," she said waving her hands, "is causing me to wonder why I even bother. You want to throw me back in jail, fine. You want to fire me, go ahead." She didn't care about office politics anymore. She wanted the charges against her to go away, and if Chaney wasn't going to make that happen, then she would. Caprice glared at him for about two seconds then turned to leave.

"Caprice," Nathan said. He tried to stop her as she stormed out of the office.

"I didn't realize she was such a hothead," Chaney said flippantly. Captain Leland shook his head. Nathan looked at his former captain, expecting him to defend Caprice. When Leland didn't speak up, Nathan did.

"She's not a hothead," he blurted out. "She's being set up, and Stevie Wonder can see that. But it seems as if all these detectives, captains, and majors can't. I'm going after her." Nathan bolted out of the office to find Caprice. He found her standing outside, leaning against the wall. "Do you realize what you did in there?" he asked.

"Yes. Who wants to be a cop anyway?" she joked. "Long hours, lousy pay, who needs it?"

"Come on, this isn't funny."

Caprice rolled her eyes and started to walk away from him. Nathan blocked her path. "Look," he said. "I know how important your career is to you."

"I can go to another department," she said.

Nathan shook his head. "And all this would follow you. When are you going to stop running?"

"I'm not running."

"Then what do you call it?"

"Cutting my losses and moving on." She pushed him away, but Nathan grabbed her arm.

"What about us?"

She sighed. "There is no us. There never was and there never will be."

Nathan clenched his jaw. "You're not getting off that easy. I know you love me, Caprice. If you didn't, you wouldn't have opened up to me, and we wouldn't have made love."

She closed her eyes and turned away from him. "If I leave, you won't have to lose your career, too."

"No," he said.

"Nathan, this isn't smart. And I do love you, that's why I'm doing this." Caprice pushed past him and ran to the edge of the sidewalk. Nathan watched her turn around and walk back to him. She bit her bottom lip and looked at him.

"I forgot I rode with you."

Nathan smiled. "So, you do love me?"

"I care about you, yes."

He shook his head. "Nah, you said you loved me, and that's why you're flushing your career down the drain."

"I misspoke," she said, trying to backpedal out of the corner she put herself in. Nathan pulled Caprice into his arms. He brushed his lips against hers. She tried to turn her head away, but she couldn't. They stared into each other's eyes. "It's you and me against the world, huh?" she whispered.

Nathan nodded, then leaned in to kiss her. Caprice accepted his kiss without hesitation or question. She wrapped her arms around his neck and pulled him closer to her, hoping to lose herself in the comfort.

Ethan looked out the living room window, searching for Donovan and his car. *What's taking him so long?* he thought. *I need my car. I hope he didn't kill Torres. He said he was just going to remind him of who he was dealing with.*

Ethan walked over to the bar in his den and fixed himself a scotch and soda. He made up his mind to end his ties with Donovan. All the death surrounding him was too much for Ethan's refined tastes. He'd rather deal with laundering money than burying bodies. Ethan downed the drink then fixed himself another. After three scotch and sodas, he returned to the front window to watch for Donovan. *He probably stole my car,* Ethan thought. He saw a car turning into his driveway. At first, he thought it was Donovan, but it was a police cruiser. *Great, what's this all about?* he thought as he opened the door.

"Mr. Washington?" the officer asked.

"That's me. What can I do for you?"

"Sir, I need you to come with me."

"Why?"

"Your car was recovered at the scene of a shooting. We have some questions to ask you."

"Maybe someone stole my car. I fail to see why you are knocking on my door in the middle of the night."

"We still need you at the station. You can come voluntarily, or we can get an arrest warrant for obstruction of justice."

Ethan sighed. "Let me grab my jacket."

When they got to the police station, Ethan was led to an interrogation room. Major Chaney was standing against the wall waiting for him. He looked Ethan up and down before nodding for him to sit down. "What's this all about?" Ethan asked.

"What was Donovan Harris doing with your car?"

"He had a flat tire on his truck, so I let him use my car."

"Really? So, he was going to Revolutionary Park to get a replacement tire?"

"I have no idea where he was going. I didn't ask for an itinerary when I loaned him the car."

"You loaned him a luxury car, but didn't ask where he was going? You're either a fool or extremely trusting."

"A car is a car."

"Donovan tried to kill a police officer tonight. What do you know about that?"

Ethan folded his arms and leaned back in the chair. "Nothing."

Chaney got in Ethan's face. "I think you're lying. Now, Donovan is in a coma. You can tell me what's going on, or we can wait for him to wake up and tell us. Either way, one of you will pay for what happened tonight."

Ethan laughed. "Let me get this straight, because I let a client and a friend drive my car, you're trying to put me in jail? What do you take me for, one of the little hood boys who is intimidated by your authority? I know the law, and if you aren't charging me, release my car so I can go home."

Chaney smirked and took a step back. "Your car's part of an investigation. But you're free to go. Just be warned, I'm going to get to the bottom of everything."

Ethan stood up and left. *Damn it, Donovan, what have you gotten me into now?* he thought as he left the interrogation room.

Nathan pulled into Caprice's driveway and shut his car off. She turned to him and smiled. "I know you think I went too far tonight," she said.

"That's the understatement of the month, maybe even the year."

Caprice rolled her eyes and grabbed his hand. "But, I think we raised some serious questions no one can ignore. Maybe this nightmare will be over soon."

"Does this mean you're going to leave the investigation alone and let the department handle it?" Nathan knew the answer was "no." She probably had something planned for the rest of the night.

Caprice yawned as she nodded. "I'm tired and hungry," she said.

Nathan looked at his watch' it was nearly 2 a.m. "Since neither of us have to work in the morning, do you want to go grab some breakfast?" he asked.

"I really should go to bed."

"Caprice, go to bed and don't play super cop anymore tonight."

"I won't. I'm too tired for that." She opened the door and got out of the car. Nathan waited until she was safely inside before he drove off. He parked a few houses down from her house to make sure she didn't try anything. *Knowing her, that door will be opening at any second,* Nathan thought.

Caprice peeped out the front window to make sure Nathan was gone. *All right,* she thought. *I'm going to get the answers I need.* When Caprice opened the door, a car's headlights blinded her. She shielded her eyes with her hand, trying to see who was in the car.

Nathan pulled back into the driveway and rolled his window down. "Where are you going?"

"Carolina's Medical Center."

Nathan hopped out of the car. "No, I can't let you do that. You've gotten in enough trouble for one night," he said as he bounded up the front steps.

"You're not talking me out of this," she said.

"I know that, Caprice, but I'm not going to let the woman I love risk her life like this. Not when I know she loves me, too." Caprice closed her eyes. *I should never have said anything,* she thought. "Nathan, I don't want to talk about that right now. I need answers."

"So do I." he said. "When you said you loved me, I know you meant it. When are you going to stop fighting it and let us love each other?"

"Nothing has changed, Nathan. I still have to clear my name."

"Caprice, Major Chaney may be a hardass, but he will find the truth. Donovan's in a coma. He can't tell you anything. If you go back to the police department, you can kiss your job goodbye."

Her lower lip quivered and tears threatened to spill from her eyes. "What if Chaney doesn't find out the truth?"

"Baby, I know you're scared, but you can't do this alone. When's the last time you slept?"

"Who has time to sleep?" she asked with a snort.

Nathan ushered Caprice inside the house and led her to the sofa. "Sit down," he ordered.

"What are you doing?" she asked as he made his way into the kitchen.

"I'm getting you something to eat and something to help you relax." Caprice kicked off her shoes, drew her knees up to her chest and leaned back on the sofa. She closed her eyes and tried to sleep, but she couldn't. Her mind wouldn't shut down. She kept thinking of more people she could question, more ways to get Ron Torres to tell the truth. Nathan walked into the living room with a mug of warm milk and a peanut butter and apple jelly sandwich.

"Caprice," he whispered as he placed the saucer and mug on the coffee table.

"I'm not sleeping," she said as she opened her eyes. "What's this?"

"Some ten-year-old comfort food," he said. "Do you remember when you were little that a PB and J sandwich would make you feel a lot better? My mom used to make me a sandwich, kiss me on the cheek, and I thought the world was a better place."

She smiled. "Things were much simpler then."

Nathan sat down beside her. "I hope you don't mind me not cutting the crust off."

Caprice leaned her head on Nathan's shoulder. "Thank you for stopping me tonight. I don't know what I expected to find at the hospital. Chaney probably would've had my bond revoked."

Nathan rubbed her arm gently. "Am I going to have to stake out this house and make sure you stay out of trouble?"

"No," she said as she sipped the milk.

Nathan shot her a questioning look.

"I'm going to let Major Chaney and the department handle this case," she said.

"I hope you don't expect me to believe that, Detective."

Caprice picked up half of her sandwich and smiled at Nathan. "You going home tonight?"

"Do you want me to stay?"

"Yes," she said. "Remember when you asked me when was the last time I slept?" Nathan nodded. "It was when I was in your arms."

He wrapped his arms around her. "So, that night wasn't the mistake you screamed it was, now was it?"

"Nathan, I'm just afraid. I feel so safe with you, and it scares me half to death. I don't want to start depending on you and then—"

He put his finger to his lips. "I told you, and I'm going to keep telling you until you believe me: I'm not that other man who hurt you, and made you feel as if you couldn't trust in love again. Caprice, I'd hurt myself before I would ever do anything to cause you a moment of pain."

She hugged him tightly and buried her head in his chest. Within seconds, she was sleeping as peacefully as a baby.

PART II

CHAPTER SIXTEEN

Three weeks had passed since Caprice was arrested. She hoped the charges against her would've been dropped by now, but the case remained active. Donovan was still in a coma and Ron Torres had disappeared, along with the truth about her gun. Things looked bleak for her. The only thing she could do was mount a defense.

She looked at her watch. Her meeting with Nina was in fifteen minutes. She grabbed her keys from the coffee table. Caprice tried to put her heart into her defense, but it was hard. She knew she was innocent; however she kept thinking about what would happen if she went to jail. She wondered how many people she would see in the woman's prison that she sent there. *I'll never make it in prison.*

When Caprice walked in the office, Nina was sitting behind her wide cherry wood desk. She looked up and smiled at Caprice. "Have a seat," she said.

Caprice sat in the leather chair across from her desk. She hoped Nina was going to tell her the DA was dropping all the charges. Nina pulled her wire-rimmed glasses off her face. "The DA called me this morning. He wants to offer you a plea. First-degree manslaughter. The maximum sentence is fifteen years."

"No," Caprice said. "I didn't kill anyone, and I won't go down for a crime I didn't commit."

Nina smiled. "That's what I thought you'd say. This is a sign the state has a weak case. If the evidence was strong, they wouldn't want to bargain."

"The state shouldn't have a case," she said. "What are they doing at the police department, anyway? I don't even think this case is about me anymore. It's about the CMPD not looking bad."

"You may have a point, Caprice. I haven't gotten any reports or anything," she said. "It's starting to piss me off."

"Nina, I didn't do this, and the evidence should show that. I'm not taking a plea."

"I don't want to give you false hope. Even with a weak case, a jury could still convict you."

"This should never even go to trial," Caprice said. She dropped her head in her hands. She fought against the tears welling up in her eyes, but lost as they began to fall. Nina handed her a tissue.

"But it might, and a jury could see you as a scorned lover with a chip on her shoulder and a gun on her hip," she said in a near whisper.

Caprice wiped her eyes. "Has Kevin Harrington completed his report on the gun yet?"

"If the DA has it, I haven't seen it. I have to wonder if they've given me all the evidence collected in this case."

"Unbelievable. It's almost as if they don't care if I'm innocent or not. It's about the department putting on a good show."

"Well, we got court tomorrow. We'll see more of the state's case, and if it is as weak as I think, I'm going to move for a dismissal. But, Caprice, don't count on us getting it."

"What would it take for this to go away?" she asked.

"A miracle or a confession from the real killer. And you have to stay out of trouble. You can't afford any more run-ins with Donovan."

Caprice closed her eyes and leaned back in the chair. "I've got to get out of here."

"Don't do anything crazy," Nina warned as Caprice tore out of her office.

Caprice got into her car and headed to the police department. She circled the block twice before deciding to head home. She knew everything was out of her hands. She was in the court system. Caprice felt hopeless and helpless, feelings she wasn't used to feeling. When Caprice got home, Nathan was sitting on the porch waiting for her.

"What are you doing here?" she asked when she got out of the car.

"I hadn't heard from you in a few days," he said. "I was just checking on you."

"I'm fine," she replied with a sigh.

"You're going to court tomorrow, right?"

She nodded and sat on the steps beside him. "Maybe whoever did this to me will come forward and confess, then I can move on with my life."

"That would be nice. Come on, let me take you some-where."

"I really don't want to go anywhere," she said.

"Come on, let's go to the lake and have lunch."

"It's a little chilly out here." Nathan grinned at her. "I'll keep you warm. I have two blankets in the trunk, and I already packed lunch."

"So, you're not taking 'no' for my final answer?"

Nathan gently kissed her on the lips. "No, Regis, I'm not. Let's go."

They hopped into Nathan's car and headed for Lake Cornelius. "Have you heard anything about Donovan or Torres?" she asked as they turned toward the interstate.

Nathan shook his head. "Donovan is still in a coma, and Torres is still missing."

"Great," she said dejectedly.

"So, why were you avoiding me?"

"I wasn't avoiding you. Sometimes I just need a little time alone."

Nathan shook his head. "I understand, but I worry about you. You have a tendency to fly off on solo missions and put your life at risk."

"I said I was going to let the department handle this investigation. The only thing I can do now is hope Nina Gilliam is as good as people say she is."

"I thought she would've gotten more cooperation from Kevin since they used to date."

"That explains the sparks that flew in the interrogation room the day she walked in," she said. "Kevin wants to bury me anyway."

Nathan parked near a boat launching dock. "Grab that basket and I'll get the blankets," he said. "And no more talk about Kevin or your case." Caprice picked up the picnic basket and walked over to the edge of the water. It was a cool Indian summer day. The sky was crystal clear and the sunlight sparkled on the water. The leaves were bursting with bright reds and oranges. It looked like a scene from a postcard. The quiet beauty of it all struck Caprice. She didn't notice Nathan when he walked up behind her.

"Don't jump," he whispered as he wrapped a blanket around her shoulders.

She turned around and handed him the basket. "It's beautiful out here."

"Not half as beautiful as you. Come over here and sit down with me."

Caprice smiled at him. "You really think I'm beautiful?"

"You get up every morning and you see that face, those eyes, those lips." He cupped her chin with his hand then brought his lips to hers.

Caprice stepped back. "Let's eat," she said.

Nathan licked his lips as he watched Caprice walk over to the tree where he had laid out the picnic blanket. She sat down and crossed her legs on top of each other. Nathan sat behind her and opened the basket. "For you, I have Concord grapes and turkey, cheese, and mustard on wheat bread," he said as he set the meal in front of her. Caprice smiled.

"I guess you paid close attention when we ate lunch together."

"I paid attention to everything you said or did," he whispered in her ear. Caprice turned around and faced him.

"Nathan, what are we doing? Is this even smart?"

"You know what your problem is? You never live in the moment. You want to analyze everything. It makes you a good detective, but for once, go with the flow, Caprice. You might enjoy the ride."

She rolled her eyes at him and leaned back on him. Nathan popped a grape in her mouth. "Isn't this better?" he asked.

Caprice nodded. "This is nice," she whispered. Nathan fed her another grape.

"I figured you needed this. Just some time away from everything."

"Now I won't spend all day thinking about tomorrow."

"I got reinstated yesterday," Nathan said.

"What? Why aren't you at work?"

"I'm taking some vacation time. Most of my cases are clear, so I figured I'd stay where I was needed."

"I do need you," she said as she turned around to face him. "I see now I can depend on you. You've been here for me every step of the way, even when I tried to push you away."

"I told you I would be."

"I know." She wrapped her arms around his neck and kissed him on the cheek.

"Bang bang," a boy, who looked to be about eight years old, hollered as he ran past them. He had a black gun in his hand.

"What the…" Nathan stood up and grabbed the little boy's arm. "What do you have there?"

"Look what I found, Mister!" the little boy thrust the gun underneath Nathan's nose. Nathan took it from his hands.

"Where did you find this?" Nathan asked.

The boy pointed to some rocks near the bank of the lake. Caprice looked at the gun. It looked like a police issued weapon, but neither of them could be sure.

"Can I have this?" Nathan asked. He fished his badge out of his pocket and showed it to the boy. "See, I'm a police officer, and this is a real gun, not a toy."

The boy's eyes widened. "A real gun?"

"Yes, and it could be loaded. I wouldn't want you to get hurt."

"Will I go to jail now?" he asked as he stared at Nathan's badge.

Nathan shook his head. "No, but who are you here with?"

"My mommy. I'd better go back over there where she is," he said pointing to a play area.

Nathan rubbed the little boy's head. "I'll walk you over there." Caprice stood up and followed Nathan and the boy over to where his mother was sitting. The petite brown skinned woman stood up.

"Jackson, what did I tell you about running off?" she asked. She looked from Nathan to Caprice. "Was he bothering you two?"

Nathan shook his head. "Ma'am, I'm Officer Nathan Wallace."

She covered her mouth with her hands. "Look, I'm not a bad mother; I turned my head for one minute and he just—"

Nathan waved his hand. "This isn't about that. Your son found a gun over near the bank."

She grabbed Jackson's shoulder. "What have I told you about guns?"

He dropped his head. "Never touch a gun."

"Well," Nathan said. "That gun may be crucial to an investigation."

Caprice held her breath. She didn't want to believe that was her gun. She couldn't afford to have her hopes dashed if it wasn't. Pulling a gun out of the lake wasn't an everyday thing. That gun could belong to anyone. *It has to be mine,* she thought.

"A murder investigation?" the woman asked. "Oh God, what have we gotten into?"

"I just need to take some information from you," Nathan said. "Just calm down."

The woman took a deep breath and looked at Nathan. "What do you need from me?"

"Just your name and number. We may need to have a lawyer talk to your son about this gun."

She shook her head. "I don't want any part of this. Next thing you know, my son and I will be on Eyewitness News dead."

"Miss, please," Caprice said. "I need your help. That gun could save my life."

She scanned Caprice's face. "You're that cop from TV."

Caprice sighed. "Yeah, and your son may have found the evidence that will clear my name."

"All right, I'm Joyce Parker," she said. Nathan began writing her information down as she rattled off her address and telephone number.

"Thank you," Nathan said.

The woman nodded and began gathering her things. "I hope it works out for you," she whispered before ushering her son away from Nathan and Caprice.

Caprice grabbed Nathan's shoulder. "Do you think this could be my gun?"

Nathan grabbed a napkin and wrapped the gun with it. "Let's find out."

Caprice ran to their picnic spot and gathered the blankets and basket. "Come on," she said as she raced to Nathan's car. When they got to the police department, Nathan made Caprice wait in the car, despite her protests.

"Caprice, it will be a lot better if I do this alone," he said. "You're still suspended, remember?"

She sighed and rolled her eyes. "I know."

"Then let me take this in. You don't need anymore trouble."

She folded her arms under her breasts and frowned at Nathan as he kissed her on the cheek. "I'll be right back," he said.

Nathan walked in and headed to Major Chaney's office.

"Inspector, I thought you were taking some vacation time," he said when he spotted Nathan.

"I am. I went to Lake Cornelius today, and a little boy gave me this." Nathan handed him the gun.

"What is this?" Chaney opened the napkin.

"It looks like one of ours."

"And, of course, you think it's Detective Johnson's."

"It could be. I brought it to you, because I'm prohibited from doing any investigation on this case."

Major Chaney rolled his eyes. "Is this woman really worth all this trouble?"

"Yes she is. I love Caprice, and I believe she's innocent. She didn't kill Damien King. I'd stake my career on it."

"For your sake, I hope that's true. I'll test this weapon and see if it's hers."

"And if it is hers?" Nathan questioned.

"Then we have to figure out how and why it washed up on the shores of the lake."

"Isn't it obvious?" Nathan mumbled.

"What was that?"

"Nothing." Nathan turned to walk out of the office.

"I still want you to back away from this case," Chaney called out as Nathan walked out the door.

"What happened?" Caprice asked when Nathan returned to the car.

"Chaney said he'll test the gun to make sure it's yours."

Caprice rolled her eyes. "I'm not feeling too confident in the department right now."

Nathan stroked her knee. "I can't say I blame you," he said as he started the car. "But the truth will come out."

Before or after I go to prison? she thought as Nathan drove off.

The doctor walked into Donovan's room and checked his vital signs. "I don't understand," he thought aloud. "His chart looks normal. He should be coming out of this coma any time."

Donovan struggled to keep his eyes closed. If he pulled this performance off, Caprice would still go to jail and the drug charges against him would be dropped.

"You're a baffling case, Mr. Harris." The doctor walked out of the room. Donovan opened his eyes. *I need to find out what's going on,* he thought. He had been in the hospital for two weeks, and Ethan hadn't visited him once. *I should get out of here and kick his ass for abandoning me. And Ron Torres is a dead man when I get out of this hospital bed. I knew he was a punk.*

Donovan tried to move his hands, but he was handcuffed to the bed. *Damn,* he thought. *The next time I get a shot at that detective, I'm not going to miss, and there will be a next time.*

CHAPTER SEVENTEEN

Morning came too soon for Caprice. She wasn't looking forward to walking into a courtroom as a defendant. Her case was moving forward, and prison loomed in her future. The phone rang as she pulled three different dresses out of the closet. She dropped them on the bed then grabbed the phone. "Hello."

"Caprice, I thought I was your best friend," Serena said.

"What are you talking about, Serena? You are my best friend."

"Then why did I read about your upcoming trial on the Internet? Damien's dead, and they think you did it. Did it ever cross your mind to call me and tell me what was going on?"

"I didn't think this would go as far as it has. Besides, how do you tell someone you're accused of murder?"

"Caprice, number one, I know you didn't do this. I mean, if you were going to kill Damien, you would've done it a long time ago. Number two, I have a ticket to Charlotte, and I'll be there at 3:30 today."

"You don't have to come down here," Caprice said. Inwardly, she was glad Serena was coming. For weeks, she'd debated on whether she should have told Serena about the situation. She didn't think Serena would find out. But

Caprice knew her friend was a news hound and surfed the Net reading newspapers.

"Oh yes, I do. I've been there for you through a lot of nonsense. You really need people in your corner right now."

Caprice smiled. "You sound just like Nathan."

"Your partner? What's that all about?"

"Since you're on your way, I'll fill you in this afternoon."

"Maybe something good did come out of this."

"Only you would say something like that," Caprice said. "I have to get ready for court."

"All right, I'll see you soon. These charges will never stick, okay."

Caprice hung up with a smile on her face. She needed Serena's visit. She hoped that by the time her friend arrived, the case would be dismissed, and her nightmare would be over. The phone rang again. *What is it now, Serena?* she thought as she answered the phone. "Yes?"

"Caprice, it's me," Nathan said.

"Hi."

"I'm coming to pick you up."

"That's really not necessary."

"It really is, because I need to see your face this morning. I want to drink my coffee with you, and I want to kiss you."

"Nathan…"

"So make sure you brush your teeth. I don't want a morning breath kiss," he said.

"Bye, Nathan." Caprice smiled as she thought about what Nathan had come to mean to her over the past few

weeks. *I don't know how I would get through this without you,*
she thought as she slipped into a brown ankle-length dress.
A few minutes later, the doorbell rang. Caprice let Nathan
in and he handed her a single stemmed red rose. She sniffed
the fragrant flower and smiled at him.

"Good morning," she said.

"Good morning."

"Thanks for the rose. It's really pretty."

Nathan pulled her into his arms and kissed her softly.
"That felt good," he said when they parted.

"I've got to finish getting dressed. Come in. There's
coffee in the kitchen."

Nathan walked into the kitchen and fixed two cups.
"What are you eating for breakfast?"

"Nothing," she called from her bedroom. "I'm too
nervous."

"You have to eat. I don't need you passing out on me."

Caprice walked into the kitchen. "I'll eat after court, I
promise." She took a steaming mug of coffee from Nathan's
hand. She took three sips before dumping the contents of
the cup in the sink.

Nathan sipped his coffee and nodded. "Come on, let's
go," he said as he set his mug in the sink.

As they drove uptown to the courthouse, Nathan held
Caprice's hand, hoping his touch comforted her. Her face
was hard to read. She showed no emotions. She smiled and
squeezed his hand in return. "What are you thinking
about?" he asked.

"Uh, the DA dropping this case."

"It might happen. The evidence they have against you is, at best, weak. David doesn't like to lose. So he'll come to his senses."

"What if he doesn't? Nathan, we have gotten people convicted on less than what they have on me. I've seen it happen. I've been a part of cases like that. Weak cases do get people convicted."

"Don't think like that," Nathan said. "We still have to get the ballistics report on the gun we found."

"Do you really think Chaney had the test run yet? He's sitting on his bureaucratic ass," she said bitterly.

"When this is over, are you coming back to the force?"

"I don't know. I've seen a side of the police department I don't like. You have to wonder, how many innocent people have gone through this because of something I missed or something that someone planted on them."

Nathan glanced at her. "You know, this doesn't happen as often as you think. Every time Cordell gets arrested, he swears up and down someone has set him up."

"And I probably sound just like him, don't I?"

"There's a difference, though. You really didn't kill Damien King. My brother is a drug dealer."

Caprice leaned back in the seat. "I hope the judge sees it that way and throws this case out with prejudice."

"Cordell's case was thrown out."

"Damnit."

"I know. I was hoping he would get some serious time behind this stunt. I don't know when he started working with Harris."

"Everything I do from now on is tainted because of this. I wonder how many of my other cases are going to be dismissed because I'm charged in a murder?"

"Caprice, you're a good cop. Your work is beyond reproach."

She shook her head. "A good officer on trial."

"Have faith everything is going to work out."

Caprice looked at him and frowned. Nathan parked in a spot marked for police vehicles in front of the courthouse. Caprice got out of the car slowly. It was 8:30 a.m. and she wasn't due in court for another half hour. She and Nathan always came to court early when they had to testify. It was a tough habit to break. Nathan wrapped his arms around Caprice. "It's going to be okay."

"I'm glad you believe that," she said as they walked into the courtroom.

Nina sat at her desk looking over the new information she had gotten from the DA. She was confident that the case would be dismissed today. The gun used to kill Damien King wasn't Caprice's. She scuffed the files into her briefcase and headed over to the courthouse.

When she got there, she ran into Kevin in the hallway. "Nina," he said flatly.

"Kevin, can I ask you a question?"

"Shoot," he replied.

"Why are you out to get my client?"

"I'm not talking about this case with you."

"Come on, Kevin, this is off the record. Have you even looked for another suspect?"

"You've seen my report. Why can't you just accept the fact that your client may be guilty?"

"I see you're still the same jerk you were when we were together. You just can't be wrong, can you?"

Kevin rolled his eyes. "If that isn't the pot calling the kettle black. You should've talked her into taking the deal."

Nina smiled wryly. "You haven't seen Chaney's report, have you? Gotta go," she said as she walked away from him. Nina walked into the courtroom and found Nathan and Caprice sitting at the defense table. "I'm glad you're here," she said.

"What happened?" Caprice asked, expecting the worst.

"I'm moving for a dismissal, and I have a good feeling we'll get it. Your gun was not used to kill Damien King. Your prints were nowhere in that room."

"Tell me something I don't know," Caprice said.

"I know you know this, now the court will too. You're going to be back at work before too long."

"I hope you're right."

Nathan squeezed Caprice's shoulder. "I told you this would work out in your favor. One day you're going to learn to listen to me."

"We haven't won yet," Caprice said.

David Thompson, the district attorney, walked into the courtroom with a stack of papers and two assistant district attorneys. He didn't look at Caprice and Nathan. The case against her was full of holes, and it would certainly be dismissed. Caprice's stellar reputation as a detective was common knowledge in the DA's office. Detective Harrington's intense focus on Caprice as a suspect was laughable, and trying to prosecute her would be nothing less than a circus.

He laid his papers on the table then walked over to Nina. "Can I speak to you for a minute?" he asked. She nodded and went with him to his table. "I'm going to drop these charges today. I don't have enough evidence to go ahead with prosecution."

"Good, that saves me from having to ask for a dismissal and preparing a motion."

"Tell Detective Johnson that I'm sorry this had to happen."

"I'm sure she's sorry, too. I wonder if she'll sue for wrongful prosecution?"

David frowned. "You'd like that, wouldn't you?"

"I don't like what this has done to her. Caprice is a good officer, and she didn't deserve this." David didn't say anything. "You know I'm right," Nina said as she sauntered over to the defense table.

A few minutes later, court was called to order. Caprice stood up and crossed her fingers. "Your honor," David said, "the state moves to drop the charges against Caprice Johnson."

"Why is that?" the judge asked.

"A lack of evidence. New reports from the police department don't place Ms. Johnson in the hotel room where the shooting took place."

"All right, Ms. Johnson, you're free to go," the judge said. "I hope the next time I see you in my courtroom, it will be on the other side of the law."

Caprice nodded then hugged Nina. "Thank you," she whispered.

"It's easy getting an innocent person off," Nina replied.

Caprice rushed into Nathan's arms. "It's over," she exclaimed.

"I'm glad. We have some serious celebrating to do tonight," he said.

"I have to go to the airport. My friend, Serena, heard about the case, and she's flying down here."

"Good, now I get to find out more about you. They say the best way to learn about a woman is to meet her best friend."

Caprice popped Nathan on the shoulder. "You know me well enough."

"But I could always stand to learn more," he whispered.

"I wonder, though, who really killed Damien."

"I have a feeling you'll find out soon."

"You know as well as I do Donovan Harris is behind this. We just have to prove it and get him off the streets once and for all."

He nodded. "Well, I guess it isn't really over." Caprice grabbed Nathan's hand and they walked down the hall.

"You know, I'm through," Caprice said as she kissed him on the cheek.

A small group of reporters pounced on Caprice as soon as they stepped outside. "Detective Johnson, the charges have been dropped. What do you have to say?" one reporter asked.

"No comment," she said.

"Come on, Detective," another reporter said. "Just one comment."

"Fine," Caprice said.

"Are you sure?" Nathan whispered in her ear. She nodded.

"For weeks, I have been living with a murder accusation. I've had to deal with the media attention, the questions from my colleagues, but all along, I knew I was innocent. Today, I was vindicated. I'm sorry for Damien King's family, and I hope the real killer is brought to justice. That's all I have to say."

Nathan ushered Caprice down the steps and to his car. "That was good."

"I know. I saw a similar speech in a Lifetime movie," she said with a giggle.

Nathan started the car. "So what's next?"

"I don't know," Caprice replied. "Should I try to get my job back or should I just move on?"

"Caprice, you know you love being a cop."

"Yeah, but who believed me when I was accused of this murder? There were more than enough people in that squad room ready to brand me a murderer."

"You're going to let that stop you from doing what you love?"

"I'm not making any decisions until I find out who killed Damien. I feel like I owe that to him and myself."

"I'll help you," Nathan said.

"I knew you would, but I don't want you to get in more trouble. I'm sure IAD is going to investigate what happened at the park, and I might get suspended again."

"You were defending yourself."

"Well, let's hope others see it that way," she said as Nathan pulled into her driveway.

He stroked her cheek. "I'll see you later, okay?"

"All right. Nathan, I...I love you," she said, then dashed out of the car.

Nathan wanted to follow her and force her to explain herself, but he saw that doe-like look on her face when she ran out of the car. He thought it was better to wait. *I love you too,* he thought as he watched her front door close.

CHAPTER EIGHTEEN

Ethan walked into Donovan's hospital room and sat in a chair beside his bed. "Your little plan is falling apart," he whispered angrily. "That detective got off because there wasn't enough evidence. Now, because of that stunt at the park, I have the police on my tail like a pack of blood-hounds. You need to wake up and fix this, Donovan. Because I will not take the fall for you."

Donovan opened his eyes and looked at his attorney. "It's about time you showed your face."

"What the…I thought you were in a coma." Ethan's heartbeat increased ten-fold.

"Well as soon as the police realize I'm not, they're going to want to arrest me," he said. "I'm faking it for as long as I can."

"What the hell am I supposed to do while you're playing a vegetable?"

"Get me out of this situation so I can wake up and get out of here. I want that woman dead."

"Now you want to kill a cop? Are you insane? The police will be all over you the minute you get out of here. You'll be in jail after this stunt." The door opened and one of the hospital security guards assigned to watch the room walked in. Donovan closed his eyes.

"I thought I heard voices," he said. He looked from Ethan to Donovan.

"I was on my cell phone, and I had the speaker going."

"You can't use cell phones in here." He pointed to a sign near the door.

Ethan threw his hand up as if to say "sorry." "I won't use it again. Do you think you can take these cuffs off my client? He's in a coma, what can he do?"

"I'll have to talk to my supervisor about that," he said. "We have our orders."

"Do that. Because this is a violation of his human and civil rights. This man is sick. Prisoners in China get treated better than this." The guard walked out of the room and Ethan turned to Donovan. "Keep your eyes closed, okay?"

Donovan nodded. "You just need to keep me out of jail so I can get rid of that cop, then I'm going to disappear." His voice was barely above a whisper. Ethan had to lean in to hear him.

"Just like that?"

"Just like that. I'll pay you one million dollars for your help."

Dollar signs danced in Ethan's eyes. A million dollars and not having to deal with Donovan Harris ever again was a deal he couldn't pass up. "What do I need to do?" he inquired. The door opened before Donovan could answer.

The doctor walked in. "Hello."

"Doctor, why have you allowed my client to be shackled to this bed this way?" Ethan asked, feigning indignation.

"The police say he's dangerous."

"He's comatose. How dangerous can he be? I'll slap a lawsuit on this hospital if you don't unchain him, now, today! The police can't possibly believe he's that big of a threat."

"I'll have to talk to the police," the doctor said as he left the room.

"All right, Donovan, once they get you unhooked, we should work on getting you out of here."

"I can get out of here on my own. Just get these handcuffs off."

"And for that, I get a million dollars?"

"Yes."

Ethan stood up and walked over to the window. He let his mind take him to a tropical getaway. The best part of his daydream was the absence of Donovan Harris.

About twenty minutes later, a security guard came to remove Donovan's handcuffs.

"I'm glad you all came to your senses," Ethan said. "Now maybe my client can heal properly."

Donovan wanted to smile. As soon as he got the chance, he was out of there, and he was going to find Caprice Johnson. *She's going to regret the day she arrested me,* he thought.

Caprice stood near the baggage claim trying to spot Serena in the crowd of thousands exiting Flight 1256 from Chicago. "Caprice!" Serena shouted when she saw her friend.

The two women embraced. "It is so good to see you," Caprice said. "The Windy City must be treating you well."

"I can't complain, and you look great yourself. Honey, I may have to move down South. The weather is lovely here."

"Yeah, right. You would have to be pried from Chi-Town. I'm surprised you didn't try to strap the Sears Tower to your back for this trip."

"You haven't seen my luggage yet. So how did it go in court today?"

Caprice smiled brightly. "The case was dismissed."

"Yes! We have to celebrate big time tonight," Serena said.

"We have to include Nathan in our plans tonight."

"Nathan? That would be your partner, right?"

"Former partner," she corrected.

"Excuse me. So now that he's included in our plans, what does it mean for the two of you? Is something serious going on? Is my friend in love again?"

"Grab your bags and we'll talk about it in the car."

Serena smiled and walked over to the baggage claim. "I'm glad you listened to me on this one," she called out.

Caprice leaned back against the wall. She closed her eyes and thought about Nathan kissing her. *I'm going to have to explain why I love him,* she thought. *I still can't believe I told him that.*

"All right, girlfriend, let's go," Serena said interrupting Caprice's thoughts.

When the two women got in the car, Serena turned the radio off and looked at her friend. "Okay, I know your case was dismissed, but tell me from the beginning what happened."

Caprice tightened her grip on the steering wheel. "Well, Damien called me, just like you said he would, and for some reason, I met with him. He had the nerve to ask me for another chance."

"Sounds like Damien-arrogance and—"

"Serena, the man is dead. Anyway, the night he was killed, we met for drinks. We had a huge argument in the bar."

"Why did you meet with him? You knew he was going to run that same old tired fifty-cent game."

"I needed closure," Caprice replied. "I thought if I got Damien out of my system, I could move on with my life. But seeing him confused me and made me angry. Part of me wanted to run into his arms and forgive him."

"Just imagine if you had. What if you had gone to his room? What if you were in that room when he was shot? Whoever killed him would have killed you, too."

"I wonder if I could've saved him that night."

"You know what my big momma used to say: when your number is up, it's time to go. Damien's card was pulled. There was nothing you could have done to change what happened. Would you have wanted to take his place?"

"I know what you're saying, but I still want to know who did it, and why. Was this even about Damien at all?"

Serena slapped her forehead with her hand. "Caprice, can you just let it go? You're off the hook. Damien's dead. Obviously, whoever killed him is still out there. Do you want to die too? Why do you always have to be the hero? You're not Mighty Mouse; you don't have to save the day."

"Serena, I owe it to Damien and myself to bring his killer to justice. I did love him at one point in my life."

"You don't owe Damien a damn thing. But I know you aren't going to rest until you find out the truth. How can Nathan put up with you?"

"Nathan's going to help me, thank you very much," Caprice said.

Serena rolled her eyes. "I forgot, two supercops."

Caprice thumped her friend on the arm. "It is so good to have you here."

"I know. You missed me, didn't you?"

The two friends laughed at their disagreement.

Nathan sat on the sofa in his den. *I wonder what's keeping Caprice?* he thought. He started to call her, but his phone rang before he could. "Wallace."

"Nathan, it's Cordell."

"What now?"

"I need some place to stay until I can get on my feet. I was hoping you would help me out."

"Call the Y."

"So it's like that?" Cordell asked.

"Do you really expect me to allow a criminal to come stay in my house? Be serious, Cordell."

"I told you, I'm trying to turn my life around."

"Are you really?" he asked.

"Yes."

"Then prove it. Help me nail Donovan Harris."

"I can't do that," Cordell said.

"Then you can't stay here. That man tried to kill Caprice and is probably behind another murder."

"You want me to get killed, don't you? I guess her life is more valuable than mine."

"Cordell, I'm not saying that, but Donovan has gone too far this time, and he has to pay."

"What's up with you and that lady copy anyway? Are you in love with her?"

"That's my business," he snapped. "Look, Donovan's in a coma. All I need from you is information. How will he even know you talked to me?"

"I don't know anything," he mumbled.

"I'm not asking you again. I can make your life really difficult, if I want to," Nathan threatened.

"All of this for some bitch? Is she worth all this trouble? Donovan will kill you, her, and me if we get too close to the truth. I'm not going out on that limb for anybody."

"Cordell, when are you going to be a man? You say you want to change your life. Now's your chance to prove it."

"All right, I'll help you," Cordell said with a heavy sigh.

"Let's meet at the Happy Face Café and talk."

"There's nothing but cops there."

"And your point is?"

"Why don't we just go to the McDonald's Cafeteria? That way it won't look obvious that I'm talking to you," Cordell said.

"Fine. Meet me there in an hour." Nathan hung up the phone and grabbed his jacket.

When Nathan got to the restaurant, Cordell was sitting at a table in the back of the dining room. Cordell looked around, making sure no one saw him and Nathan together. Even though he wanted to prove to his brother that he was trying to change, he didn't want to risk being sighted by some of Donovan's people talking to a cop. Brother or no brother, Nathan was a liability to Cordell.

"You look nervous," Nathan said when he sat down across from his brother.

"Look, what do you want to know?"

"All right, I need to know who would kill for Donovan."

"There was a girl who works for him, Sabrina Jones, I think. She was ruthless, and she did a lot of contracts."

"As in murder for hire?" Cordell nodded. "Where is she now?" Nathan asked.

"Hell if I know. She worked directly with Donovan. I saw her once or twice. I wasn't that deep into the business."

"How did you get involved in this? What were you thinking?"

"I was thinking I needed some cash. Who do you think is going to hire a three-time convicted felon? Nobody paying real money wants to hire me. Hell, I paid my debt to society, and these motherfuckers still want me to suffer. With my record, I couldn't be legit like you."

"You have no one but yourself to blame, Cordell," Nathan said.

"Here we go again with this bullshit. Why don't you come down off your high horse and look at the real world? I'm a black man with a criminal record. Everybody turns their back on me."

"That's bullshit and you know it. You use your past as a reason to continue to screw up your life. How many times have I lined up jobs for you? How many times have I called in a favor to get a charge against you reduced? I'm tired of it and you. When you grow up, your life will be better. Fast cash don't last."

Cordell rolled his eyes. "Oh, I get it, if I straighten up and fly right, I can be just like you, little bro, huh?"

Nathan shook his head. "I'm glad Mom and Dad don't have to be here to deal with you. This would kill them."

Cordell leaned back in his seat. "You get on my fucking nerves with your holier-than-thou attitude," he bellowed. "You ain't no better than me. I'm sick of this. I'm not helping you or that bitch with shit!" He jumped up from the table, nearly knocking the vinyl chair over.

Nathan started to go after his brother, but he had enough information to get the ball rolling. He looked at his watch. Caprice should be back from the airport by now, he thought. Nathan wanted to rush to the police department and run a background check on Sabrina Jones, but he knew Caprice would want in on it.

After all, he thought, this is her case and her life.

CHAPTER NINETEEN

Nathan knocked on Caprice's door just as the sun set. He turned around and watched the Carolina blue sky turn lavender then burnt orange. Nathan was a little nervous about meeting Serena. He always had anxiety about meeting a girlfriend's sistafriend. Her opinion could make or break a relationship.

Wait a minute; she isn't mine yet, I don't think, he thought as the door opened. He looked at the cocoa brown sister who opened the door. She was short with a head full of jet-black dreadlocks. She had a pair of piercing brown eyes that twinkled in the waning sunlight. "You must be Serena," Nathan said.

"And you must be Nathan. Come in. I've heard a lot about you."

"All good, I hope."

She smiled. "Caprice, Nathan's here."

Caprice walked out of her bedroom. "Hey," she said.

Nathan smiled approvingly at her outfit—a black skirt that stopped mid-thigh and a white shirt with black Chinese letters on the front. Nathan looked down at her knee-high black leather boots. "Wow, you look hot."

"That's an outfit I brought her from the Windy City. Took your breath away, didn't it?" Serena said as she sauntered off to the kitchen.

Caprice dropped her head and giggled. "She's crazy."

"I like her. She has style," he said, admiring Caprice's outfit.

"You want to stop drooling? You've seen me in less." Caprice grabbed his hand and led him to the sofa.

Nathan grinned as he thought about her naked body in his arms. "That's hard to do. You look so delicious." Nathan licked his lips and pulled her into his arms. He stroked her cheek. "You know we need to talk."

Caprice sighed. "I know."

"So, you love me." His eyes gleamed with excitement.

"Nathan, I'm so confused about what I'm feeling right now, but I have very strong feelings for you."

"It's really simple, Caprice, either you love me, or you don't. I know I love you with every fiber of my being."

She swallowed hard as she looked into his eyes. "I do love you, and that scares me."

"Why? There's nothing to fear."

"Yes, there is. You don't know my track record with men. It all starts off lovely, but it always ends up with me being heartbroken and devastated."

Nathan squeezed her hand. "Not this time. I told you, I'll never hurt you. I don't tell a woman I love her if I don't mean it." He kissed her gently on the lips. "I want you to trust me and believe that this time it's different."

Tears welled up in her eyes. Nathan took her face in his hands. Caprice wrapped her arms around Nathan's neck and pulled him closer to her. He ran his hands down her back.

"Ahem," Serena said, announcing her presence known in the living room. Caprice and Nathan parted. "I thought we were going out? You two look like you want to be alone. I'm ready to do what Lucy Pearl said and dance tonight."

"All right, let's go," Caprice said as she stood up and smoothed her skirt.

"Where are we going?" Nathan asked.

"Let's go to that new R&B club uptown," Caprice suggested. Serena shrugged.

"This is your world; I'm just going along for the ride. But let me lay some ground rules," she said, pointing her index finger at both of them.

"Here we go," Caprice said and rolled her eyes upward.

"No shop talk, supercops. Now we can go."

Nathan smiled at Serena. "You're a funny woman."

"I try. And one other thing, I'm asking all the questions tonight."

"Let's get out of here before I have to strangle this girl," Caprice said.

Nathan walked out ahead of the women. "He's cute, girl," Serena whispered. "I see what it means when they say 'nothing is finer than being in Carolina.' "

"Shut up," Caprice hissed. They broke out into laughter like two elementary schoolgirls.

It was after midnight when Donovan decided to test his legs. After three weeks of lying flat on his back, he had to get a feel for walking again. Gingerly, he strode to the door and peeked out. The guard sat outside the room sleeping. He shook his head. *I can take him out, steal his uniform and get the hell out of here. He probably goes to sleep the same time every night,* he thought. Donovan walked back to the bed. It was time to devise a plan. He needed to call someone and have a car waiting for him when he made his escape. He knew he couldn't call Ethan. The police were watching him like a hawk. *Cordell—he owes me a favor. I'll call him tomorrow.* He slid back into the bed and laid on his back. He looked up at the ceiling and thought about what he was going to do when he saw Caprice. He wanted to catch her in a dark alley. She'd be walking alone, thinking she was going to meet someone to get information about him. Donovan would be standing in the shadows, smoking a Newport. To blend in with the darkness, he'd wear a black raincoat and black boots, clothes he could throw away after he was done.

"Hello," she would say. "Is anyone back here?" She'd walk closer, following the smell of the cigarette smoke. "I know someone's here. It's me. You called me out here. You said you had some information for me about Donovan Harris."

That's when he would pounce. He'd step out of the shadows and into a sliver of light coming from a dim street lamp. "We meet again, Detective," he'd say. "And I know you're alone this time. Did you ever find that gun?"

"I…I thought you were in a coma." Her voice would waver with fear. Her hands would shake.

"You thought wrong. Did you think I was going to let a bitch like you bring me down?" He'd flick his cigarette butt in her face, and then laugh as she wiped the hot ashes away. "I gave you a chance to let me go. You'd still be on the police force, and that man would still be alive. But you wanted to be big bad Betty Brown. How bad do you feel now? You're out here all alone, no gun, and no backup."

He'd watch fear flicker in her eyes. *What is he going to do next?* she would think as he stepped closer to her. "Yeah, you're going to die tonight, slow and painful." Donovan would pull a three-inch lock-blade knife from his coat pocket and hold it in front of her face as he grabbed the back of her neck. She'd be paralyzed with terror. A scream would die in her throat. Then, with the skill of the neighborhood butcher, Donovan would slash her throat. As the blood gushed from the gash, he would jab the knife into her stomach over and over again, losing count of the stab wounds. He'd drop her lifeless body to the ground and watch her twitch until she bled out. Just to make sure she was dead, Donovan would kick her in the face with the toe of his boot. Still, he wouldn't be satisfied with her being stabbed to death. He'd pull out his gun, with the silencer attached, and empty the clip into her body. Then he would walk away, tossing the bloody coat and shoes in a dumpster. He'd get in his car, drive to the Charlotte-Douglas International Airport, and take a flight to New York. From there, he would go on to a tropical island in the South Pacific.

Donovan smiled at his fantasy, then drifted off to sleep.

Nathan sat at the bar in the club watching Serena and Caprice talk. They seemed to forget he was with them as they caught up on old times. He couldn't remember a time when he saw Caprice this relaxed. She was a new woman.

"Do you miss Chicago at all?" Serena asked her friend.

"Not as much as I used to," she replied, glancing at Nathan.

Serena followed her eyes and smiled. "I wouldn't miss it either," she said. Then she turned to Nathan. "What are your intentions with my friend?"

"Excuse me?" he said, taken a little off guard by the question.

"Serena, chill out," Caprice warned. Serena waved her hand in her friend's face to shut her up.

"Nathan, my friend here tries to be hard, but she is really a softie, and I think this Carolina living has made her lose some more of her edge. So I get to be the hard-nosed city girl. Don't hurt my friend, because I'll have to come after you."

"Is that a threat? You know you can get arrested for that," he joked.

Serena snorted. "I know people, too. But seriously, Caprice and I have been friends forever, and from what I can see, you're a good man, and you care about her. I just want Miss Thing to be happy."

"So do I," Nathan replied.

"Hello. Remember me?" Caprice said. "I'm still here. Don't talk about me like I'm in the bathroom."

"Ignore her," Serena said. "And answer my question."

Nathan glanced at Caprice, who looked as if she was going to die from embarrassment. "I have nothing but the most honorable intentions for your friend."

Serena smiled. "I like the sound of that. Well, I'm going to leave you two and hit the dance floor."

"But you can't dance," Caprice joked.

"No one knows me here, so it doesn't matter," she said with a bright smile. Before she walked out on the dance floor, a tall brother with a bald head and a caramel complexion stopped her and asked for a dance.

Caprice turned to Nathan. "Honorable intentions, huh? What exactly do you mean by that?"

"You'll just have to find out." He eyed her hungrily. Watching her at the bar being relaxed and smiling turned him on. Nathan stroked her leg. "You have the softest skin."

"Stop it," she whispered with a giggle.

"I'll try, but I can't promise I will. Being this close to you just makes me want to reach out and touch you all over."

Her breath caught in her chest. "You know, I can come to your place tonight once we drop Serena off at my house. She's probably tired from her flight."

"Not the way she's dancing out there," Nathan replied. Caprice looked at her friend and dance partner bump and grind to the Isley Brothers' classic "Between the Sheets."

"Let's go out there and show them how it's really done," Caprice whispered. Nathan stood up and extended his hand to Caprice. They walked out on the dance floor as Ron Isley sang "ooh baby baby." Nathan pulled Caprice into his arms and held her close. He rocked his hips from side to side. She followed his rhythmic lead. Nathan spun her around and dipped her. Then they started dancing cheek to cheek again. When the song ended, neither one of them noticed for a few seconds.

As the opening cords of "Jamaica Funk" began to play, Nathan looked at Caprice and smiled. "It's getting hot on this dance floor." Caprice nodded and they headed back to the bar. The desire to make love was as thick as a humid Carolina summer.

"Nathan," she began.

"Yeah?"

"Have you found out anything about Damien's killer?"

"Didn't Serena say no shop talk tonight?"

"She isn't sitting up here listening, now is she?"

"I found out some information earlier tonight. We need to find a Sabrina Jones. She's done some contract killing for Donovan in the past."

"Sabrina Jones?"

"Yeah. You know her?"

Caprice shook her head. "No, I don't think so. Have you checked her background yet?"

Nathan shook his head. "Not yet. But don't worry; I'll do it tonight since I won't be otherwise occupied."

"You're so bad." Caprice kissed him on the cheek.

Serena returned to the bar after she and her dance partner finished dancing to three other songs. She smiled at Caprice and Nathan. They were sitting so close to each other, not even air could come between them. "I wish I had a camera," she exclaimed.

"Dancing queen comes off the floor. I'm shocked," Caprice said when she turned around.

"Girl, that man was foine! But I'm going back to Chicago in a few days; it would never work out. You two, on the other hand, I know there had better be a bride's maid's dress in my future."

"You're jumping the gun just a wee bit, don't you think?" Caprice said.

"Excuse me," Nathan said as he stood up. "I have to go powder my nose."

"I didn't run you off, did I?" Serena called out.

Nathan laughed and headed to the bathroom.

"Don't let that man get away," Serena said when he was gone. "He's sexy, considerate, and did I mention sexy?"

"I won't let him go."

Serena pulled at her ear. "I'm sorry, but do I hear Ms. Pessimist being optimistic about a relationship? Lord, that man has worked wonders on you."

"No, he just kept his word. That's the only thing I've ever wanted from anyone."

Serena sat on a bar stool and propped herself up on the bar with her elbow. "Does this mean that you've dropped this all-he-is-going-to-do-is-hurt-me attitude?"

"For now. I'm not going to sit here and say Nathan is definitely the one, but I feel like he could be."

"Well, I'm happy for you. If you would give up this quest to find out who killed Damien, I would be ecstatic."

"That's not going to happen," Caprice said.

"You have to borrow trouble, don't you? Everything would be perfect if you'd let this Damien thing go, Capri. I'm being serious."

Caprice smiled as she watched Nathan walk over to them. He wrapped his arms around her waist. "You guys done talking about me?" he asked.

"Who said we were talking about you?" Caprice replied. Nathan kissed her on the back of her neck.

"My ears were burning. Can I buy you ladies some breakfast?"

"A true southern gentleman," Serena said. "Do you have any brothers?"

Nathan laughed uncomfortably. "Trust me, you can do better than my brother," he said as he ushered the two women out of the club. Caprice squeezed Nathan's hand. She knew how difficult it was for him to deal with Cordell.

The three of them headed to The International House of Pancakes for a quick bite to eat. Caprice and Nathan sat beside each other and held hands. Serena couldn't help but smile at them. She was happy for her friend. After everything she went through with Damien, Serena knew Caprice would never open up to another man again.

CHAPTER TWENTY

After three days in Charlotte, Serena was preparing for her return to Chicago. "He's good for you," Serena said as she and Caprice said their goodbyes at the airport. "Just make sure this investigation doesn't get either of you killed."

"You worry too much."

"I have to. Sometimes I think you have no fear, except when it comes to falling in love."

"I'm getting over that. Nathan's helping me in that area."

"Well, get back to that man, okay? I'll call you next week." The two women hugged, then Serena headed for the boarding gate. Caprice turned around and headed to her car. With Serena gone, she and Nathan could put more work into their investigation. She had an address for Sabrina Jones, but she hadn't checked it out yet. And even though Nathan told her not to go there alone, she drove to Statesville Avenue.

Caprice pulled into the driveway of the Twin Oaks Apartment complex. She looked down at the piece of paper with Sabrina's address written on it. This is the right place, she thought. Caprice leaned over, reached into her glove box and pulled out a .38 revolver. She dropped the gun in her jacket pocket then got out of the car. The roof of the porch sagged like a wet towel. The wooden steps were grey and rotting. Caprice nearly fell through a step as she walked to Sabrina's door. She knocked on the door with authority, but stopped short of identifying herself as a police officer. No answer. She knocked again, harder. Still no answer. Caprice looked around to see if anyone was watching her. The coast looked clear. She reached into her purse and grabbed a credit card then jimmied the lock open.

"Hello," she called out as she walked into the apartment. She had her hand in her jacket pocket on her gun. The apartment smelled musty, as if it hadn't been occupied in weeks. She coughed several times until she got used to the smell.

"What am I looking for?" she thought aloud. Caprice examined the huge entertainment center in the corner of the living room. There was nothing there except a twenty-five-inch TV, a DVD player, a stereo, and a video camera. Caprice sat down on the dust-covered brown leather sofa and went through the papers and magazines on the oak coffee table. All she found was a few bills, a pre-approved credit card application, and a flyer from a neighborhood church. She dropped the papers on the table in a heap.

In the kitchen was a list of phone numbers taped to the side of the refrigerator. Instead of names, there were initials and numbers. Caprice looked at the list-E, D, R, A, W. She ripped the list down and dropped it in her purse. She went through the caller ID box. Most of the calls came from private callers and unknown numbers. Caprice picked up the phone and hit the redial button. The phone rang three

200 CHERIS F. HODGES

times before Donovan Harris's voice mail picked up. Why did she call Donovan? she thought as she walked into the bedroom.

When Caprice got to the bedroom, she searched Sabrina's dresser drawers. She found condoms, a box of bullets, and a file folder. *Looks like I hit the jackpot,* she thought. She opened the folder and found papers with her name on them. *What's this?* Caprice read through her own life history—her last address in Chicago, her address in Charlotte, her police service record. She tucked the folder under her arm and looked deeper into the drawer. She found a FedEx receipt from Donovan Harris.

What is this all about? I bet this is how they found out about Damien and me. I can't believe the nerve of these bastards. Caprice continued to look for clues about Damien's murder. After coming up empty-handed, Caprice decided to head to Nathan's with her findings. *When I find this Sabrina Jones, she's going to pay for what she did.*

Ethan walked into Donovan's hospital room and sat beside his bed. "You awake?"

"Yeah," he replied without opening his eyes.

"Everything is set. I got in touch with Cordell, and he said he'll be here at 1:30 a.m."

"Good."

"I want my money up front," Ethan said.

"You'll get your money when I get out of here."

"Look, I have put myself at risk for you for the last time. If I don't have my money within the next three days, I'm going to stop helping you."

Donovan opened his eyes and turned to Ethan. "You have a death wish, don't you?"

"No, I'm just sick of your bull. I want out."

"You can join Sabrina in a dirt nap. I said you'd get your money when I get out of here."

"That's another thing, you don't have the upper hand right now. I would get a sweet deal if I turned state's evidence against you."

"And disbarred. Hell, you'd end up in a jail cell, and I'd make damn sure you wouldn't last a month. One thing you should know by now is I don't make idle threats. I make promises."

Ethan stood up and turned toward the door. "Cordell will be here at one-thirty. I hope you have your stuff together."

Donovan smirked. He knew Ethan's words were empty. The last thing he wanted was to be disbarred and arrested. Donovan closed his eyes and waited for the doctor. Everything in the hospital was done on a schedule. So predictable, so easy to exploit. Donovan knew he'd have to get rid of Ethan too. So many people to kill and so little time, he thought as the doctor checked his vital signs.

The door to the room opened. Who is that? Donovan thought.

"Doctor, I'm Inspector Wallace with the Charlotte-Mecklenburg Police Department," Nathan said.

"What can I do for you?"

"I need to know how this patient is doing. When do you expect him to come out of this coma?"

"That's the million-dollar question. Mr. Harris could wake up at any time."

Nathan looked at Donovan. "What happened to the cuffs?"

"It was a little 'barbaric' according to his lawyer. He threatened to sue if we didn't take them off. Besides, he's in a coma. He can't hurt anyone."

"This man is very dangerous, and I wouldn't be surprised if he's faking it." Nathan searched Donovan's face for movement.

"He's not faking anything," the doctor said. "If he wasn't sick, then we would know. Even when he wakes up, he won't be able to walk out of here."

Nathan's eyebrow shot up as he looked at the doctor. "Just know this, if he wakes up and escapes, lives will be in jeopardy. Can you live with that?"

Nathan knew Donovan and Ethan were up to no good, and he was going to find out. His cell phone rang as he headed to his car in the parking lot.

"Wallace."

"Where are you?" Caprice asked.

"Leaving the hospital. What's going on?"

"I need to see you. I have some interesting information about Sabrina Jones and Donovan Harris."

"Do I want to know how you got this information?"

"Umm, let's pretend this is the Army. If you don't ask, I won't tell."

Nathan chuckled. "All right, I'm on my way home now."

"I'll be waiting for you when you get here."

Nathan turned off the phone, got into his car, and sped home. Whatever Donovan was planning, he had to stop it before it started. *He's going to want revenge, and Caprice is probably at the top of his to-do list,*, he reasoned. *I can't let him get to her.*

When Nathan arrived at his house, Caprice was sitting on the front steps. Nathan walked over to her and kissed her on the cheek.

"What were you doing at the hospital?" she asked.

"Checking on Donovan. He's still in a coma."

"Really?"

"Yeah. I think he's faking it, though. Why would he be in a coma for this long because of a little bump on the head?"

"I know what you mean," she said. "But there was definitely something going on with him and Sabrina Jones. The last call she made on her home phone was to Harris."

"You broke into her house?"

"Didn't I tell you not to ask?"

"Caprice, all jokes aside, that woman is a killer. She could've walked in the house and shot you."

"But she didn't. It looked as if she hadn't been there in weeks. Maybe she made so much money from killing Damien and setting me up that she could disappear. We have to find her now."

Nathan unlocked the front door. "Come in so we can talk about this," he said. Caprice walked in behind Nathan, noticing his heavy and angry steps. She could tell he was upset about what she did by the way he walked.

"Look," she said, "I know what I did was wrong, but I needed to know if she had anything to do with all of this crap that has happened in my life."

"What you did was not only wrong, but dangerous. You aren't above the law. This evidence isn't admissible in court. You didn't help the case, Caprice. You put all of our work in jeopardy."

"I know the damn law," she sighed.

"I can't tell."

"You want to bring me up on charges, Mr. IAD?"

"That's not fair. I said I'd help you with this, but I didn't say I'd be an accessory to a burglary."

"I don't need your help, your judgment, or you!" Caprice stood up and stormed out of his house. Nathan ran after her but couldn't stop her from driving off.

"Damnit!" he swore as he watched her speed away.

CHAPTER TWENTY-ONE

Caprice drove down the street like a flaming bat out of hell. She couldn't believe Nathan's reaction to what she did. *It's not like I'm an official cop anyway,* she thought. *And I don't think I want to be one anymore.* She slowed her car down as she turned into one of the residential neighborhoods with speed bumps. *Maybe I should go back to Sabrina's and see what else is in her apartment.* Caprice turned her car around and headed toward Statesville Avenue. When she got to the apartment complex, Nathan was sitting on the hood of his car. *What is he doing here?* she thought as she parked her car and slammed the door.

"I knew you'd come back here," he said.

"So?"

"Caprice, do you really want to throw your career away like this? Let's just acknowledge you made a mistake coming here the first time and move on. We can work around how you found whatever information you have."

"Nathan, I told you I was going to do whatever I had to do to find out who killed Damien and set me up. If you can't handle it, then step aside, and let me do this my way."

"Is that what you want me to do? You want me to stop helping you so that you can write me off as another man who broke a promise to you?"

Caprice rolled her eyes. "I'm doing this my way, okay?"

Nathan grabbed her hand. "No, you're not. Don't make me cuff you."

"I wish you would," she said, as though issuing a dare.

"Don't test me," Nathan said forcefully.

Caprice rolled her eyes and jerked away from him. "So, what do you suggest we do?"

"I put an APB out on Sabrina Jones. If you'd waited before having your temper tantrum, you would've known this."

"I don't need your condescending tone, Nathan. Had you not jumped on my case, I wouldn't have stormed out."

Nathan sighed. "Caprice, lets hold the blame game for later and look for Sabrina."

Caprice pulled out the list of numbers she took from Sabrina's apartment and handed it to Nathan. "We need to put names with these numbers."

Nathan took the list and pulled Caprice into his arms. "I don't want this to come between us. We can't keep butting heads over this."

"Well, what do you suggest?"

"For now, let's just follow what we have and try not to break any more laws." Caprice frowned at him. "Come on," he said. "You can't go breaking into people's apartments anymore."

"Fine," she said, pulling out of his embrace.

"Have you heard anything about your suspension?"

"Captain Leland called a few days ago, but I didn't call him back. It's kind of hard to want to go back in that squad room, knowing so many of my fellow officers believed I was a murderer."

"A lot of us didn't believe it at all."

"You don't count. Thom didn't even have my back. If I were a man would things have been different?"

"So, now the department is sexist?" he asked incredulously.

"Did I say that? But if the pig nose fits, oink oink."

"You can't be serious," Nathan said. "Caprice, no one knew much about you or your past, but I find it hard to believe that everyone thought you did this."

"Whatever," she said.

"Let's get out of here," Nathan suggested.

"You know what, I'm going home. I need to be alone." She walked over to her car and drove away. Nathan watched her car speed down the street. *All right, Caprice, I'm tired of chasing you today,* he thought as he got into his own car.

Donovan sat up in his bed; he could sense it was midnight. The quiet hum of the hospital let him know it was time to put his plan in motion. He grabbed the phone and called Cordell.

"Yeah?" Cordell said.

"Is everything set?"

"You got the cash?"

"Yeah," Donovan answered.

"Then it's a go. I'll be parked in the emergency room parking lot. I'm driving the rental car like we discussed."

"Make sure you take the license plate off before you get here."

"I got it."

"Don't be late. One a.m., that's when there's no one on the floor."

"All right, fine," Cordell said with a sigh.

"Good. I've got to get out of here. There are a few people who have lessons to learn. I have scores to settle, and I'm going to enjoy this."

"I hear you," Cordell said.

When Donovan hung up the phone, he unhooked the cord from the receiver. He looked out the door at the guard who was settling into his seat for a nap. Go to sleep, he thought, get comfortable. Donovan walked back to his bed and sat on the edge of it. He imagined meeting up with Caprice in an alley again. He was lost in his fantasy when he heard the guard snoring. He slowly opened the door, hoping not to wake the man. He wrapped the telephone cord around the guard's neck and dragged him inside his room. The guard struggled to scream and free himself from Donovan's grip, but Donovan was too strong. The man passed out and Donovan tossed him on the bed like a sack of potatoes. He stripped him of his uniform. The pants were a size too big, but as late as it was, no one was likely to notice. He draped his hospital gown over the man and then pulled the covers up to his chin. He checked the man's pulse. He was dead. Donovan looked at his watch. It was now 12:30. He had to get down the corridor before the night nurses did their rounds. Donovan tied the black shoes he took from the dead guard's feet and slithered out of the room. The halls were empty, just as he expected them to be. *All right,* he thought as he walked through the emergency room exit doors. *Where are you Cordell?*

A black Ford Taurus pulled up to the curb. The window was rolled down.

"You ready?" Cordell asked.

Donovan nodded and ran over to the passenger side of the vehicle and got in. "I was getting ready to worry."

"I told you I was going to be here. Where are we going now?"

"I have a safe house off South Boulevard," he said. "I don't think the police know about it."

"Cool," Cordell said.

"I need you to make a phone call for me."

"To who?"

"Detective Caprice Johnson. I need you to tell her you have some information about me and you want to meet with her."

"I don't know if I can do that. I know her. She arrested me too, remember."

"She would believe you. I know your brother's a cop. Maybe she'll think you're giving up the thug life and trying to score points with your brother. Just get her to agree to meet you, and I'll take it from there."

"All right," Cordell said.

"That bitch is going to pay for ever messing with me," Donovan snarled as Cordell drove.

CHAPTER TWENTY-TWO

Caprice still fumed from her argument with Nathan. *He has some nerve,* she thought. *What right does he have to judge me?*

The telephone rang, interrupting her thoughts. "Hello?"

"Caprice, it's me."

"Nathan, it's late; I'm tired."

"We need to talk," he said.

"Not tonight, okay?"

"You're mad, right?"

"Mad? What right do I have to be mad? You pretty much told me that I brought all of this on myself, and I should run back to the department and beg for my job."

"I never said that! You're twisting my words. Are you sure you're not a reporter?"

"I don't have time for this. Why don't you just leave me alone?"

"Then make time for it, because I don't want to go to sleep with this hanging over us."

Caprice hung up the phone. She didn't want to hear Nathan's apology. The phone rang again. She didn't answer. *I'm going to bed,* she thought as she looked at the clock. It was nearly 1 a.m. Before she could get into bed, there was a knock at the door. Caprice walked to the front door and pulled the curtain back. Just as she expected, Nathan was standing there. She opened the door.

"What do you want?"

"I'm not going to lose you."

She rolled her eyes.

"Do I have to stand out here all night?" he asked.

Caprice stepped aside and let Nathan in. "It's late," she said. "I don't have the energy to listen to you tell me you're sorry for what you said earlier."

"I'm not sorry for what I said. I meant it. You crossed the line in this investigation, that's a fact. But I understand why you felt like you had to do it, even though you could've come to me before you went to extremes. We could've gotten a search warrant for Sabrina Jones's place."

"I wasn't thinking, but I don't need you judging me. What's done is done."

"Caprice, I wasn't judging you. I was stating a fact. As an officer, you shouldn't have broken into her apartment. Your case has been dropped, and you haven't made any kind of effort to see if you will be reinstated. You're obsessed with this case. Have you thought about just letting this go? Let me and the department handle this."

"Hell no, Nathan! This is my life, and he was my fiancé!"

"What is this really about? Did you still love Damien King? Is this about you or him?"

"I think you need to leave," she said as she opened the front door wide. "I don't have to explain anything to you!"

Nathan grabbed her hand and closed the door. "Just tell me something. Are you using this as an excuse to pull away from me? I still love you, and your mood swings aren't going to change that. I'm worried about you."

Caprice turned away from his penetrating gaze. Why was she so angry? Was she trying to do what Nathan accused her of? *Maybe I just can't be what Nathan needs right now,* she thought.

He reached out and stroked her face. "What are you thinking?" he asked. "Just let it out. Talk to me, sweetheart."

"Maybe this is about us. Nathan, this just isn't going to work."

"That's because you won't give it a chance."

She sighed heavily. "I've given it a chance, and I just can't do this, Nathan. Maybe it's time for us to stop fooling ourselves. We shouldn't be together."

"Why not? Give me one good reason why I should walk out that door and put you out of my mind."

Caprice shook her head from side to side, hoping to clear her mind. "I don't want to be at odds with you. I loved our friendship, and it has changed."

"But I thought it changed for the better. Caprice, we connected on a deeper level."

"Whatever, Nathan."

"Maybe we should just pull up on this case. We should let the department handle this," he said.

"No. Are you going to tell me that if the shoe was on the other foot, you'd just let this go?"

Nathan dropped his head. "Probably not."

"Then don't expect me to," she said.

"I'm not going to argue with you about this anymore. If this is how you want things, then fine." Nathan stood up and headed toward the door. He turned around and looked at Caprice. She didn't really want him to go, but it was for the best. At least that was what she told herself. Caprice wanted Nathan in her life, but not this way. She wanted what they had before love complicated everything. But she knew the line had been crossed and there was no going back.

Nathan grabbed the doorknob, and Caprice fought the urge to stop him. When he walked out of the house, she knew he was walking out of her life.

Caprice jumped when the door slammed behind Nathan. *What have I done?* she thought as she listened to his car start up. Caprice ran to the door and opened it, but Nathan was halfway down the street. The phone rang.

"Nathan?" she said, desperation straining her voice.

"Nah, it's not Nathan."

"Who is this?"

"I have some information about Donovan Harris that I think might interest you."

"Once again, I'm going to ask. Who is this?"

"It's Cordell."

"Why in the hell should I believe anything you have to say?"

"I know you think I'm lowlife garbage, but I'm trying to change. That's why I want to tell you about Donovan. He's planning something big."

"Why didn't you call Nathan about this? Donovan's in a coma, so how is he planning anything?" Caprice asked, suspiciously.

"No, he isn't. He's playing the cops and the doctors. I know for a fact he's faking it."

"Tell me what you know."

"I want to talk to you face to face."

"Then let's meet tomorrow."

"Nah, I'm getting the hell out of town tomorrow. I can meet you tonight or not at all. "

"Where do you want to meet?" she asked.

"At that twenty-four-hour pizza place on Central Avenue."

"Are you sure we can't do this in the morning?" Her instincts were telling her not to go, but her obsession with the case overrode good sense.

"I can leave with my information. Either way, I'm out of here in the morning."

"All right, all right," she said. "I'll be there in fifteen minutes."

Nathan couldn't sleep, despite all of his attempts. He ended up tossing and turning in the bed. He couldn't help but think about Caprice and their argument. If she wanted him out of her life, then he had to oblige. His phone rang. Who is this? he thought as he rolled over and picked up the phone from his nightstand.

"Yeah."

"Nathan, it's Caprice."

"What?"

"Never mind, I don't know why I even called you."

"Caprice, it's late, and the last time I talked to you, you were telling me to get the hell out of your house. So what can you possibly want now?"

"I got a strange phone call from your brother," she said.

Nathan sat up. "I'm listening."

"He said he had some information about Donovan, and he wants me to meet him in about ten minutes on Central."

"I don't like the sound of that," Nathan said.

"Do you think you can come with me?"

"What? You want my help?"

"Forget it, Nathan."

"No no, I'll go with you. Let me get dressed."

"All right, I'll meet you there."

Nathan hopped up and slipped into a pair of jeans that were hanging on the foot of his bed. *Cordell, what in hell are you getting us into?* he thought as he pulled his sweatshirt over his head.

Donovan tapped a fresh pack of Newports against the steering wheel of the car. He pulled at the tab to open the cigarettes and shook the pack again, causing a cigarette to fall out. He held it between his fingers and smirked as he reached into his pocket for a lighter. He stuck the cigarette between his lips and lit it. He inhaled sharply, then exhaled smoke. Donovan opened the door and got out of the car. He walked along the side of the restaurant and hid in the shadows. Every time a car passed he looked for Caprice. Finally, she drove into the parking lot. She got out of her car and scoured the parking lot for Cordell. "Yo!" Donovan called out. Caprice turned around and looked for the voice.

"Who's there?" she asked. She slipped her hand in her pocket.

"A, yo!" he said again.

Caprice headed for darkness, the stench of cigarette smoke indicated someone's presence.

"Cordell, is that you?"

Donovan exhaled smoke again. "Hey, you want to talk to me or what?"

"Cordell, I don't have time for these damn games; it's late," she snapped.

Donovan stepped into the dim light. "Surprise."

"What the…I knew you weren't in a coma. You lying son-of-a-bitch!"

He smirked and reached out to grab her, but Caprice pulled her gun out of her pocket. "I've been itching to blow you away, Donovan. Just give me one reason."

"You don't have the guts." He stepped toward her. "Shoot me." He pressed his chest into the barrel of the gun. Caprice stepped back.

"Why are you trying to ruin my life?" she asked.

"Trying? I've taken your career, your man, your safety. I have ruined your life. I gave you a chance to stop this, but you wanted to be a hero. Did you think I was going to let you make a name for yourself off me?" He snorted and dropped his cigarette.

"You have some nerve, you and Sabrina Jones. I know she killed Damien."

Donovan shrugged his shoulders. "Prove it."

"I will, when I find her."

"Do you think I'm going to let you get out of here?" Donovan laughed. "You're really going kiss your ass goodbye tonight."

Caprice wrapped her finger around the trigger and stepped forward. "Who has the gun?"

Donovan sucked his teeth.

"Don't move," she ordered.

He didn't listen, he reached in his back, and pulled out his own gun. "What are you going to do now? I got a gun, too."

They stood there, like two cowboys in the old west, guns cocked and loaded. Caprice took a half step back and Donovan took a step forward. He put his finger on the trigger. Caprice did the same. Donovan fired and missed her by half an inch. Caprice shot back, hitting him in the shoulder. He winced in pain.

"Drop the gun, Donovan!" she yelled.

"Burn in hell," he said before shooting her in the leg.

Caprice fell to the ground and rolled away from him. She attempted to shoot him, but she missed, and the bullet crashed through the front window of the restaurant.

Screams poured from inside, and the six customers dove to the floor. Donovan hobbled over to Caprice and kicked her injured leg. She screamed in pain. He kicked her in the face three times, then pointed the gun at her head.

"This isn't how I dreamed about killing you, but I guess this will have to do," he said before spitting in her face. Caprice brought her free leg up and kicked Donovan in the family jewels. He doubled over in pain. She kicked him in his bowed head. He dropped his gun and fell to the ground. Caprice took the opportunity to try and stand up, but her leg hurt too much. She inched toward the door of the restaurant.

"Stop!" Donovan yelled. He had picked up his gun again. He fired another shot at her, barely missing her back. Caprice turned around and shot him again in the right arm. He screamed as he dropped the gun and fell to his knees. One of the patrons in the restaurant opened the door and pulled Caprice inside.

"Call 9-1-1," she said before passing out.

The closer Nathan got to the pizza shop, the louder the sirens became.

"What happened here?" he said.

He looked to his left and saw all the emergency medical vehicles and police cars in the parking lot of the pizza parlor. Caprice, he thought as he whipped his car in the lot. He put the car in park and hopped out without turning the ignition off. He ran over to a patrol officer.

"What happened?" he asked.

"What's up, Nathan?" the officer said.

Nathan nodded. "What happened?"

"Detective Johnson got shot."

"What? Who shot her? Was it Cordell Wallace?"

"No, it was Donovan Harris."

"That slick motherfucker! I knew he was faking that coma. Where is he?"

"Back in the hospital. She popped him twice in the shoulder and arm. She should have killed the bastard."

"Where is she?" Nathan asked frantically.

"She's in the hospital, too. She passed out before EMS got here."

Nathan started to his car.

"Wallace!" Kevin Harrington called out. "What do you know about this?"

"I just got here," Nathan replied.

"Come on, man, I know you and Caprice are tight. Why was she here?"

"For some pizza, maybe? Kevin, I got to get to the hospital and see how she's doing." Nathan sprinted back to his car and sped out of the parking lot. He headed to Carolina's Medical Center's emergency room. When he arrived, he ran up to the desk.

"I need to find Caprice Johnson," he said to the nurse. She looked down at the list in front of her.

"Ms. Johnson has been taken to surgery. Are you a relative?"

Nathan pulled out his badge and showed it to the woman. "Yeah, she's a police detective, and I'm her partner."

"She's up on the fourth floor. When they're done with the surgery, she'll be taken to recovery. There's a waiting—"

Nathan was at the elevator before the nurse finished her statement. As he rode up the elevator he fumed over his brother's hand in the situation. *Cordell set her up. I'm going to kill him! How could he do this to her?*

The doors parted, and Nathan nearly ran off the elevator. He didn't know where to go or who to look for. He sat down underneath the TV in the corner of the waiting room. Every time a doctor walked through the waiting area, Nathan stopped him or her and asked about Caprice. Finally, after two hours, a doctor came out asking for Ms. Johnson's family.

"Yes," Nathan said, nearly running into the man.

"We removed the bullet from her leg without any problems. There was no damage to any arteries."

"Okay."

"She did have a broken nose. It looked as if she was badly beaten."

Nathan clenched his jaw. "When can I see her?"

"She was sedated, but she should be coming out of it. I can take you back to her room if you like."

Nathan nodded and followed the doctor to the recovery room. Caprice looked so small in the bed. Her face was pale, her eyes closed. He stroked her hair. He was stunned by her bruised face and bandaged nose.

"Oh baby," he whispered. "I'm sorry I was late. I'm going to make Cordell and Donovan pay for this."

"Nathan," she said hoarsely. Her eyelids fluttered like hummingbird wings. She struggled to breathe.

"Shh shh. Don't talk."

"Donovan isn't in a coma."

"I know."

"He did this, all this to me."

"Just go to sleep, okay? I'll be right here when you wake up."

"You're too good to me," she said before drifting off to sleep. Nathan kissed her forehead then settled into a chair beside her bed.

CHAPTER TWENTY-THREE

The first rays of the morning sun beamed through the blinds in the hospital room. Caprice opened her eyes and looked at Nathan's sleeping frame in the chair beside her. His hand rested on her thigh. She struggled to sit up without disturbing him. Her right leg was in a cast. Caprice's head was pounding. She moaned slightly then touched the bandage on her nose. The door to her room opened and a nurse walked in.

"Good morning," she whispered. "Your husband was so worried about you last night."

"Husband?"

The nurse pointed to Nathan, and Caprice smiled. "He's not my husband."

"He should be. Don't let this one slip away, girl. Any man that loves you enough to sleep by your bedside is very special."

Caprice smiled at the nurse as she took her vital signs. She'd heard those words before. She turned again to Nathan, who was beginning to wake up. He cleared his throat and sat up. "Hi," Caprice said.

"How are you this morning?" he asked. His voice was heavy with sleep.

"Better than you sound."

The nurse smiled at them as she took the blood pressure cuff off Caprice's arm. "I'll bring some breakfast in here for you two." Nathan nodded and thanked the woman as she left the room.

"You stayed here all night?" Caprice asked.

"Where else would I be?"

"You were pretty pissed off with me earlier. I thought you would've gone home after you saw I wasn't going to die."

"Nothing else is important. It was a stupid argument. I'm just glad you're all right."

"We have to stop Donovan before he gets away again."

"He's not going anywhere. Donovan's got two shots in him." Nathan felt his blood pressure start to rise. He was going to make sure Donovan paid for hurting Caprice. And Cordell. His reckoning was on its way. He stood up and walked over to the window. "I have to take care of something," Nathan said. "I'll be back soon."

"All right," Caprice replied. She was drifting off to sleep, because her pain medicine was kicking in. Nathan looked back at her as she walked out the door. He smiled at her sleeping frame. *I'm going to keep you safe,* he thought.

Cordell knew it wouldn't be long before Nathan came for him. He rushed around his one-bedroom apartment, stuffing clothes into a tattered black duffel bag. *I wonder if Donovan really killed that lady cop. If he did, I hope he got away, because Nathan is going to be full of fire,* he thought.

After Cordell had everything packed, he headed for the door. When he opened it, Nathan greeted his brother with a jab to the face, knocking him backwards.

"What the…" Cordell stammered, and Nathan grabbed him by the collar, nearly lifting him from the ground. He shook his brother, then punched him again. Cordell tried to block the punch, but Nathan's anger infused him with superhuman strength. He continued to pummel Cordell. Nathan threw him on the sofa and stood over him.

"Caprice almost died because of you," Nathan spat. "Do you even care? Donovan tried to kill her, and you set her up!"

"I didn't know what would happen. He said he just wanted to talk to her."

"Aw, bullshit," Nathan said as he punched his brother again.

Spittle and blood trickled from Cordell's bottom lip. He pushed Nathan off him. "I wasn't even there," Cordell explained.

"You called her and told her to meet you there. Now, why in the hell are you helping Donovan Harris?"

"I needed the money," he exclaimed. "I didn't know he was going to hurt her. I just needed the money."

"That's no excuse." Nathan pulled his handcuffs out of his back pocket.

"What the hell are you doing?" Cordell's eyes widened as Nathan grabbed him and slapped the cuffs on his wrists.

"You're under arrest."

"For what? Ouch, those cuffs are tight," Cordell shrieked.

"I don't give a damn," he snapped. Nathan jerked him up and pushed him into a wall.

Both Cordell's mouth and nose were bleeding. He struggled to walk out of the apartment. Nathan shoved him several times as they walked outside. He pushed him in the back seat of his car. "What are you charging me with?"

"Shut up." Nathan drove to the police department. He parked in the prisoner intake lot then snatched Cordell out of the car. "Let's get something straight, if you want to stay out of jail, then you're going to go inside and tell Kevin Harrington everything you know about Donovan Harris and Damien King's murder."

"I don't know anything," he replied. "You haven't even read me my rights!"

"Do you think I believe that?" Nathan forced himself not to hit Cordell again. "And you have the right to remain silent. Anything you say can and will be used against you in a court of law. You have the right to an attorney. If you can't afford one then the court will appoint one to you at no cost. Now talk! Tell me the truth. What do you know about Donovan's involvement in Damien's murder?"

"I am telling the truth, damnit. I had nothing to do with a murder. I don't even know who Damien King is!"

"And I'm sure you had nothing to do with last night either. Caprice was shot because of you. If anything else happens to her, I'm going to forget that I'm a cop and come after you and Donovan." He pushed Cordell through the entrance, leading him to Kevin's desk. "Sit down," Nathan ordered.

"Wallace," Thom called out. "How's Caprice?"

"She's doing better," he replied flatly. Thom didn't notice his tone.

"Tell her there are better ways to take a vacation," he said. Thom looked at Cordell. "What's going on?"

"He has something he needs to tell Kevin." Nathan glared at his brother, daring him to say anything to contradict him.

"What happened to his face?" he asked.

"He walked into my fists," Nathan said without a trace of a smile. Thom threw his hands up and walked away from the brothers.

"I ought to sue you for police brutality," Cordell said when they were alone.

"Shut up before I show you what brutality is."

Kevin walked over to his desk and looked from Cordell to Nathan. "What's up?" he asked.

"This suspect has some information about Harris, the King murder, and the shooting last night."

Kevin raised his right eyebrow. "Really?" He leaned down and got a better look at Cordell's face. "Somebody must really hate you. What happened to your face?"

"Ask him," Cordell replied.

"Shut up and don't make me say it again," Nathan barked.

Kevin sat behind his desk and grabbed a notepad. "What do you know about the shooting last night?"

"Nothing," Cordell said. Nathan smacked him in the back of the head.

"Nathan, chill out," Kevin cautioned. "Come on, Cordell. Tell me what you know. We can do this informally or you can lawyer up. This will just make things harder for you in the long run."

Cordell leaned on the desk. "Donovan called me and told me he wanted to get the lady cop alone. All I did was call her and set up a meeting."

"How did Donovan get out of the hospital?"

"I picked him up. I didn't know he was under arrest or anything."

"So you helped him escape from the hospital. Then you lured a police officer into a trap?"

"That's not how it happened."

"That's what I'm hearing. Is that what you're hearing, Nathan?"

Nathan nodded. "That's exactly what I'm hearing."

"What's this, a set-up?" Cordell asked. "Anything I say now ain't gonna be admissible in court. You said this was informal. I want a lawyer!"

"No, a set-up is what you did to Detective Johnson. You can make this hard or easy," Kevin said as he leaned across his desk and got in Cordell's face. "Cooperate and I'll keep you out of prison. Lawyer up and you can spend some time with the sheriff and his boys across the street."

"Yeah, whatever," Cordell said as he leaned back in the chair and sucked his teeth.

"Look, we don't like it when one of our own gets shot by scum like Donovan Harris. Now, if you can give us specific detailed information about what Harris's plans are for Detective Johnson, you'll probably get a walk."

Cordell looked from Kevin to Nathan. "All right, all right," he said. "I'll talk."

Nathan sat down beside Cordell. Kevin pulled out a tape recorder and pressed the red record button. Cordell began spilling his guts about what Donovan said in the hospital. He told Kevin how he called Caprice while he was at Donovan's safe house in south Charlotte. He wanted to meet her at the pizza parlor because of the dark alley.

"I didn't go. I took my money and went home. I was planning to leave town today."

"So, you took the money and planned to run?" Kevin said.

Nathan seethed with anger. He stood up and walked over to an empty desk a few feet away from Cordell. He feared if he was any closer to his brother, he'd kill him in the middle of the squad room.

"Yeah."

"What do you know about Damien King?" Kevin asked.

"Who?"

"Now you want to play dumb," Kevin snapped.

"He's not playing," Nathan called out.

"The only thing I know about is what happened last night," Cordell said.

Kevin shook his head. "I don't believe you. If I don't believe you, I can't work with you." He turned the tape recorder off and waved for a uniformed officer. "Take him down to lock up." The officer grabbed Cordell by the arm and led him away. Kevin turned to Nathan. "What do you think about what your brother said? Do you think he's telling the truth about Damien King?"

Nathan shrugged his shoulders. "To be honest, I don't know what to think about my brother. Maybe he doesn't know anything about Damien King, but he could find out. He already has an in with Donovan."

Kevin rubbed his chin. "I'm still not convinced Donovan Harris had a role in Damien King's death."

Nathan rolled his eyes at Kevin. "You still think Caprice did this, don't you?"

"I know you don't want to hear that, but it's the truth. She had motive, she argued with him, and she was the only person in Charlotte who knew him. Why would Donovan Harris want to kill him? King had no criminal record and no drug ties. He was a businessman. There was no reason for Harris and King to cross paths."

"I can't believe you. You're willing to believe a police officer killed a man when you have a strong lead in your face!" Nathan's anger had become an inferno of rage.

"Just because you're thinking with your crotch and not your head, it doesn't mean I'm going to do the same thing. I'm following the evidence, and there's nothing here that points to Donovan Harris."

"Go to hell, Kevin." Nathan stood up and walked out of the squad room.

Kevin sat down and thought about what Nathan said. Had he really spent so much time trying to prove Caprice was the killer that he overlooked the Donovan Harris link? He looked out over uptown Charlotte's skyline and wondered who really killed Damien King.

Donovan knew there was no way he was going to be able to get out of the handcuffs this time. *That woman must be part cat, because she has nine lives,* he thought as he stared at the ceiling. The door to his room opened and Nathan walked in. He stood near the foot of the bed and glared at Donovan.

"What?" he snapped.

"I could forget I was a cop right now and smother you with a pillow," Nathan said in a low, angry whisper. "But then I'd be a murderer just like you. You're going down for that security guard you killed on your last escape attempt. And then you shot a police officer. How stupid are you?"

"Get out of my room."

"Let me warn you, if you do anything else to hurt Caprice, I'm going to kill you. Make a note of it."

"Are you threatening me, officer?" Donovan asked sarcastically.

"No, I'm promising you. Hurt her again and you can kiss your ass goodbye."

Nathan turned and walked out of the hospital room. Donovan glared at the door. *He wants to play hero; he can get it too,* he thought as he relaxed against the pillow. *I need to get in touch with Ethan. Somehow he has to get me out of this hospital..*

Three weeks had passed since the shooting on Central. Caprice was walking on crutches, but she still hadn't been released from the hospital. She was going stir crazy as she sat in the room.

Nathan walked in her room and smiled at her. Caprice was sitting in the recliner chair with her leg elevated on the bed. "This is cute," he said. "You look so helpless."

"Shut up!"

"I heard that someone has been an impatient patient."

"I'm chomping at the bit to get out of here."

"I know. When did the doctors say they were going to release you?"

"Maybe today."

"You're looking much better."

"Thanks," she said as she rubbed the smaller bandage on her nose. "Now, if I could get this cast off."

"In due time, grasshopper."

"Knock knock," the doctor said as he walked in.

"Are you letting me out of here today?" she asked.

"Yes. You can rehab your leg at home."

"At my home," Nathan interjected.

"No, Nathan, I can't do that."

"That's not such a bad idea. You might need some help until you get used to the crutches and walking around with the cast," the doctor chimed in.

Caprice folded her arms across her chest and started to say something, but Nathan cut her off. "Don't worry, doctor, I'll take care of her."

The doctor nodded. "I'll send the nurse in with the discharge papers."

When the doctor left, Caprice turned to Nathan. "Why did you do that? I want to sleep in my own bed. I've been in here for weeks."

"Caprice, when are you going to stop acting like you don't need anybody? You can barely walk. How are you even going to maneuver around your house right now?"

She knew he was right, but she didn't want to admit it. "I'm fine. See." Caprice tried to stand up, but she fell into his arms. Their lips were dangerously close but neither of them made a move to kiss.

"You're coming home with me. Don't make me have to handcuff you."

"You keep threatening me with handcuffs, don't you?" He helped her steady herself then led her to the bed.

Nathan smiled. "Don't knock it; you might like it."

A nurse walked into the room and handed Caprice her discharge papers. "Here you go," she said. "Just sign at the X."

"So, after I sign this, I'm free?"

"You make it sound like you were in prison," the nurse said with a giggle.

She turned to Nathan. "Take care of her, sweetie."

"I will," he replied.

"You like this, don't you?" Caprice asked once the nurse left the room.

"Like what?"

"Playing my knight in shining armor."

"Well, if I'd known that all it took for you to admit you need someone was for you to get your leg in a cast, I would've broken it a long time ago."

"There you go." She rolled her eyes. "Get me out of here. I hate the smell of this room." Nathan went to Caprice and scooped her up in his arms. She wrapped her arms around his neck and kissed him on the cheek.

"Thank you for doing this for me," she said. "I know I haven't been the easiest person to get along with lately. I wouldn't have blamed you if you wanted to wash your hands of me."

"I'll agree with that. But you have to know I wouldn't give up on you that easily."

"But these last few weeks, you've been right here by my side. You even got Kevin off my back. I really appreciate what you've done for me."

Nathan stroked her back. He wanted to tell her that he loved her, but he didn't want her to feel uncomfortable. And it seemed like every time he mentioned love she would freak out. Nathan scooped her up into his arms.

Maybe this time together is what we need, he thought as he carried her out to a wheelchair.

When Nathan and Caprice got to his house, he carried her across the threshold even though she wanted to use her crutches. "Are you going to carry me to the bathroom when I need to go?" she asked when he set her down on the sofa.

"If you want me to, but you're on your own at three in the morning."

"Gee thanks." She smacked him on the arm.

"Seriously, though, how's the leg?"

"Itching like crazy, but it doesn't hurt as much as it did."

"I should've been there. If I had been on time, I could've stopped Donovan from hurting you."

"Nathan, don't do this to yourself. It's over; I'm not dead, and Donovan's in jail."

"For now anyway. I know Cordell better testify against him."

"I can't believe your brother set me up. Have you found Sabrina Jones?"

"Don't start. Sabrina isn't important. We have to get your leg healed and you back on the force."

"Don't you start," Caprice said. "I told you, I'm not sure if I want to go back."

"Are we going to have this argument again?"

"No, because I'm too tired to argue with you, Nathan."

"Good," he said.

Caprice leaned in and kissed him on the cheek. Nathan wrapped his arms around her, and she rested her head on his shoulder.

CHAPTER TWENTY-FOUR

Donovan paced around the jail cell. He had been there since the judge denied him bail two weeks ago. He hated being cooped up like a chicken. The sheriff's deputies were keeping a watchful eye on him. *I have got to get out of here,* he thought. *That woman isn't going to get away with what she did to me. And Cordell, he's going to kiss his ass goodbye. I should have known better than to trust him. After all, his brother is a cop. This way, I'll get Wallace where it hurts most. His girl and his brother are going to die.*

Donovan had already put the word out that Cordell's days were numbered. Even though he was in jail, he still had his connections. The jailhouse underground communication system worked quickly. Even though he could have ordered a hit on Caprice, he was going to wait, because she was his. No one would kill her but him. Donovan had already heard that the hit was set. He knew that by the end of the day, Nathan was going to be shedding tears for a dead brother.

"Harris," one of the guards shouted as he walked by the cell. "Your attorney is here." He opened the cell, handcuffed Harris, and then he led him to the visitation room.

Donovan was pissed off with Ethan. He hadn't seen him since the bail hearing. *He'd better be getting me out of here,* he thought as he sat down across from Ethan.

"Hello, Donovan," Ethan said.

"Am I getting out of here?" His voice was forceful and demanding.

"No. The district attorney has fast-tracked this case. We're going to trial in a few weeks."

"What?"

"Donovan, you messed up beyond anything I can fix. You need to take a plea. A jury will bury you."

"I don't think so. I have things I need to take care of now. You have to get me out of here. I'm not taking a deal"

"Do you want to spend the rest of your life in jail? That's where you're heading."

"It's your job to help me beat these charges," Donovan spat.

"There's nothing I can do this time. There are witnesses who saw you shoot Detective Johnson. You broke her nose. The dead guard was in your hospital bed. You left a trail of evidence."

Donovan shrugged his shoulders. "So? She attacked me, and she wasn't even a real cop. She's suspended. Besides, that bitch isn't going to be around long enough to testify against me."

"The state has Cordell Wallace as a witness."

Donovan banged on the table. "That doesn't matter. Cordell will never make it to the trial."

"It's over. The best you can hope for is a plea bargain."

Donovan leaned back in the seat and closed his eyes. "Always remember this, it ain't over until the fat lady starts belting out a melody."

Ethan shook his head and stood up. "Whatever you say, Donovan." He waved for the guard and walked out of the room.

Caprice woke up around noon. She sat up in Nathan's guest room and rubbed her cast. Her leg felt like thousands of fire ants were crawling around inside of it. She moaned in distress. Nathan knocked on the door.

"Caprice, are you up?"

"Yeah, come in."

He sat on the side of the bed. "Are you all right?"

"Just fine," she said as she swung her legs over the bed slowly. She reached for her crutches. "I can't believe I slept so late."

"Do you want some breakfast or anything?"

"Not really."

"Come on, you have to eat. I'm supposed to take care of you. I can't have you going back to the doctor nothing but skin and bones. "

She stood up on the crutches and attempted to walk to the door. Her steps were awkward, nothing like the confident swagger that she was used to.

"I hate these things."

Nathan laughed at her as she struggled with the crutches.

"You think this is funny, right?" she asked.

"Not really. I know this is killing you, Ms. I-got-to-do-everything-for myself."

Caprice sucked her teeth. "What's wrong with wanting to be independent?"

"Nothing. I think that's one of your sexier qualities." Nathan walked over to her and stood in her face. Their faces were so close, they shared the same air. Caprice inhaled Nathan's woodsy cologne. She had to admit to herself that he was a comfort to her. Without him, she didn't know how she would've made it through the shooting and everything else that had happened to her recently.

She smiled at him. "I have to go take a shower."

"All right," he said. "When you're done, I'll have brunch waiting for you. And you are going to eat."

She kissed him on the cheek. "Thanks."

Nathan watched her walk out of the bedroom.

About twenty minutes later, Caprice and Nathan were sitting in the den munching on cheese and salsa omelets and fruit salad.

"This is good," she said. "I didn't know you had culinary skills like this."

"There's a lot you don't know about me."

"Maybe it's time for me to learn."

Nathan smiled and wiped some strawberry juice from her chin. "I think so."

"I'm sorry for everything I've put you through lately," she said. "I know I was pushing you away. It's just the way

I feel for you scares me. It seems like every time I fall in love, I get hurt. I don't want that."

"Don't be afraid to love me. Because I'm not afraid to love you with all my heart."

Caprice set aside her plate. "So, what are we going to do about finding Sabrina Jones?"

Nathan sighed and rolled his eyes. "You really know how to kill the moment, don't you?"

"Come on, Nathan, you know—"

He silenced her with a soul-scorching kiss. It caught Caprice off guard, but she went with the flow. She wrapped her arms around him as he leaned her back on the sofa. Caprice was lost in his kiss. All her fears and reservations about loving Nathan blew away like dust in the wind. Nathan's hot hands roamed her upper body. He slid his hands underneath her T-shirt, his fingers danced across her sculpted stomach. Caprice's body was hot like a summer's day from Nathan's touch. She nearly forgot about her cast until she heard the glasses crashing to the floor. She'd inadvertently knocked them over with her leg. Nathan looked up, and the couple broke out in laughter.

"I guess I made that mess, huh?" she said through her laughter.

Nathan let her go. "I'll clean it up." He walked into the kitchen and grabbed a broom. When he returned into the living room, Caprice was standing near the television on her crutches.

"This is so embarrassing," she said.

"Come on now, you've done worse. I saw you in a blonde wig."

"Thanks," she said with a laugh.

"And I remember those nights we were in a surveillance van, and you would knock over the coffee and the doughnuts."

"Excuse you, that was you, not me, butterfingers," Caprice corrected.

"All right, so it was," he said as he swept the shards of broken glass into the dustpan. "I was just nervous about being that close to you."

"Oh, stop it."

"I'm serious. When they teamed me up with you, I thought it would never work. I figured this big city detective is going to come in here with a know-it-all attitude. Then I met you that first day and your beauty, your strength, and your poise blew me away. You didn't think you were better than anyone else. You came in wanting to know how we did things, not telling us how you did things in Chicago. I've always respected that about you. Then I got to work with you every day, and it was hard not to fall in love."

Caprice could feel her eyes watering. "Please, stop it," she whispered.

Nathan walked over to her and pulled her into his arms. "I can't stop how I feel about you. You make me happy and angry all at the same time. I never knew any woman could do that." He brushed his lips across hers. "And some day soon, you're going to believe in our love too." Little did he know, she was already starting to do just that.

Cordell stood outside of Nathan's house. He wanted to say something to his brother, but what? He rang the doorbell and waited for Nathan to answer. When the door opened, he was shocked to see Caprice standing there. She glared at him and called out for Nathan.

"Look, I'm sorry," Cordell said. "I really didn't think anything this serious would happen." She shot him a questioning look then hobbled off, leaving him standing at the door. Nathan looked up and saw Cordell standing in the foyer. "What in the hell are you doing here?" he demanded.

"I want to talk to you. I didn't know Caprice was staying here."

"Get out of my house," Nathan said as he pushed his brother toward the door.

"Listen, I know I was wrong for trying to set her up. I didn't want her to get hurt."

"You're not making any sense. You knew Donovan wanted to kill her. Get out, Cordell, and don't come back. I don't have a brother anymore." Nathan pushed him out the door and slammed it in his face.

Cordell glared at the closed door. *I'm sick of his judgmental ass,* he thought as he walked away from the house. Cordell knew he should've been grateful to Nathan for getting some of the more serious charges against him dropped. He was surprised Nathan had done anything to help him after the fight they had.

But, he wanted his brother's respect. As Cordell turned to head to his car, shots rang out. He dropped to his knees as bullets riddled his body. A black sedan sped down the street.

Nathan opened the door and saw Cordell lying in the driveway. "Caprice, call 9-1-1!" he yelled. He ran to his brother's side. "Damn, C, don't die on me." Cordell's blood seeped though Nathan's jeans as he cupped his brother's head in his hands. "Come on, Cordell, fight."

Cordell began coughing up blood.

"Who did this to you?" Nathan asked.

He coughed again. "Do...Donovan." His body started to grow cold. "Cordell, come on, fight this!" Sirens broke the silence. The emergency medical vehicle pulled into Nathan's driveway, and two police cars pulled in a few seconds later. But they were all too late; Cordell had stopped breathing. Nathan howled like a wounded beast as he pounded the pavement until his fist bled.

"You're dead, Donovan," he said with a trembling voice.

CHAPTER TWENTY-FIVE

Nathan sat in his darkened bedroom, still trying to digest Cordell's death. Despite their differences, he didn't want to see Cordell end up like this.

Caprice hobbled into his room and sat down on the bed beside him. She gently placed her crutches on the floor. She touched his shoulder. Nathan turned around and looked at her. They didn't exchange words. He just dropped his head in her lap. She stroked the nape of his neck gently.

"I can't believe he's gone," Nathan whispered.

"I know." Caprice was having a hard time mustering up any sympathy for Cordell, but her heart broke for Nathan.

Nathan wrapped his arms around her waist and squeezed her tightly. "Cordell and I didn't get along, but I didn't want him to die."

Caprice kissed him on the top of his head. "It'll be okay."

"Donovan is behind this. I can feel it."

"We have to stop him, Nathan."

"I'm going to stop him. No matter what I have to do, he's not going to slip away this time."

"What if he was gunning for one of us? I mean, it isn't like he hasn't tried to shoot me before."

Nathan sat up. "I know. You really need to stay out of it this time, Caprice. I'm not playing, and I'm going to keep telling you this over and over again. We've seen how dangerous this man is now. He had my brother killed right in front of my house."

Caprice pushed away from Nathan. "I know you aren't going to sit here and order me around."

"I don't want anything else to happen to you. I already lost my brother," Nathan said. "And with that cast, what can you do to help anyway?"

"I may not be able to go out there, but I can and will do something," she said.

Nathan stood up and ran his hand over his face. "I don't want to fight with you right now. Just give me some time to be alone, okay?"

Caprice stood up. "Fine." She took the crutches from him and started for the bedroom she had been sleeping in. She walked in and sat on the bed. The deep scowl on her face illustrated her anger and frustration. She was trying to be understanding, but once again, Nathan had gone too far. *I'm going home,* she thought as she gingerly stood up and began gathering her things. One of her crutches fell, knocking over a lamp on the nightstand. She swore inwardly as she tried to pick the lamp up.

The loud crash sent Nathan rushing into the room. "What happened?" he asked as he picked up the lamp.

"I was packing," she said.

"Why?"

"It's time for me to leave."

"Come on, Caprice, you don't have to leave."

"Nathan, you need your space, and obviously, I'm in your way. I'm just giving you what you want—time alone."

"Why do we always have to do this? Everything doesn't have to be a fight."

"You make it that way, because you have to be in control of everything."

Nathan raised his right eyebrow. "I have to control everything? Caprice, you're in a cast now because you wanted to run the show! You got shot because you wanted to pull the strings. Don't tell me I'm the one with a control problem. I have gone along with you long enough, and look what it's gotten us."

"Are you blaming me for Cordell's death? This was all my fault? Is that what you're saying?"

"In a way, it is," Nathan revealed.

"Go to hell, Nathan," she shouted.

"You had to go out there," he said. "You had to go out there and try to meet with Cordell to get something on Donovan. If you had allowed the department to handle this investigation, we might have been able to get him, and my brother would still be alive."

"Your brother set me up. Is it my fault that he worked for Donovan? Cordell was just another one of his casualties. I hate to be cold, but that's just the way it is. I had nothing to do with it."

"I know that," Nathan said as he turned his back to her in hurt. "I don't want you to end up like Cordell. I'm just trying to protect you. I couldn't protect him, but—"

"Nathan, Cordell didn't want to be protected. And I don't need to be protected."

"Yes you do, and if you think I'm going to let you walk out of this house, you're mistaken. Donovan could have someone waiting for you outside your house, waiting to take you out."

"Donovan is in jail."

"Has that ever stopped him from getting someone killed? He was in jail when Damien died; he was in jail tonight when Cordell was killed. What makes you different? If anything, you're an easier target," he said and whirled around to face Caprice. "I said I needed to be alone tonight. I didn't say I wanted to live the rest of my life without you."

"I can't do this, Nathan. I can't have you second-guessing me and everything I do."

"I'm not second-guessing you. My brother just died, Caprice. I'm hurting right now."

"And I'm sorry about that, but we have to do something," she said.

"Not we, me."

"Nathan, you need my help. I can lure Donovan to us."

He turned his back to her. "I'm not changing my mind about this. I want you to stay out of it." He slammed out of the room. Caprice dropped down on the bed. She immediately put aside everything Nathan had said. She was going to take Donovan Harris down.

Night turned into morning, and Nathan and Caprice walked around the house on eggshells. When they sat down to eat breakfast, they barely said two words to each other. Caprice's bags were packed, and she was leaving as soon as she got a chance. Nathan stared at her as they ate.

"Caprice," he said in a low whisper.

"What?"

"I'm sorry about last night."

"There's nothing to apologize for."

"I don't want to argue with you today."

"Then don't."

"I talked to Major Chaney, and he wants to put you in protective custody."

"You did what?"

"Caprice, I know that as soon as I walk out that door, you're going home. If that's what you want to do, fine, but you will not be there alone."

"I don't like people making decisions about my life," she snapped. "And I don't want anyone watching over me. I'm a cop; I can take care of myself."

"I'm just trying to make sure you still have a life."

"Fine," she said as she folded her arms across her chest.

"You don't have to leave," Nathan said. His voice was in a near whisper. "I don't want you to leave, but if you go, then it's straight to protective custody."

Caprice nodded. "Fine, home it is then."

"That's your choice." Nathan was disappointed. He wanted her to stay. He needed her to stay. *I can't make her do anything she doesn't want to do,* he thought as he stuffed a fork full of eggs in his mouth.

"Who's going to be guarding me?"

"Kevin."

"What? And how long ago was it that he wanted to put me in jail?"

"That's the same thing I thought."

"Is Chaney trying to punish me?"

"You could stay here," Nathan said, fearing he sounded desperate.

Caprice narrowed her eyes at him. "We've had that discussion already, and I don't want to have it again."

"Fine," he replied. "I'll drop you off. Are you all packed?"

His nonchalant tone rattled Caprice. "Yes." Caprice pushed away from the table. Nathan handed her the crutches. She snatched them from his hands and hobbled off to the guest room.

It was about 1 p.m. when Caprice arrived at her home. Kevin's scowl told them this was the last place he wanted to be and that their tardiness wasn't appreciated. Nathan pulled into the driveway and rolled down the window. "Kevin, how long have you been here?"

"Long enough," he said.

This is going to be great, Caprice thought as she opened the passenger side door and hopped out. She held on to the side of the door as she reached for her crutches from the backseat. Nathan got out of the car to help her, but she slapped his hands away. "I don't need your help," she said.

He stepped back. "Fine."

"Trouble in paradise?" Kevin asked as Caprice made her way up the front steps.

Caprice glared at him and fought back the sarcastic comment on the tip of her tongue. Kevin took note of her mean stare and smiled mockingly.

"I want to be here as much as you want me here," Kevin said.

"Then leave." Caprice opened the front door and her mouth dropped open. The inside had been ransacked. It looked as if blood had been splattered on the walls. Her house looked like a scene from a B-horror movie. Caprice didn't realize she was that vulnerable. She turned to head down the steps.

"What's wrong?" Nathan asked.

"Someone has been inside," she said. Kevin pulled out his gun. He ordered Caprice and Nathan to stand back.

"You're not staying here," Nathan said as they watched Kevin enter the house.

Caprice didn't want to agree with him, but it was now obvious that her home wasn't safe. So she relented. A few minutes later, Kevin walked out of the house with a note in his hand.

"This is a message from Donovan," he said. "Take it to the station and lock up here. I'm taking Caprice some place else."

"Make sure you inform the brass," Kevin said. He looked at Caprice. "Detective, I'm sorry about all of this." Caprice nodded. For the first time since the trouble started, Caprice realized that she really couldn't handle all this alone. She knew Donovan wasn't going to be happy until she was dead. Nathan drove her to a safe house the police used to protect witnesses. She stole a look at Nathan as he turned onto Shamrock Road.

"I'm sorry," she said with a sigh.

"What was that?"

"I'm not going to repeat it. You were right, though. I can't handle this by myself."

"Now you believe it. Donovan is dangerous and there is no limit to what he will do."

"This isn't going to be over until either I'm dead or Donovan is."

"I have to radio the station and let them know we're here," Nathan said as he picked up the radio.

"Are you going to stay here with me?" she asked.

Nathan looked at Caprice. He saw a deep fear in her eyes, a look he'd never seen before. Caprice was always in control. Nathan wasn't used to seeing her this way, not even when she was accused of Damien's murder.

"I'll stay," he replied as he squeezed her hand. "What did you see in that house?"

"I…I don't want to talk about it."

"We have to find Sabrina Jones so we can keep Donovan off the streets. I'm going to have Kevin look for her too. Is that okay with you?"

"That's fine. I know we need help on this," she said. "Donovan isn't going to get away with anything he's done to you. Not Damien's murder, not breaking into your house…"

"And not killing your brother," she said softly.

Nathan nodded. "He's caused a lot of pain, and as long as I have a badge, he's got it coming."

Caprice didn't say anything when they got out of the car. She didn't object to Nathan helping her with her crutches or her bags. When they got inside, Nathan turned on all the lights and set Caprice's things down.

"This house is ugly," she said as she dropped down on the dusty plaid sofa.

"Hopefully, you won't be here that long."

"I have to get off these crutches," Caprice said as she rubbed her leg.

"Don't rush it. I'll wait until Kevin gets here, then I have to go take care of something."

"I need a nap," Caprice said as she attempted to stand up. She ended up falling into Nathan's arms. He held her against his chest. "You can let me go."

"I don't want to." Nathan's lips brushed against Caprice's. Just as they were about to kiss, the front door opened and a uniformed officer walked in.

"Sorry," he said turning his back when he saw them.

Caprice grasped Nathan's shoulder and stood up. "It's okay," she said. "I'm the person you're babysitting."

"I know, Detective Johnson."

Caprice grabbed her crutches. "Just call me Caprice," she said as she headed to the back bedroom.

Nathan walked over to the officer. "I'm heading out for a little bit. Don't let her leave, and don't let anyone in besides me and Detective Harrington."

"Yes, sir," the officer said as Nathan left.

When Nathan arrived at the Mecklenburg County Jail, he stared contemptuously at Donovan's sleeping frame. He wanted to reach through the bars and strangle him. Donovan was a waste of human flesh who deserved to die,

Nathan reasoned. *But I'd be no better than him if I killed him.*

"Harris!" Nathan yelled.

Donovan awoke and looked up at Nathan. He smiled sardonically as he stood up. "What the hell do you want?"

"Answers."

"Talk to my lawyer."

"I'm talking to you, you piece of garbage."

"I know my rights. I don't have to take this from you."

"Who killed my brother?"

Donovan giggled. "How in the hell would I know? I've been locked away from society. And Cordell was my friend."

Nathan took a deep breath and stepped back from the cell. "Don't you dare mention his name! I know you had him killed, and I'm going to make you suffer for it. You're going to pay for this and what you did to Caprice. Time's almost up. I just might take my badge off and forget I'm a cop the next time I see you." He turned and headed out the door.

CHAPTER TWENTY-SIX

Caprice woke up from her nap and walked into the living room of the safe house. The officer who was supposed to be watching her was asleep on the sofa. *Great,* she thought when she spotted him. *Anybody could just stroll in here and kill us both.*

"Hey!" she shouted.

The officer sat up and wiped a stand of drool from the side of his mouth. "Huh?"

"I feel so safe with you around," Caprice said snidely.

"Sorry, Detective. It was just so quiet here."

"Why don't I make us some coffee?"

"There's no food in here. Somebody forgot to restock after the last time this place was used."

"Great," Caprice said as she sat down on the sofa. "Have you heard from Inspector Wallace?"

"No, ma'am," he said. "I'm going to walk around the perimeter and make sure it's secure."

Caprice nodded. When the officer left, she headed for the kitchen. The only thing in the cupboard was a molded loaf of bread. *Some safe house,* she thought as her stomach rumbled. Caprice returned to the living room. As she sat down, the door opened and Nathan walked in with several bags of groceries.

"God bless you," Caprice said.

"Hungry?"

"Yes."

"Where's the rookie?"

"He's outside checking the perimeter."

"Fell asleep, didn't he?" he asked.

Caprice nodded and Nathan laughed. "Let me get you something to eat."

"Did you find out anything about Sabrina while you were gone?" Caprice asked.

"No," he called out as he unpacked the groceries. "Don't worry, though, I'll find her."

"She probably killed Cordell and broke into my house."

Nathan nodded. "I don't want to talk about that right now. How's your leg?"

"I'm ready to get out of this damn cast."

Nathan took her leg and placed it on his lap. "Just relax."

"Yes sir." Caprice kissed Nathan on the cheek. "Thank you for not giving up on me. I know I've been hard to deal with."

"You think?"

She playfully rolled her eyes. "I've been hardheaded about this whole thing from the beginning. I know you were just trying to help me. If I had listened to you, I might not be in this cast now."

Nathan stroked her face. "Caprice," he murmured. He leaned in and kissed her. Caprice wrapped her arms around Nathan's neck. "I love being this close to you," he said.

"I just wish it wasn't here."

"You're not leaving this place until we get to the bottom of the break-in and find Sabrina. She might be the one who's after you. I can't have anything else happen to you. I know you don't need my protection, but you got it."

"The old knight-in-shining-armor routine, huh?"

"All I need is a white horse," Nathan joked. Caprice kissed him gently on the lips to thank him. Her tender gesture caught Nathan off guard. He kissed her again, this time with more fire and depth. The front door to the house opened, and the officer walked in.

"Oh oh, I'm sorry," he said as Caprice and Nathan parted.

"Why don't you take off for little bit?" Nathan suggested to the rookie. "Go grab some dinner and have a patrol unit drive by here." The officer nodded and headed out the door, nearly bumping into the frame.

Caprice fought back a laugh. "You know, when he gets back to the station, he's going to tell everybody about us," she said.

"Do you have a problem with that?"

She shook her head. "I don't care who knows that I love you."

Nathan smiled. "I'm glad to hear that because I want the world to know how I feel about you."

"You think we can get something to eat?" she asked. "I am a little hungry."

"So am I, but not for anything in that kitchen," Nathan said seductively.

"Nathan…" she cooed.

"All right, I'll fix you something to eat." Nathan let her go and walked into the kitchen. He fixed both of them tuna salad sandwiches and chips. He set the paper plates on the table in front of her. Nathan was about to sit down to eat when he heard a noise at the back door.

"Did you hear that?" he asked. Caprice nodded her head yes. Nathan drew his gun, and headed to the back door. Slowly he opened the door and pointed his gun in the face of a masked man trying to pry the door open. "Freeze, asshole. Drop the crowbar, now!"

The man followed Nathan's orders then threw his hands up. "Who are you?" Nathan demanded. The man didn't answer. "Caprice, call 9-1-1," Nathan shouted.

"No no," the man said. "I'll talk, just don't tell Donovan."

Nathan snatched the mask off Ron Torres. "You son-of-a…Get in here!"

"Donovan told me if I didn't help him, he would kill me. He found out I set up that meeting in the park. He was going to kill me that night. He told me if I could get to the detective he'd let me live."

Nathan fought the urge to slap Ron. "Did you break into her house again?"

Ron nodded. Nathan narrowed his eyes at him. "What were you planning to do here?"

"Just scare her. I saw the cop leave."

"You're under arrest!" Nathan grabbed his arm and reached for his handcuffs.

Ron tried to wiggle out of Nathan's grasp. "Man, if I go to jail, I'm dead."

"Sounds like a personal problem."

"I know who killed your brother!"

Nathan let him go. "What?"

"I know who Donovan had kill Cordell."

Nathan pulled Ron into the house and led him into the living room.

"What's going on?" Caprice asked as she looked from Nathan to Ron.

"Ron broke into your house," Nathan said.

"You snake," Caprice said. "What are you, an idiot?"

"I was just tryin' to stay alive," Ron said.

"So you trashed my house?"

"It was either that or Donovan killin' me for talkin' to you. I told you that night Donovan was going to find out and try to kill me."

Caprice rolled her eyes at him. "Am I supposed to care?" she asked as Nathan shot her a let-me-handle-this look. Caprice stepped aside.

"You said you knew who killed Cordell," Nathan said. "Talk or I'm calling for a car."

Torres rubbed his chin then sighed. "Donovan, you know, he got people who owe him favors. When he got arrested for trying to pop her, he called me and Lewis Carter."

"Lewis Carter?" Nathan asked.

"Yeah, he had beef with Cordell anyway."

"That robbery ring." Nathan shook his head. Cordell's first major conviction was for his involvement in the South Park robberies. He and three other men were breaking into posh stores and houses in that historic neighborhood. The residents of South Park had old money and when they found out the burglars were caught, they wanted the book thrown at them.

Torres nodded. "He always thought Cordell sold him out."

Nathan dropped his head. He was the reason Cordell didn't spend as much time in prison as his three cohorts. "What happened?" he asked through clenched teeth.

Caprice touched Nathan's elbow. "Are you sure you want to do this?" she whispered.

"I have to," Nathan replied. He nodded for Torres to continue.

"Donovan paid us to kill Cordell so he couldn't testify. We followed him and found him outside your house."

"Who pulled the trigger?" Nathan asked.

"Lewis."

Nathan stood up and walked to the front door. He ran his hands over his head. "You and Donovan are nothing but wastes of flesh," Nathan growled. He turned around and looked at Ron with fire in his eyes. Within a blink of an eye, Nathan had lunged at Ron and grabbed him by the throat. "He was my brother, and you all shot him down like a dog in the street."

Caprice stood up and grabbed Nathan's arm, fearful of his loss of control. "Nathan, stop it!" Ron was beginning to turn blue and lose consciousness.

Nathan let him go and Ron fell to the floor. "Get up," Nathan demanded. Caprice grabbed Nathan's radio and called for a squad car. Ron slowly rose to his feet and

Nathan cuffed him. "One more question," Nathan said. "Where is Sabrina Jones?"

"I…I don't know," Ron gasped.

Nathan threw him against the wall. "Where is Lewis?"

"He's stayin' at Donovan's."

Caprice looked up at Nathan. "Let someone else go," she said.

"What?" Nathan snapped.

"If you go after this Lewis person, you'll do something you may regret."

Nathan couldn't believe what he was hearing from Caprice, the same woman who wanted to take Donovan Harris down alone. Was she saying that out of concern or because she didn't care if Cordell's killer was caught? After all, he was the reason she was in a cast. Nathan closed his eyes and realized Caprice was right. He was angry, and if he saw Lewis, he might kill him. He had nearly killed Ron.

There was a knock at the front door. Nathan looked out and saw Kevin and two uniformed officers standing there.

"Trouble keeps finding you two," Kevin said as he grabbed Ron.

Caprice narrowed her eyes at him. "I wonder why, Detective?"

"Take the prisoner to the car," Kevin said to one of the officers. "Be sure you advise him of his rights." Then he turned to Caprice. "If you have something to say to me, say it."

Caprice stood up. "I know for a fact Donovan has officers on his payroll. Are you one of them? How else would Ron know about this place?"

"I don't have to take this sh—"

"She does have a point," Nathan chimed in.

"If I was working for Donovan, Caprice would be dead or in jail. If you don't trust me, have me taken off this case. Both of you are getting on my damn nerves."

Caprice rolled her eyes, unconvinced by Kevin's indignation. His enthusiasm about putting her in jail, his unwillingness to look for other suspects, it was all starting to make sense.

"Nathan, get me out of here and don't tell anyone where we're going," she said. Kevin stormed out the front door.

Nathan turned to Caprice. "You can't seriously think Kevin is working for Donovan," he whispered.

"I wouldn't put it past him. How helpful has he been these last few months? He wouldn't even consider the possibility that someone other than me killed Damien."

"I think you're a tad paranoid," Nathan said.

"And you're entitled to your opinion," Caprice replied sarcastically.

Nathan shook his head. "So, where are we staying tonight?"

"The only option we have is a hotel," she replied. "It's too dangerous to go anywhere else."

Nathan and Caprice got into his car and headed for the Ramada near the airport.

CHAPTER TWENTY-SEVEN

Donovan stood near the gate of the jail recreation yard, hoping to find a way to break out. If he did get out, that detective was toast. Donovan watched the guard patrolling the gated area. *I can take him out, but I wonder how long would it take the rest of these fools to catch on?* he thought as he paced back and forth. The whistle blew signaling the end of the prisoners' recreation time. Donovan filed in with the other inmates. He didn't have much time to plan his escape. His trial was tomorrow. *Wait,* he thought, *I can get our of here when they take me over to the courthouse.* Donovan took a seat in the cell with a smile on his face. *All I have to do is slip out of there when the judge calls for the morning recess.* He stood up.

"Guard, I need to talk to my lawyer."

"All right, Harris," he replied as he walked over to Donovan's cell. He opened the door and led him to the pay phone.

Donovan dialed Ethan's number. "Ethan Washington."

"It's me."

"What is it now, Donovan?"

"Is that deal still on the table?"

"Are you serious?"

"Yes."

"I'll call the DA and let him know."

"Now, if I take this deal, we still go to court, right?"

"Yes, you'll still have to answer to your charges," Ethan said.

"Okay, cool."

"What are you planning?" Ethan asked with growing suspicion in his voice.

"The less you know, the better."

"Donovan, I'm not going to be a parry to any more of your…"

"Goodbye, Ethan." Donovan hung up the phone then quickly picked it up again before the guard could notice he had finished talking to his attorney. He dialed his home number.

"Yo," Lewis Carter said.

"Is that how you answer the phone?"

"My bad, D, I didn't know it was you."

"Lewis, I need you to be in the court room tomorrow morning at 9 a.m. You need to create a diversion so I can get out of there."

"Aight, bet."

"Have you heard from Ron?"

"Not today. I know he was on that cop's tail."

"Good. Did he do the job?"

"Yeah, he did it. He got in there and ransacked the place and covered everything with blood."

"Great, I hope she got the message," Donovan said. "They moved her to some safe house, and Ron followed her out there."

"Good. Look, I got to go before they realize what's going on. Make sure you're in court tomorrow."

"Aight, I'll be there."

Donovan hung up the phone and headed back to his cell.

Nathan walked into the police department and headed straight for Kevin's desk. "Hey, man, I'm sorry about the other day," he said.

"Whatever," Kevin sighed.

"Look, I know you didn't have anything to do with what happened. Caprice is just on edge."

"And? She can't go around hurling accusations about me. I've never done anything besides my job. I know she's sore because I investigated her, but she needs to get over it."

"Did you get the warrant for Donovan's house?"

"Yeah, right here." Kevin handed the paper to Nathan. "You know Donovan is going to court today. I heard he was going to take a plea."

"'What?"

"That's what I heard," he said. "Carole in the DA's office let it slip."

"Wow. I wonder why he's taking a deal."

"Who knows?"

"I'm going to roll out and start this search."

"Nathan, I'm not working for Donovan, and no matter what Caprice says, I was never out to get her."

"Any luck on finding Sabrina Jones?"

Kevin shook his head. "It's like she dropped off the face of the earth."

Nathan sighed. "We have to find her. She is a key part to all of this mess."

"Yeah well, this mess is getting on my nerves. We still don't know who killed Damien King."

"I know who didn't do it."

"We got the point, all right. Caprice didn't do it. Let's move on."

Nathan rolled his eyes. "What do you have against her?"

"Nothing. I just don't…Never mind."

"Nah, say it."

"I wanted her job; that's all. She came here, and they put her in vice. I had been waiting years for that assignment. I'm not saying she isn't good at her job, but it's hard getting beat out of a job by a woman." Nathan raised his eyebrow at Kevin. "I know it's petty," Kevin said. "And I don't wish her any harm. I'm just old school, y'know?"

"It's called sexism, y'know?" Nathan replied.

"Don't forget you weren't thrilled to have her as your partner, either."

'That's true, but it wasn't because she was a woman."

"Sure," Kevin said. "'Whatever."

"Listen, I have to get out of here and do this search."

"Is she really worth it? I mean, you put your career on the line for her and—"

"Trust me," Nathan said. "She's well worth it." He turned and headed out the door. Nathan and two officers arrived at Donovan's house at 10:30 a.m. Nathan banged on the door and got no answer. "Charlotte-Mecklenburg Police! Open up," he yelled as he banged again.

Nathan nodded for the officer with the battering ram to break the door down. Once the officer got the door open, Nathan and two other cops walked in with their guns drawn. "Police," Nathan called out as he and the other officers checked to see if anyone was in the house.

"All clear," an officer said.

"All right," Nathan said. "You take the first floor, McNally, you take the second floor, and I'll take the basement."

The three officers split up and began searching. Nathan headed for the basement, and the smell of something rotten caused him to cough. There's a body down here, he thought as he walked over to a stack of boxes. He went through them, not turning anything up. A blue tarp in the corner caught Nathan's eye. He pulled it back and saw the decomposing body. "Get a medical examiner down here now," he screamed into his radio. "We got a body down here."

Within seconds, a medic and two other officers were running into the basement. "What's going on down here?" he asked.

"There's a badly decomposing body in here," Nathan said. "I don't know who it is or how long it's been down here."

"I guess this is evidence of a murder, huh?" an officer said.

"Looks like it," Nathan said. "Let's get an ID on this body as soon as possible. We have Donovan this time."

Caprice sat in the doctor's office and closed her eyes as he began to cut her cast off. She hoped her leg had healed properly. She was tired of needing help to get from point A to point B. "Ms. Johnson, the leg looks good," he said. "I need to X-ray it to make sure the bone healed properly."

Caprice nodded. "Will I be able to walk without these crutches?"

"You should be, but I wouldn't sign up for the *Charlotte Observer* marathon right yet," the doctor replied with a laugh. "I'll have the nurse come up and take you down to X-ray."

Caprice wiggled her foot. She felt as if she could walk miles. *This is great,* she thought. *I'll be walking soon, and I can find Sabrina Jones.* After Caprice's leg was X-rayed, she was given a clean bill of health.

She headed to the police station to show Nathan that she was walking again. She pulled up to the department and looked at her watch. *He's probably in court. Donovan's trial started this morning,* she thought.

Caprice sat in the back of the courtroom and looked for Nathan. Donovan was sitting at the defense table with his attorney. *That son of a bitch,* Caprice thought as she looked at him.

"Your honor," Carole Young began, "the state has accepted a plea agreement from Mr. Harris, who has pleaded guilty to second-degree murder and misdemeanor assault on a government agent."

"Mr. Harris, please stand," the judge said.

Donovan stood up and looked back at Lewis then he looked up at the judge.

"Mr. Harris, according to the plea agreement with the state, the court could decide to sentence you to up to seven years in prison for assaulting a police officer. You could also be sentenced to fifteen years for second-degree murder. These sentences could run concurrently. Have you entered into this plea on your own free will?"

"Yes, your honor," Donovan said.

"As a part of this plea agreement, you have to answer to your charges. Please tell the court what happened on the night in question."

Donovan cleared his throat. "The night in question?"

"Mr. Harris, don't test the court's patience," the judge warned. Lewis stood up and coughed violently. One of the bailiffs rushed to Lewis's side, taking everyone's attention from Donovan, except Caprice's. He wasn't cuffed, and she knew how dangerous he could be. More bailiffs rushed to Lewis as he faked a seizure.

"What's going on?" the judge asked.

"We need a doctor," a bailiff called out.

The judge banged his gavel and called for a recess. As he headed to his chambers and the bailiffs attended to Lewis, Donovan made his escape.

"Somebody get Donovan!" Caprice screamed as she watched him run out the side door. A short, overweight bailiff tried to run after him, but Donovan was long gone by the time he made it outside. Unsure of herself, Caprice didn't chase after him. She didn't want to hurt her leg again. She walked quickly to her car. Now that Donovan was on the loose, she was in trouble. *I have to find Nathan,* she thought as she got into her car and started it.

Donovan hopped in the car waiting outside the courtroom. He was surprised Lewis got the distraction right. It was so easy for him to get out of the courthouse. He drove by his house and saw the police cars parked out front. *Damn,* he thought as he continued to drive. *Where can I go? I have to find some place quick. I can't call Ron. The police are going to look there first. That detective's house, perfect. I'll be*

waiting for her when she gets there. Donovan smiled diabolically as he headed in the direction of Caprice's house.

Caprice rushed into the police station and ran to Nathan's office. "Where's the fire, detective?" Chaney asked.

"Donovan Harris escaped from the courthouse this morning. Where's Nathan?"

"He's searching Harris's house." Chaney reached for his radio. "Adam 1-2 to Baker 4," Chaney said, calling Nathan on the radio.

"This is Baker 4," Nathan said.

"Harris escaped from court this morning."

"Well, we have to find him. There's a corpse in his basement."

"What?"

"A decomposed body. It looks like a female."

"Ten-four. We need to get an APB out on him. He should be considered armed and dangerous."

"Where is Caprice?"

"She's standing in my office."

"Don't let her out of your sight. Donovan will be gunning for her."

Chaney turned to her. "You're stuck with me," he said. "Inspector Wallace said you have to stay here."

Caprice shook her head. "I can't stay here, I have to find Donovan."

"You're still suspended. If I have to arrest you, I will."

"What will the charges be?"

"Pissing me off. Now sit down. Donovan has tried to kill you before. I'm sure he'd try it again. Do you have a death wish? You don't have to prove how bad you are."

"I'm not trying to prove anything. I'm tired of hiding. This is between me and Donovan, and I'm putting an end to it today." Caprice stormed out of the office.

Chaney followed her and grabbed her arm. "Detective! If you walk out that door, I can't guarantee your safety."

"I'm just going to have to take that risk," Caprice said as she snatched away from him. "I'm taking my life back."

Nathan knew Caprice was going to be going after Donovan after he talked to Chaney. Instead of going back to the station, he headed to Caprice's house. He pulled into the driveway at the same time Caprice did.

"Nathan," she said when she spotted him. "What are you doing here?"

"Saving your life, more than likely."

"Nathan, do you…"

"I knew you were going to fly out of the station ready to kick some ass. I thought you agreed that you needed help on this."

"This isn't going to be over until Donovan and I have it out."

"This is not 'Shootout at the okay Corral,' " Nathan shamed.

"But it's my life!"

"And I want you to keep living. Get in the car and let's go. We can form a plan together and stop Donovan before he comes after you. It's only a matter of time before he does." Caprice rolled her eyes, but she got into Nathan's car. Neither of them realized that they were being watched from the front window of her house.

Why did he have to come here? Donovan thought. He would've had a clear shot at Caprice if Nathan hadn't showed up. She would have walked into her house and never seen it coming. Maybe he would have tied her up and tortured her a little bit.

I wonder how long will it be before they come back, he thought as he walked into the kitchen. Donovan boldly fixed himself a sandwich and sat at the dining room table. He ate slowly, hoping Caprice and Nathan would return. He pulled a gun out of his pants and set it on the table.

CHAPTER TWENTY-EIGHT

Nathan drove Caprice back to the police station as she sat with her arms folded across her chest. Nathan glanced at her familiar scowl and hoped to offer some consolation. "I know you're mad," he began.

"I'm not mad. I'm just sick of this," she said.

"It's going to be over soon. We'll find Donovan."

"Then what? What will we do? Arrest him again then watch him escape? This isn't going to end until one of us is dead, and it damn sure isn't going to be me."

"What do you want to do, have a shootout with Donovan in the middle of the street? Are you willing to risk everything just to get even with him?"

"I'm willing to risk everything to live again. Do you know what it feels like to constantly have to look over your shoulder? Nathan, I'm tired of it and I'm not going to take it anymore. And don't tell me you're going to protect me."

Nathan shrugged. "I won't make that mistake again," he replied.

Caprice rolled her eyes. "Do we have to have this talk again?"

"No, we don't have to talk at all," he said.

"What's your problem?"

"Your cowgirl attitude is my problem. Do you want to die? Donovan killed Cordell and almost got you. You aren't Wonder Woman, Caprice."

"Nathan, if I was a man, would you have such a problem with me doing this?"

"Now this is the talk I don't want to have again. You can't keep thinking that I doubt you. Caprice, I love you, and I don't want anything to happen to you. When are you going to get that through your head? I lost my brother. I don't want to lose you."

"Nathan..."

He stopped the car abruptly in the middle of the street; then he leaned over and grabbed her chin. "I love you so much that I ache inside when I think about something happening to you." He captured her lips with his. Caprice returned his kiss. They were oblivious to the honking horns of the cars behind them. It was as if time had stood still in the car. Caprice wrapped her arms around Nathan and held on to him as if her life depended on it. Finally, Nathan heeded the horns and backed away from Caprice. "Let's go some place where we can be alone. We don't have to be the ones to find Donovan today," he said.

Breathless, all Caprice could do was nod. She couldn't explain what was happening; all she knew was she needed and wanted to be with Nathan desperately.

When he arrived at his house, he noticed for the first time that Caprice no longer had a cast. "I see why you want to take over the world. You got your legs back."

"Shut up," she replied as they walked into the house. Nathan held his arm out, stopping Caprice from entering right away. He walked in, flipped on the light and pulled his gun from his holster.

Caprice walked in and stood behind Nathan as he put his gun back in place. "Paranoid?" she asked.

"No, just cautious, much like you are with your heart," he replied.

Caprice rolled her eyes at him. "I have to be that way for a reason."

Nathan pulled her into his arms. "Not with me you don't." He ran his finger over her petal soft lips. "It's okay to let go. It's okay to be in love with me, because I'm totally in love with you."

Caprice melted in his arms. "Nathan, I love you; I do, but…"

"Shh," he replied bringing his finger to his lips. "All you have to do is love me." Nathan brought his lips down on top of Caprice's and quieted all her doubts.

She tugged at his shirt. "Make love to me," she whispered breathlessly. Nathan stepped back from Caprice and pulled his shirt over his head. Then he walked over to her and unbuttoned her shirt. He peeled it from her body, slowly and deliberately, running his hand across her smooth skin. Then he unhooked her lace bra, exposing her breasts. He took them into his big warm hands and massaged them until her nipples peaked. They were as hard as diamonds. Caprice tingled underneath his touch, feeling the tiny jolts of electricity run wild through her nervous system. He took his time, gently sucking and biting her nipples. Caprice stroked the back of his neck as he feasted on her succulent breasts. Nathan dropped to his knees and pulled Caprice closer to him. With his teeth, he unbuttoned her jeans and slid them down her legs. He slipped his hand in her satin panties and massaged her most sensitive spot. She moaned in delight as Nathan slowly entered her with his finger. With his other hand, he removed her panties. Caprice's knees began to shake as Nathan pressed deeper into her. An unintelligible whisper escaped her throat as he replaced his finger with his tongue. Nathan gently pushed Caprice back on the sofa.

"You taste so good," he whispered as he kicked out of his slacks.

"I want you so much right now," Caprice moaned. She pulled a thoroughly aroused Nathan on top of her and ground against him. He felt as if he was going to burst being this close to Caprice. He needed to feel the valley of femininity around him. He wanted to become one with her, never wanted the feeling to end. He reached up and squeezed her breasts. He left a trail of kisses down her taut stomach.

Caprice arched her back, pressing her body closer to Nathan's lips. She was burning up. She wanted Nathan as much as he wanted her. "Nathan, Nathan," she called out between shallow breaths. "Please, I need you."

He looked up at her and smiled. Nathan reached down and pulled a condom from the wallet in his pants pocket. He slid the prophylactic on his erect penis then turned to Caprice. He spread her legs apart, licked his finger and then entered her with it.

She was weak with desire. Her body shivered with anticipation when Nathan removed his finger and thrust his throbbing manhood deep into her.

A husky moan escaped his throat. "You feel so good," he groaned.

Caprice mumbled incoherently as they began a slow and sensual bump and grind. She wrapped her legs around his waist, giving him all the room he needed to press every hard inch of him into her. "Oh, Nathan," she screamed as he clutched her bottom, pulling her closer to him. Caprice wrapped her arms around his neck, losing herself in his love. She could barely breathe; the heat between them was like an erupting volcano.

"Caprice, Caprice," he exclaimed as he began to climax.

She moved up and down underneath him, creating a friction that felt so good to both of them. Like a high tide crashing against a rocky shore, they reached the peak of sexual desire. Nathan collapsed on top of her. His heart was beating a thousand times a minute. Sweat covered their bodies. She didn't want him to let her go. Neither of them had the energy to move.

Nathan sighed and looked down at Caprice with a satisfied smile on his face. She seemed to be his mirror image, their heartbeats and breathing in perfect sync. Caprice gently stroked his back before kissing him sweetly on the lips. This was right, she thought. This wasn't a mistake. At that moment, her heart swelled with love for Nathan. Nothing else mattered in that moment. Everything was perfect. She forgot about Donovan and everything else going on outside Nathan's living room as they held each other and drifted to sleep on the sofa.

CHAPTER TWENTY-NINE

Caprice and Nathan stayed tucked away in his house for two days. They passed the time by making love every morning and night. They needed this time away from the stress of the real world. This time together gave them a chance to connect on a deeper level.

"What do you want for breakfast?" Caprice asked when she and Nathan woke up.

"You."

"Be serious."

He pulled her into his arms. "I am."

Caprice gently pushed him away. "I'm going to say something you don't want to hear."

Nathan groaned. "This is about Donovan, isn't it?"

Caprice nodded. "We have to get out there and find him and Sabrina."

Nathan sat up in the bed and looked at Caprice, who had already swung her legs over the side. "All right, what do you suggest we do?"

"We know Donovan is going to be after me. I say let's give the man what he wants."

Nathan shook his head. "Are you out of your mind? You're not putting your life in danger to find that maniac."

"Every day Donovan is out there on the loose, I'm in danger, and as much as I'd love to, I can't stay in your house forever."

"You can, you just don't want to. Seriously though, I understand what you're saying, but there has to be another way."

Caprice stood up and walked over to the window in the corner. "Nathan, this isn't going to be pretty or easy. Donovan is a cold-blooded killer. And yes, one of us might get hurt, but we have to go after him."

"I don't want you to be his victim again, Caprice."

"I won't be," she said confidently.

"You don't know that."

"Nathan, I don't want to fight about this. We have to get out there and find Donovan and Sabrina."

Nathan sighed and stood up. "I knew it was going to end soon." He wrapped his arms around Caprice's waist. "These last few days have been paradise."

Caprice turned around and kissed Nathan gently on the lips. "They have, but it's back to the real world now."

Nathan groaned. "All right, all right. Let's do this." He dropped his arms and walked into the bathroom. A few minutes later, the two were on their way to the police department. "You know, we found a body in Donovan's house."

"He is a sick bastard."

"It could easily have been you."

"Do you have to start this again? Have you forgotten that I'm a trained police officer, just like you?"

Nathan ignored her comment. "They should have an ID by now."

"Don't gloss over what I said," Caprice snapped. "You're just like every other male cop. You think that because I'm a woman I can't handle myself."

"For the love of God, don't start this, Caprice. Every time we start working on this case, we fight and I don't want to do that. For the record, I know you can handle yourself. But can't you understand that I want you to stay alive? Can't you understand how much I love you?"

"So am I supposed to give up the battle so you can keep your watchful eye on me?"

"No, but not once have you tried to get your job back. You've been so hell-bent on getting Donovan—"

"I have to clear my name. There are people who still think—"

"I don't give a damn what people think, and you shouldn't either!" he bellowed. "You're a good cop, and anyone who thinks you had something to do with Damien King's death doesn't deserve a badge."

Caprice turned her head away from Nathan as tears began to fall from her from her eyes. "I wanted Damien dead so many times. I hated him. That night, I probably could have killed him. He made me so angry. I was hurting because he played me for a fool so many times, and I was so close to letting him back in my life. That made me angry. I felt like I was weak, and I hate being weak."

"But you didn't pull the trigger. You didn't kill him, because you're not a criminal," Nathan said softly.

She wiped her eyes and sighed. "This has to be over. I need my life back."

"We're going to get it back." Nathan stroked her knee tenderly.

When they got to the police department, Caprice and Nathan walked into his office. He flipped through the stack of messages on his desk until he found one from the medical examiner's office. "All right, let's find out who that stiff was in Donovan's basement."

"Probably a pizza boy who shortchanged him."

Nathan smirked as he dialed the phone. Caprice picked up Donovan's file and began flipping through it. Maybe there is a clue in here about where he is, she thought.

"This is Inspector Wallace. You got news for me?"

Caprice looked up at Nathan as his eyes widened and his jaw dropped. "You're kidding me," he said.

"What?" Caprice mouthed.

"All right," Nathan said then hung up the phone. "Well, we found Sabrina."

"That was her in Donovan's basement." Nathan nodded. "There's more news," he said.

"What?"

"The bullet they fished out of her came from your gun." Caprice's eyes widened. Was she going to face another murder charge?

Now people were going to think she worked for Donovan. Nathan waved his hand.

"Donovan's and Sabrina's fingerprints were on the gun."

"We have evidence linking Sabrina to stealing the gun and Donovan to the murder," she said with a satisfied smile. "Let's go get him."

"We don't know where he is."

Caprice stood up. "Then we're going to go out and find him. Donovan isn't going to get away again."

"You're the boss," Nathan said as he followed her out the door.

Donovan had been holed up in Caprice's house for three days. He was starting to go stir crazy. *When is that bitch coming home?* he thought.

He peeked out the front window for passing police cars and saw none. *I'm out of here,* he thought. As he reached for the doorknob, he heard a car pull into the driveway. Donovan ducked behind the sofa with his hand on his gun. Whoever walked through the door was going to get shot. He just prayed it was Caprice. He listened as the key entered the lock.

The door opened. He heard Caprice and Nathan. The lights came on. "Wow," Nathan said when he saw the damage in her house. "Ron did a number on this place."

"Yeah," she said wistfully. "I need to have someone come in and get the blood and gore off the walls."

Nathan looked around and spotted a shoe near the loveseat, a man's shoe and not one of his. He grabbed Caprice's arm and whispered in her ear. "Donovan's in here."

She looked up at him with a question in her eyes. Nathan drew his gun and pointed to the shoe. Caprice gritted her teeth then walked over to the loveseat. She picked up the shoe and tossed it at the sofa.

"Donovan, show yourself!" she screamed. He stood up and pointed his gun at the side of her face.

"I should've known you wouldn't come alone," he said. "Drop the gun or she dies."

Nathan pointed his gun at Donovan. "It's over, Harris. We found Sabrina's body. You're already in enough trouble. You want to add another murder to your charges?"

Donovan cocked the revolver and reached for the trigger. Nathan shot him in the shoulder, causing him to drop the gun. Caprice lunged at him, grasping his throat. "You son of a bitch!" she screamed as she choked him.

"Caprice, get off him," Nathan said as he grabbed her shoulder, trying to stop her from killing Donovan. She let him go, and Donovan coughed, trying to breathe again. Nathan cuffed him and radioed for a backup unit and EMS.

Caprice looked at Donovan as they waited for the others to come.

"Why did you do this?" she asked.

"Go to hell," he spat.

"Don't waste your time," Nathan said. "We got this snake this time, and he's not going to slither away."

Donovan smirked, but his confidence was fading. He was sloppy and he was caught, but he was going to have to get out of this. He knew all was lost when he heard the sirens. Nathan grabbed his arm and pushed him toward the door. "Let's go."

Caprice watched the EMS workers patch up Donovan's shoulder then load him in the back of a patrol car from her front porch. She closed her eyes and took a deep breath.

Nathan walked up the front steps and pulled Caprice into his arms. "Come on, we've got to head to the police station," he said.

"I hope this is over."

"It is," Nathan said as Caprice squeezed his hand as they headed to his car. "Caprice, don't be nervous. Once we get this thing behind us, your life will be back to normal."

"What is that?" She smiled weakly.

Nathan opened the passenger side door for Caprice. "Come on, Detective."

Donovan's arrest was the top story on the evening news. Ethan sat glued to his TV. He knew it was time to get out of town. He didn't want to represent Donovan in this mess. He was a murderer—and everything else he was accused of. Ethan went into his bedroom, pulled his luggage from the top of the closet and began stuffing clothes in it. Before he could finish packing, the phone rang. Don't answer it, he thought as he looked at the extension in his room. The phone continued to ring; then the answering machine picked up.

"This is Ethan Washington. Please leave a message or call my service at 704-555-3942," the machine played back.

"Ethan, pick up the damn phone. I called your office, and they said you were at home," Donovan growled into the phone. Reluctantly, Ethan picked up.

"What is it?"

"I need you to get to the police department."

"Donovan, you might want to find new representation."

"Oh, hell no. You're not getting out of this."

"I am out of this," Ethan said. "I'm not getting involved. They found a body—"

"Yeah, a body I told you to get rid of. You got me into this, so you're getting me out of it. If you don't, I'm going for a plea and tell the DA everything you've ever done," Donovan threatened.

"You really think anyone would believe you? You made this mess; you get out of it the best way you can." Ethan slammed the phone down and continued to pack. He knew he'd signed his own death certificate. *All he has to do is make a phone call. I've got to get out of Charlotte tonight,* he thought as he zipped his suitcase. He headed to the front door and opened it. Caprice and Nathan were standing on his door step.

"Taking a trip?" Caprice asked.

"What are you two doing here?" Ethan asked.

"We want to talk to you," Nathan replied.

"Well, as you can plainly see, I'm heading out."

"With your client in jail again? Don't you have a trial to prepare for?" Caprice probed.

"Another associate will handle that. Why is it any of your concern?"

"Because we know you've been helping Donovan in his activities," she said. "Is that why you're running now? Did you turn Donovan down, and now he has a hit out on you?"

"I'm going to a legal conference in San Antonio."

Caprice and Nathan shot Ethan a "yeah right" look. They both knew that if he stayed in Charlotte, he would be another victim. "When Donovan needs you most, that seems a little suspect to me," Nathan chimed in.

Caprice nodded in agreement. "Why don't you show us your plane ticket and hotel reservations?"

"Why don't you show me a warrant?" Ethan said. Nathan smiled and pulled a blue document from his jacket pocket.

"You're not the only one who knows the law," Nathan quipped. He and Caprice walked into the house. Ethan followed them.

"What are you looking for?" he asked.

"It's in the warrant," Caprice said. She glanced around the foyer before walking into the living room. "You have a nice place here. And they say crime doesn't pay."

"I don't have to take this," Ethan shouted. "I know my rights."

"I'm sure you do," she replied as she opened his entertainment center and began looking through its contents.

"Tell me something, what does Donovan have on you? I mean, you seem too smart to be a stooge for a criminal."

Ethan looked at her and frowned. "Do I look like a common hood? I'm not saying anything to you about anything until I talk to my lawyer."

"Look," Nathan began, "we can do this informally, or you can lawyer up, and we can file charges. How does obstruction of justice, accessory to murder, accessory to assault on a government official, conspiracy to commit murder, and just being an asshole sound to you?"

"It sounds like I'm going to need a lawyer. I know how you cops operate with your 'informal' interrogations."

Caprice turned to Ethan. "We could actually give a damn about what you've done. We want Donovan."

"Have you ever heard of attorney-client privilege?"

"As an officer of the court, you have a duty to report any crimes your client committed," Caprice said. "He used your car the first night he tried to kill me."

"And?" Ethan stated.

"This isn't getting us anywhere," Nathan said. "We can just bring you in."

"And put you in the cell right next to Donovan. How long do you think you would last? A day? An hour?"

"No, please don't do that," Ethan said with rising desperation. "Look, I'll tell you whatever you want to know. This has gone on long enough, and I'm tired of it."

Caprice and Nathan looked at each other and then turned to Ethan. "We're listening."

Ethan began to recount Donovan's schemes. Caprice ran her hand across her face and frowned. "What kind of deal can I get?" Ethan asked after what seemed like forever.

"That's up to the DA," Nathan said. "We need you to come down to the station and make an official statement. If you cooperate fully, then I'll put in a good word for you."

Ethan nodded and stood up. "I'll do what I have to do," he said. "I don't want to be associated with this mess anymore."

Nathan led Ethan out of the house, and Caprice followed behind them. Nathan glanced back at her as he loaded Ethan into the backseat. "Are you okay?" he asked.

She nodded. "This wasn't your fault," he said. "You were doing your job. You had no control over Donovan's actions."

"I know," she said. "If Damien had let our relationship die, he'd be alive."

"You didn't have any control over that either. Damien did what he wanted to do, and Donovan tried to make you pay for arresting him. You didn't do anything wrong, and I don't want you to think you did."

"You're right," Caprice said as she got into the car.

When Nathan and Caprice got to the police department, they turned Ethan over to Major Chaney. "Let's get out of here," Nathan said to Caprice.

"Good, I don't want to deal with this anymore."

"Why don't we go get something to eat and turn off all the phones?"

"That sounds like heaven," Caprice said. "Do you think this is actually going to stick? What if Donovan kills Ethan before this even goes to trial?"

"I'm sure they will put him in protective custody."

Caprice put her arm around his waist. "I need you to hold me," she whispered.

Nathan squeezed her tightly. "This will be over soon. Donovan has a lot to answer for."

"Including Cordell's death."

He nodded. "I've been trying not to think about that. I want to wring Donovan's neck, even though I know Cordell brought this on himself for dealing with that snake."

"He still didn't deserve to die," Caprice said.

Nathan sighed. "I know; I know. I never thought I would say this, but I miss Cordell. We never really got along, but I miss him calling me, even if it was just to save his ass. I wanted to protect him, but he wouldn't let me."

"You can't protect someone who doesn't want to be protected."

"I know that," he said. "So I'm trying not to blame myself for what happened."

"But it's hard, isn't it?"

"Let's go," Nathan said as they walked out the door.

CHAPTER THIRTY

A week passed after Donovan's arrest. Even though Caprice was completely cleared of any suspicion of murder, she hadn't checked into getting her job back. Caprice still wasn't sure if law enforcement was for her anymore. She was wrestling with herself about the entire situation. She no longer felt accepted by her fellow officers. She kneeled over the porcelain tub in her bathroom and scrubbed as she thought about going back to work. Her money was dwindling, so she would have to do something soon. Caprice stood up and wiped sweat from her brow with the back of her hand. *What am I going to do?* she thought as she looked at her sparkling clean bathroom. She didn't want to ask Nathan about her job. She knew what he would say. He didn't understand why she hadn't gone back to work yet anyway. *I haven't talked to Serena in a while,* she thought as she walked into her bedroom and picked up her cordless phone. She dialed her best friend's office number.

"This is Serena."

"Don't we just sound so professional," Caprice teased.

"I am a professional. What's going on?"

"Oh nothing, I was just thinking about how long it's been since we talked."

"I've been meaning to call you and see how things were going."

"Well, we found Damien's killer," Caprice said. "She was dead too."

"Whoa. Well, at least that part of your life is over now, and you don't have that cloud over you anymore. How is Mr. Nathan?"

"He's okay. His brother, Cordell, was shot and killed."

"Damn, there is death all around you guys," she said. "This is wild. You didn't get hurt in all of this, did you?"

"I had a broken leg, but I'm fine."

"Caprice, with all of that stuff that was going on, why are you just now calling me? You love keeping me in the dark."

"Because you would have been worried, and I didn't want you thinking about it. Besides, I could only take one overprotective person in my life at a time."

"You must mean Nathan."

"Yes. He can be worse than an overbearing mother sometimes."

"Well, you two are supercops, so he should be used to it."

"I haven't gone back to work yet. I'm not sure if I want to," Caprice revealed.

"What? You love police work. Ever since I've known you, you've been talking about being a cop. What are you waiting on?"

"Serena, I feel like it's my fault that Damien was killed."

"No, it wasn't, and I'm sure you heard this before. Damien was a hothead and that's what got him killed. Stop doubting yourself and get your badge back."

"When did you get so smart?" Caprice asked.

"I know how much you love being a cop. You shouldn't give that up for anyone, especially not Damien King. You deserve your job, and you're good at it."

"All right, I guess I'll go talk to my captain."

"And tell Nathan I'm sorry about his brother."

"I'll do that," she said then hung up the phone. Something inside of her was pulling her away from police work. Caprice sat on the side of the bed and stared out the window trying to figure out her next move.

Nathan drove slowly to his brother's gravesite. He needed to make peace with Cordell. Nathan reflected on the last time they spoke. They both were angry and said things they shouldn't have. As Nathan pulled into the cemetery's driveway, he wished he could take those final angry moments back. Nathan parked his car and walked to Cordell's head stone. He knelt and ran his hand across the cold, gray slab.

"What's up, bro?" Nathan whispered. "I never thought the last time we talked would be the end. I know I was upset with you because of what happened with Caprice. It seems like we've been fighting for the last five years, but I did love you. I wanted you to do better, change your life. You were too smart for this. Maybe I should have been more supportive, then you wouldn't have gotten involved with Donovan. I miss you, C. You were all the family I had left. I'm glad I have Caprice in my life, but it doesn't make losing you easier."

He looked over at his mother and father's headstones. "I'm sorry, guys, I failed." Nathan dropped his head in his hands and started to sob silently.

A warm gust of wind blew over him, carrying a message of assurance from his mother. Nathan stood up and wiped his eyes with the back of his hand. He returned to his car, feeling a little better, but he had to make sure Donovan paid for killing Cordell and everything else he did.

I just hope Caprice makes up her mind and comes back to work, he thought as he looked back at the three graves. *You would have liked her, Mom and Dad. You would have loved Caprice.*

When Nathan got to the police department, he walked into Chaney's office. "Major, we need to talk," Nathan announced.

"I'm glad to see you came to work today," he replied flippantly.

"When is Detective Johnson going to be offered her job?"

Chaney leaned back in his seat and folded his arms across his chest. "I haven't decided yet. She's a hothead, and I'm not sure if she should get her job back."

"If it wasn't for Caprice, Donovan Harris would be on the streets. There would be three unsolved murders and—"

"Look, Inspector, don't come in here and try to tell me how to do my job. There is still an investigation into her actions."

Nathan rolled his eyes. "Her actions got a cold-blooded killer off the street. What's there to investigate?"

"Get out of my office."

"She's a good cop, and you know that. If she doesn't come back, then the department loses."

"This is the last time I'm telling you to get out of my office. Are you so blinded by this woman that you want to sacrifice your career for her? I am your superior officer, and I will not take much more of this insubordination!"

"Fine," Nathan snapped. "I'm just trying to stop you from making a colossal mistake, but it's your decision." He stormed out of Chaney's office and sat at his desk. Nathan picked up the phone and called Caprice.

"Hello," she said.

"Hi, beautiful."

"Where have you been all morning?"

"I had some things I had to take care of. I went to visit my family."

"That must have been rough on you. You should have called me, I would have gone with you."

"I needed to go alone. I had some stuff to get off my chest. But I was thinking about you."

"That's sweet."

"Caprice Johnson, when are you going to fight for your job?"

"Don't start that again," she said with a sigh.

"I'm going to keep starting it until you get in here and talk to Leland and Chaney. I know what your career means to you."

"Maybe it doesn't mean as much as I thought it did. This whole thing has changed me, Nate. If what I do is going to put people around me in danger, maybe I shouldn't do it."

"Now you know this is not the norm. How many other drug dealers have you arrested without a hitch? Donovan was a horse of a different color, but look who stopped him."

"Stop it," she said. "I don't need the ego boost."

"Well, I have to go, but I wanted you to know that I love you, okay?"

"I love you too."

When Caprice hung up with Nathan, she decided that it was time for her to make a decision about her future with the Charlotte-Mecklenburg Police Department. She grabbed her jacket and ran to her car. *I'm going back,* she thought as she headed uptown.

Caprice walked into the department with her old confident swagger. She headed straight for Leland's desk.

"Captain," she said.

"De…Caprice, what can I help you with?"

"We need to talk," she said.

"Have a seat."

"I've been going back and forth on this, and I've come to a decision about my future here."

"Lee's hear it," he said. Leland held his breath. Caprice was one of his best detectives, and he needed her skill and expertise.

"I want my shield back, and I want to rejoin the police department."

Leland smiled and leaned back in his chair. "What took you so long, Detective?" He opened his desk drawer, pulled out Caprice's badge and handed it to her. "Welcome back. I need you on my team."

"Thanks," Caprice said as she took her badge.

"Before we make it official, I'm going to have to talk to Chaney. He has a major stick up his ass about you, but you brought Donovan down, and if he doesn't reinstate you, me and the rest of the vice unit will walk out of here and go work in Gastonia or Rock Hill."

Caprice smiled. "Thanks, I really appreciate that," she said. "I have something I need to take care of. I'll be right back."

"Don't get suspended again," Leland cautioned.

Caprice walked down the hall to Nathan's office. She walked in and closed his door. "What are you doing here?" he asked.

Caprice pulled out her badge. "I'm back. On the force, that is," she said happily.

He pulled her into his arms and kissed her with an intense passion. Caprice's knees were weak when he let her go. "Well, I guess I should have done this a long time ago," she said when she caught her breath.

"Chaney and I had it out about you today."

"Will you stop putting your neck in the noose for me? I'm a big girl."

"I know that, but if I want to help my woman out, I'm going to do it," he said.

"I'm not going to argue with you."

"Good, because I'd rather make love to you."

She stroked his cheek. "So would I."

"Meet me tonight at my place. I have a special treat for you."

Caprice smirked. "I'll be there," she said as she turned to walk out the door.

"Detective, we need to talk," Chaney said when Caprice opened the door.

"Okay," she replied.

Caprice followed him to his office. He motioned for her to sit down.

"Welcome back. Your suspension is lifted, and you are reinstated."

"Thank you."

"There are conditions," he said. "You're on probation. If you step out of line one time, you're fired."

"I understand."

"You're a good cop, and that's the only reason I'm doing this. You and Wallace did great work bringing Donovan Harris in. I know you put your life at risk, and you upheld the oath you took at the academy. I appreciate that."

Caprice nodded and kept her sarcastic comment to herself. This man is so anal, she thought as she listened to him drone on and on about what she did and how it was wrong but effective.

"In the future, if you are suspended don't do any police work."

"I'm not going to be suspended again," she said confidently.

"Let's hope not. You can return to duty tomorrow morning."

Caprice stood up. "Thank you, Major."

"I may be wrong about you, and I hope that's the case," he said.

Caprice walked into the vice unit's office again, where she went to her desk and ran her finger over a stack of old case files. "Hey, Johnson." Thom said when he saw her hovering over her desk. "I hear you're coming back tomorrow."

"News travels fast around here."

"It sure does. Man, you couldn't have come back at a better time."

"Really?" she asked. "You act like you've been suffering or something."

"I have. They teamed me with a rookie who knows about as much about investigating as Santa Claus."

"It can't be that bad."

"Trust me, it is. I hate first-year detectives, but I'm getting my partner back tomorrow. I was worried you were going to quit since they tried to pin that murder on you."

Caprice bit the inside of her cheek. "It's going to take a lot more than that to get rid of me. Look, I'll see you tomorrow." She turned to leave the squad room.

"Johnson," Leland called out. "You can't leave without this." He held out a new service gun. "Try to keep up with this one."

"I think I might sleep with it," she joked as she stuck the gun in the back of her jeans.

Later that evening, Nathan prepared for Caprice's visit. Finally, there was something for both of them to celebrate. After months of pain and sadness, there was good news in their lives. The nightmare with Donovan was nearly over. He was in jail under maximum security until his trial. They didn't have to look over their shoulders for flying bullets and hired killers.

Nathan lit two tapered candles on the dining room table then lit three cylinder-shaped candles on the coffee table in the living room. In his bedroom, he lit the rose-scented candles surrounding the bed and a juniper-scented incense stick. He ran his hand over the pillow-soft down comforter on the bed. *I hope she likes this*, he thought. Nathan had ordered dinner from Morton's Steakhouse. He wanted tonight to be extra special. He wanted the evening to feel magical. He placed the food on the table then looked at his watch. She should be here soon, he thought as he looked around to make sure everything was perfect.

Like clockwork, the doorbell rang at 8 p.m. Nathan greeted Caprice, who wore a knee-length pink strapless dress with a matching wrap and three-inch stiletto sandals. She looked like a princess. Nathan inhaled sharply.

"Breathtaking," Nathan said.

"Thank you," Caprice replied as she walked in. Nathan took her hand and pulled her into his arms. Caprice leaned in and kissed him gently on the lips. "You know, you really didn't have to go through all this trouble for me."

"Yes I did, Detective. Come over here and sit down," he said as he led her to the dining room table. "For you, I have grilled chicken breasts with butter and garlic, tender California blend vegetables, and cheese biscuits."

"Did you cook this?" she asked.

"No. I ordered it from Morton's. I had other things to think about."

"And I was about to be impressed. What's for dessert?"

"You'll see after dinner, now eat."

"Yes sir," she said in mock salute. Nathan sat across from her and smiled as he cut into his medium rare ribeye steak. "This food is good," she said. Then she dropped her knife and fork on the side of her plate. "But I want my dessert now."

"What would that be?" he asked.

Caprice stood up, walked over to Nathan and took his fork out of his hand then sat on his lap. "I want you." She picked up his napkin and wiped his mouth before kissing him. She darted her tongue in his mouth, savoring the taste of it. Nathan ran his hand down her svelte body. He pushed away from the table and swooped Caprice into his arms.

"I'm all about giving the people what they want," he said as he carried her to his bedroom. The scene in Nathan's bedroom was like one from a romantic movie. She smiled lovingly at him.

"You did all this for me?" she asked.

"I wanted to make tonight special," he whispered.

The flickering candles made her skin glow. Nathan gently laid her on the bed and looked at her. "You are so beautiful," he said as he ran his fingers though her hair.

She reached up and stroked his cheek. "So are you," she replied. Caprice tugged at Nathan's pants, pulling him on top of her. "Make love to me."

Nathan slid his hands underneath her dress and discovered her lack of panties. He smiled. "So, I just wasted my money on food, huh?"

Caprice grinned and arched her back to kiss him on the lips. Nathan unzipped her dress and slowly slid it off her body, uncovering her raw essence. She reached up and snatched Nathan's shirt open and ran her hands across his smooth chest. He unbuttoned his slacks and kicked out of them. Caprice rolled over on top of Nathan and straddled his frame. She kissed his neck, slowly moving down his chest, gently nibbling on his nipples. She slipped his boxers down his legs.

Nathan was aroused by her touch. His manhood was throbbing against her thighs. Nathan clutched her bottom, pulling her closer to him. Their lips were drawn together. Nathan gently bit her bottom lip as he reached over and grabbed a condom from the nightstand. He couldn't take being so close to her anymore; he had to feel her warmth wrapped around him. He quickly rolled the condom down on his erect penis as Caprice continued to kiss his neck, clouding his mind with desire. Nathan rolled over so that he was on top of Caprice. He lovingly looked down at her body. "I love you," he whispered.

"I love you, too." Her breasts heaved up and down as she stared into Nathan's eyes. He pressed his pulsating shaft into Caprice's body. She moaned in delight, spreading her legs and grabbing the bed sheets. Nathan brought her breasts together and drew each one to his mouth, all the while gyrating his hips against Caprice's.

"You feel so good," he whispered in her ear.

Caprice's words stuck in her throat. She clutched Nathan's back as she felt the twangs of an orgasm beginning to attack her nervous system.

Nathan slowed his pace, wanting to share the climax with her. Caprice tightened her body around his. Nathan could feel his body shivering with an impending orgasm. He muttered incoherently as he and Caprice came. They clutched each other's sweaty bodies. She buried her face in his shoulder as he squeezed her closer to him.

"Um, I could stay like this forever," she whispered.

"I want you to."

They held each other close and drifted off to sleep.

PART III

CHAPTER THIRTY-ONE

THREE MONTHS LATER

Donovan was led to the courtroom with shackles on his hands and feet. Two bailiffs were assigned to sit next to him when he got to the defense table. This time, no one was going to let him slip away. He looked at the public defender sitting beside him.

"Are you sure you don't want to take a plea?" he asked Donovan.

"I'm not pleading to anything, and if you don't get some of these charges dismissed, you will live to regret it," Donovan hissed.

"Are you threatening me? I'm not Ethan Washington; I'll gladly walk away."

"Look, I don't want to go to jail."

"Have you seen the evidence against you? Jail is the least of your worries. You're looking at death row."

"You're fired!"

"What?"

"I'll represent myself," Donovan announced.

"Fine," the attorney said throwing up his hands. "I'll let the judge know."

"Good," Donovan said as he leaned back in his seat.

"I just want you to know you're a fool. You're facing the death penalty. This isn't a joke. Are you sure you want to fire me?"

"I did it, didn't I? I know what this case is about," Donovan said. He turned around and watched Caprice and Nathan walk in the courtroom. He sneered at them. *They ruined my life, and if they think this is over, they should think again,* he thought.

Caprice's eyes locked with Donovan's. She shuddered inwardly when she got a good look at him. He was so cold, so evil. She looked away and tried not to show any fear.

Nathan squeezed her hand. "It's okay; this will be over soon," he reassured.

"I hope so," she said.

"The DA has an airtight case, and Ethan is on our side. Donovan is all bark and no bite now." Caprice nodded.

"You're right. He isn't important at all." They sat down behind the district attorney's table as the judge called the court to order.

"Mr. Harris, I trust there won't be another disappearing act," the judge cautioned.

"Your honor, if it pleases the court," Donovan's attorney began. "My client has fired me and wishes to represent himself." Hushed whispers floated through the courtroom's gallery.

Donovan stood up. "Mr. Harris, this is highly irregular," the judge said. "Why are you firing your attorney?"

"With all due respect, your honor, this man is incompetent and has yet to mount a defense for me. I feel that I can do better by myself."

"Well, I don't. Your attorney will not be removed from your case," the judge said.

"It's my right—"

"Sit down, Mr. Harris. This circus has gone on long enough. There will be a trial in this courtroom, and it won't be a comedy of errors. Ms. Young, is the state prepared to continue, I mean, begin this trial?"

Carole nodded. "Yes, your honor, we are."

Caprice looked over at Donovan and fought back a smile. She knew his stunt was an attempt for a mistrial. He turned away from Caprice, seemingly accepting his defeat. But she wasn't going to be fooled by Donovan again. The last time he was in this courtroom, he was pleading guilty one minute and gone the next. She was going to make sure history wouldn't repeat itself.

Caprice would have shot Donovan in the back to keep him from escaping again. She kept a close eye on him as the assistant district attorney made her opening statement. Donovan stared straight ahead as Carole Young painted him as psychotic, drug-dealing killer. Caprice shuddered as she thought about how close she came to death at Donovan's hands.

Nathan patted her hand reassuringly. "Soon, honey," he whispered.

She nodded.

Caprice was the first witness the state called to the stand. Even though she had testified in hundreds of other cases, she was nervous about this testimony. She took a deep breath as the clerk of the court swore her in. "Detective Johnson, please state your name and occupation for the jury," Carole said.

"Detective Caprice Johnson, I work in the vice/narcotics unit of the Charlotte-Mecklenburg Police Department."

"Have you ever seen the defendant, Donovan Harris?"

"Yes."

"How do you know him?"

"My unit has investigated Mr. Harris for about a year-and-a-half. And he tried to kill me on a few occasions."

"Objection," Donovan's attorney shouted.

"Overruled," the judge said. "Continue."

"Please explain what you mean by Mr. Harris tried to kill you?" Carole asked.

"After he was arrested by my unit, Mr. Harris began a campaign to discredit me as an officer, and he shot me in the leg. The second time he tried to kill me was in my house after he escaped from this courtroom."

"When you arrested Mr. Harris on the initial charges, what if anything, did he say to you?"

"He told me that I had messed with the wrong person."

"What happened next?"

"My gun was stolen, and I was implicated in the murder of my ex-fiancé."

"Through the department's investigation, was it determined who killed your ex-fiancé?"

"Yes, Donovan Harris ordered the killing of Damien King and the theft of my gun."

"Objection!" Harris's attorney shouted once again. "Assuming facts not in evidence. Are we supposed to just take her word for it because she is a cop?"

"Sustained," the judge said. "Show some proof, counselor."

"If it pleases the court, your honor, if you give me a little more time, I will show proof."

"Thin ice. I'll allow it for a few more minutes but make your point quickly," he said.

"Thank you. Detective, how was it discovered that Donovan Harris was behind the death of Damien King and your attempted murder?"

"An investigation was launched by the department. In the course of that investigation, everything led back to Donovan."

Carole walked over to the state's table and pulled out a stack of reports. "Are these the findings of that investigation?"

"Yes."

"Your honor, I'd like to submit state's exhibits one through fifteen," she said.

Donovan's attorney dropped his head for a split second. He looked at Donovan, begging him to take a plea before it was too late. The reports were damning, to say the least.

"I have no further questions," Carole said.

"You may cross examine," the judge said to Donovan's attorney.

"Your honor, I need a moment to confer with my client," he said.

"Why don't we take a fifteen-minute recess so you can get yourself together?" the judge said, obviously annoyed.

The bailiff called for everyone to rise. Caprice walked off the stand and glanced at Donovan and his attorney. They seemed to be arguing. She walked over to Nathan.

"You're doing great," he said.

"I wonder what his attorney is planning."

"Don't think about it. Just continue to tell the truth." Meanwhile, Donovan's attorney motioned for Carole to come over to his table. She walked over with a confident smile on her face. "I bet he wants a plea bargain," Nathan said. "If he doesn't take one, he's going to get the needle for sure. That won't be such a bad thing, either."

"I just want him off the street. And death would be too easy for that scum. Taking his power away would be a fate worse than death for Donovan. I want him to rot in prison for the rest of his life without any power."

"I'm going to get a cup of coffee. You want something?" Nathan asked.

Caprice shook her head. "I'm okay." Nathan walked out of the courtroom and Caprice turned her attention to the defense table. She watched the intense conversation. Carole returned to her table. "What was that all about?" Caprice demanded.

"Donovan is going to spend the rest of his life in prison. He copped a plea to conspiracy to commit murder, assault on a government official, and two counts of second-degree murder. When the judge comes back, we're going to let him know, and this will finally be over for you. The only thing we'll have to do is fill out the plea-change paper work."

Caprice held her breath. She felt like breathing would wake her up from this dream. She had her life back now.

Carole touched her shoulder. "Are you all right?"

"I just can't believe this is finally over," she replied.

"It will be as soon as the judge accepts the plea."

A few minutes later court was reconvened.

"Your honor," Carole said. "The defendant has entered a change of plea."

The judge frowned. "I figured as much. Have the motions on my desk by five. Bailiff, take the defendant into custody. We will discuss sentencing at nine tomorrow morning."

Donovan stood up and was led out of the courtroom. Caprice watched him as he was carted away. She closed her eyes exhaled loudly. She went out into the hallway to find Nathan, who was walking toward the courtroom sipping on a cup of steaming coffee.

"It's over," Caprice exclaimed.

"What happened?"

"Donovan pleaded to two counts of second-degree murder, assault on a government official, and conspiracy to commit murder. He's going to spend the rest of his sorry life in prison."

Nathan set his cup on the floor and hugged Caprice tightly, lifting her off the floor. "You did it," he said when he put her down.

"No, we did it." Caprice stroked his face.

"Let's get back to the station," he said. "You put Donovan Harris away. I see a medal in your future." Caprice playfully smacked him on the shoulder and they walked out of the courthouse hand in hand.

Caprice walked into the vice squad room and quietly sat at her desk. Thom spotted her first. "So what happened?" he asked. A few of the other detectives who were at their desks turned around and looked her way.

Caprice smiled. "Harris is going to spend the rest of his sorry life in jail."

"Yes!" Thom said. "We finally got that bastard."

"Excuse me? We?" she joked.

"There you go. You know you couldn't have done this without me."

"Congrats, Johnson," one of the other detectives chimed in. "Although, if Donovan had screwed with my life the way he did yours, he'd be dead."

"I thought about it, but I'd rather see him suffer in prison. Just another inmate in an orange jumpsuit," she said.

"I don't know," Thom said as he offered Caprice a doughnut.

"IAD would have cleared that shooting in a minute." Caprice snorted.

"Not IAD at the Charlotte-Mecklenburg Police Department as long as Major Chaney is leading it." Thom laughed and took the pastry Caprice turned down. "I thought you guys were best friends."

"Yeah, right. Look, I got work to do," Caprice said.

"So when's the wedding?" Thom asked in a near whisper.

"What?"

"You and Nathan have gotten real close these last few months."

"Nobody's getting married," she said with a nervous laugh.

"Whatever you say, but I'm a detective too, and I detect love between the two of you."

Caprice rolled her eyes. She didn't want to admit it, but she wouldn't mind being Mrs. Nathan Wallace. Caprice, however, hadn't thought about marriage since her relationship with Damien. *No,* she told herself, *this will just become complicated. Nathan and I are fine just the way we are.*

"Earth to Caprice," Thom said. "Can you hand me the Reilly file?"

"Oh sure. Sorry," she said as she handed him a manila folder.

Caprice stood up and walked over to the copier to clear her head. She loved Nathan, but Caprice still had her fears about being in a serious relationship. She kept waiting for the other shoe to drop. *If we just take this one*

*day at a time, everything will be fine. There is no need for us
to change things,,* she thought as she returned to her desk.

Nathan walked past the entrance of the jewelry store
twice before finally walking in. His heart was beating a
thousand times faster than normal. *This could be a
mistake,* he thought. *How do I know Caprice is as madly in
love with me as I am with her? She might throw this ring in
my face and tell me to go to hell. But after all we've been
through, she wouldn't do that. But she could always say "no."*
Nathan frowned as he looked at the assortment of rings.

"Can I help you sir?" the clerk behind the counter
asked.

"Yeah," Nathan said. "I think I'm going to ask the
woman of my dreams to marry me."

"Well, I have the right ring for you," the clerk said
with a smile on his face. He unlocked the glass case and
pulled out a tray of engagement rings. "What is she, a
princess cut, solitaire, or marquis?"

Nathan looked at the rings and he had no clue.
"Which is which?" he asked.

The clerk smiled and began to show him the difference in the stones. "The solitaire is classic and classy. But
a lot of women like the way the light shines on a marquis-
cut stone."

Nathan picked up a brilliant cut three-stone engagement ring. It was set in white gold. He held the ring up to
the light and marveled at its shine. "This is the one," he

said in a near whisper. Nathan looked into the diamond and it looked like a white starburst on the inside. It reminded him of Caprice's attitude, hot and cool.

"That is a beautiful ring," the clerk said. "It's 1.5 carats. She's going to love it."

"I hope she does."

"What size does she wear?"

"I'm not sure. You know, I haven't really thought this out all the way. Maybe I should talk to her before I buy the ring."

"Why not buy the ring and let it talk for you? It can always be sized later."

Nathan looked at the ring again. The diamonds on the side of the main stone twinkled like bright stars in the night sky. He had to get that ring for her, and he had to make her his wife. Nathan pulled out his wallet and handed the clerk his credit card. He held his breath as the clerk ran the card through the machine. He was making a big investment in love. Nathan silently hoped he was doing the right thing as the clerk handed him the receipt to sign.

"Good luck to you, Mr. Wallace."

Nathan nodded then walked out the door. He tucked the ring box in his pocket and headed for his car. Now for the hard part, he thought as he pulled out his cell phone and dialed Caprice's desk number.

"Detective Johnson."

"Hello, sweetheart," he said.

"Nathan," she said dropping her voice to a whisper.

"I guess there are people around you."

"You-know-who is staring in my face as I speak."

"Tell Thom I said what's up."

Caprice laughed. "I'll do that."

"Do you have dinner plans tonight?"

"No. Why?"

"Because we have something to celebrate tonight."

"You know, I was thinking of ordering a pizza and watching an old movie."

"Is that what you call a celebration?"

"You're welcome to join me," Caprice said. "As a matter of fact, I insist that you do."

"That sounds good," he said.

"I have to take off. Thom and I have to go serve a warrant."

"Then I'll see you at seven."

"Ciao," she replied.

Later that night, Nathan and Caprice curled up under an afghan and watched *The Color Purple*. They'd just finished chomping down on pepperoni pizza and barbecue chicken wings. Nathan dozed off as the movie played, but Caprice followed every scene, even reciting some of the lines with the actors.

"Nathan, you're snoring."

"Huh, oh," he said as he wiped his mouth. "Sorry about that."

Caprice turned the DVD player off. "So what do you want to watch? *SportsCenter*?"

"I'd rather watch you taking your clothes off and walking into the bedroom in front of me."

"You are so nasty," she said slapping him on the shoulder.

"You asked; I answered. I mean, how many times have you seen *The Color Purple*?"

"Anyway," she said throwing her hand up in his face. "This is my favorite movie. This is how I unwind."

"There's a better way, darling."

Caprice eased onto Nathan's lap. "And just what would that be?" she asked. Nathan grabbed her hands before she could slip them around his waist. Caprice leaned back and looked at him quizzically. "What's that all about?"

"I pulled a muscle at the gym today."

"Seems like you have something to hide." She narrowed her eyes at him.

"Now what would I hide from you?"

"I don't know. You tell me."

Nathan sighed. "Okay, I am hiding something. I was waiting for a more romantic time to do this, but..." Nathan reached into his hip pocket and pulled out the small black velvet box. Caprice froze; her breathing practically stopped.

"Caprice, I love you with all my heart. You mean the world to me. We've been through a lot these past few months. So I want to know if you will be my wife?"

"I...I don't know what to say," she replied as she slid off his lap and sank in the sofa beside him.

"Just say 'yes,'" Nathan said. He opened the box, showing Caprice the ring. She looked at the diamond as tears welled up in her eyes. Caprice saw the joy flickering in his eyes. She closed the box and stood up.

"Nathan, I can't do this."

"What?"

"I can't marry you. This isn't something I want to do."

"What do you mean, this isn't what you want?" Nathan asked. "Caprice, I thought we were in love."

"I do love you, but I'm not trying to marry you. Not now." Nathan felt like he had swallowed a piece of lead. He mistook the look on her face for happiness. "So, what does this mean for us?"

"Why do things have to change?" she asked.

"Because I love you, and I want to take our relationship to another level. Why don't you want to marry me?"

"I just don't want to get married," she said, turning her back to him. "I thought we were happy the way we are."

"Forget it. I think I'm going to go home and let you finish watching your movie." Nathan bounded to the door. Caprice followed behind him, but he slammed the door in her face. She ran her hand across the door and broke down sobbing.

CHAPTER THIRTY-TWO

Nathan threw himself into his work after Caprice turned down his proposal. He tried to take his mind off her rejection, but at the most unexpected moment, that night would pop back into his head. He was tempted to pick up the phone and call an old girlfriend over, but what would that accomplish? Added drama.

"Inspector Wallace," Chaney said, breaking into his thoughts. "I need to see you in my office."

"What is it?" Nathan asked when he walked in.

"What's going on with you lately? You've been snapping at people, and I'm getting complaints about you."

"I'm doing my job, and people don't like it. They'll get over it."

"No, you need to get over whatever's bugging you. You aren't above being investigated yourself. I know you've had some trying times, but don't take it out on those around you. Do you need some personal time?"

"No, I don't. I have a stack of cases on my desk that I need to go through," Nathan sighed.

"Then you need to do them as a professional. Have you talked to anyone since your brother's death?"

"No."

"I want you to go see Dr. Edenson."

"I don't think so."

"That wasn't a request," Chaney said. "You need to handle whatever is going on in your life."

Nathan rolled his eyes and walked out of the office. He sat at his desk and rubbed his hand across his face, urging himself to get it together. Nathan vowed not to let Caprice affect him, but she was all he could think about.

Caprice stared at the phone. She wanted to call Nathan, but what would she say to him? How could she explain that she still loved him and wanted to be with him? She called him three times after that night, but he wouldn't take her calls. She wanted to go to his office, but what would happen if she did? Would he kick her out? She knew she couldn't bear it if he did.

"Johnson," Leland called out.

"Yes, Captain?"

"You want to add a few more pages to this report so I can understand what the hell happened?" He slammed the barely completed report on her desk.

Caprice looked up at Leland. She wanted to say something, but the scowl on his face kept her silent. She looked down at the report. *Damn*, she thought. "Ah, Captain, I filed the wrong paperwork." She picked up the completed report and handed it to Leland.

"Johnson, what's wrong with you? Is this post-traumatic stress from that Harris catastrophe?"

She shook her head. "I've been a little distracted lately."

"Obviously. Get it together, Johnson."

"Yes, sir," she said. Caprice dropped her head on the desk when Leland left. *Damn,* she thought. *I have to fix this now.* Caprice stood up and started toward Nathan's office. She knocked on his door then walked in. "We need to talk," she said.

"I have nothing to say to you," he said.

"Nathan, I never said I didn't love you."

"No, you said you didn't want to marry me. It sounds the same to me."

Caprice closed her eyes then shut his door. "Look, the last time I was engaged, it didn't work out."

"That was then. That was Damien. If I haven't showed you anything else, I showed you that I am nothing like him. I'm not going to keep paying for someone else's crime. I've been nothing but good to you, Caprice. I have never loved a woman as much as I love you. And I've never felt this kind of pain because of a woman either."

"And I love you. I'm just not ready to be married. I'm afraid."

"Afraid of what?" Nathan boomed. "Are you afraid to be happy? I'm tired of playing savior, Caprice. When you decide you're ready to love me all the way, then you come back, and I may be here."

She dashed out of his office, fighting back the tears. Nathan's words stung her like a swarm of African killer bees. There was truth to what he said. Caprice was standing in the way of her own happiness.

Days turned into weeks as Caprice and Nathan continued avoiding each other like the plague. If she saw him walking down the hall, she would turn and go the other way. He'd do the same if he saw her first. Thom noticed it one day when he and Caprice returned to the station from a stakeout.

"What's that all about?" he asked.

"What are you babbling about?"

"Nathan saw us and ran from us like we were a pair of rabid dogs."

She shrugged her shoulders. "We have a report to write. I don't have time to worry about Inspector Wallace."

"Inspector Wallace? That's certainly formal."

"Thom, we have a report to file. Focus on that, and stay out of my business."

"Fine," he said as he walked away from her. Caprice shook her head. Every time she saw Nathan run away from her, it broke her heart. *I have to get out of here,* she thought. *I'm going back to Chicago.*

Caprice got to her desk and picked up the phone to call Serena.

"This is Serena."

"Hey, girl."

"Caprice, what's going on?"

"Nothing much. Listen, I'm thinking of coming to Chi-town."

"You and Nathan?"

"No, just me. I have some vacation time I need to use before I lose it."

"Uh, you and Nathan are still together, aren't you?"

"Nathan and I are going in different directions right now," she said, trying to avoid having to explain things to her friend.

"What do you mean?"

"I don't want to talk about it, okay? Do you think I can crash with you next week?"

"Of course. *Mi casa es su casa*," Serena said. "But I want to know what's going on."

"We'll talk when I get there. I'll call you later with my flight plans."

"I'm worried about you, Capri."

"Don't be. I'm fine."

"Okay, I have another call coming in. I'll see you soon." Caprice hung up the phone and looked down at her computer screen.

Leaving felt like the right thing to do because staying and watching Nathan turn away from her was torture. After Caprice and Thom finished their report, she called U.S. Airways to book a flight to Chicago. She was going to leave in two weeks.

"Will this be roundtrip or one-way?" the ticket agent asked.

"One-way," Caprice said.

"Moving to the Windy City, huh?"

"Yeah," she replied.

"I hear the winters are brutal there."

"The fall is kinda brutal here," Caprice said in a near whisper.

"What was that?"

"Nothing," she said. Caprice confirmed her ticket and hung up the phone. She wondered if her old position in Chicago was still open. When she left, her captain said she could have her job back if she wanted it. Now seemed like the best time to return. She would probably even get a promotion.

"Taking a trip?" Thom asked.

"You are so damn nosey," she said.

"You need a vacation. So I'm glad you're going away. When you come back, I hope you're calmer."

Caprice rolled her eyes and sucked her teeth. "Who says I'm coming back?"

"What?"

"You know, this place has been nothing but trouble for me. I get set up for murder, a drug dealer tries to kill me, and…" She stopped herself. "I'm just really missing Chicago, and I'm going back."

"You can't do that. What about you and Nathan?"

"I'm going to get some coffee. You want something?"

Thom shook his head. When she walked away, he picked up the phone and called Nathan.

"Inspector Wallace," Nathan growled when he answered the phone.

"Damn, you're in a nasty mood too, I see."

"What's up, Thom?"

"Let's have lunch."

"I don't have time today. I have too much work to do."

"We need to have a serious conversation. Did you know Caprice is going back to Chicago?"

"What?" Nathan exclaimed.

"Yeah, she just told me. I don't know what's going on with the two of you, but I know both of you have been miserable these past few weeks. You guys need to fix whatever is wrong so both of you can have better attitudes."

"If she wants to leave, it's on her. I have to go." Nathan hung up the phone.

Nathan hopped out of his seat and stomped down the hall. He spotted Caprice at the coffee machine. He couldn't let her go, not when she had his heart in her hands.

Nathan watched her for about ten seconds before he cleared his throat to let her know he was standing there. Caprice almost dropped her cup when she saw him.

"Hey, um, I think we need to talk," he said.

"There's nothing left to say. You've made yourself clear," she said, hoping he didn't hear how her voice was shaking.

"I hear you're moving back to Chicago."

"There's no reason for me to stay here."

"Are you sure about that?" he asked. "I mean, you're building a heck of a career here."

Caprice rolled her eyes. "Is that the only reason I should stay? I can build a career anywhere."

Nathan shook his head. "It's your life. Do what you feel is best."

"Do I have a reason to stay here, Nathan?" she asked.

He shrugged his shoulders. "What am I supposed to say? Do you want me to put my heart back out there so you can step on it again? You know how I feel about you."

"I thought I did." She turned and walked away.

Nathan fought the urge to follow her. He wanted to tell her that he didn't want her to leave and he did love her and it didn't matter that they weren't getting married. But his pride held him back. Nathan sighed and walked back to his office. *If she wants to go, there's nothing I can do about it,* he thought.

CHAPTER THIRTY-THREE

Caprice sat on her sofa replaying her encounter with Nathan in her head. He seemed so cold to her. *He doesn't care if I leave,* she thought. Nathan's attitude cemented her decision to return to Chicago. The only thing she had to do now was stop loving him. But as hard as she fought not to fall for him, it was going to be that much harder to rid herself of the feelings she had now. Even though she didn't want to, Caprice had come to depend on Nathan. His presence in her life made her happy. She slept better in his arms. His sweet words of encouragement brightened her day. Seeing his face made her believe everything would be all right. But something held her back from marrying him. She couldn't put her finger on what it was. Maybe it was the baggage she carried from her relationship with Damien. But Nathan had proven to her over and over again that he was nothing like Damien. His love for her wasn't conditional.

He wouldn't have asked me to marry him if he didn't love me. I guess I ruined everything, she thought as she walked over to her front window and stared into the night sky. If her life were a movie, there would have been an answer in the stars, Caprice mused.

She thought about all the good times she and Nathan had together. There were so many. Even when they dealt with Donovan, things weren't that bad. *I'm not going to do this to myself,* she thought as she walked away from the window and back to the sofa. She wanted to call Nathan and tell him she still loved him and that she didn't want things to end between them. *Hell, he could call me,* she thought defiantly. *Obviously he isn't sitting at home pining away about me.*

Across town, Nathan sat at the bar in the Marriott sipping on his third beer. He didn't want to go home to an empty house filled with memories of Caprice. He could smell her in his sheets. Since they broke up, Nathan would wake up in the middle of the night, half expecting her to be there. Now she wants to go back to Chicago. *I guess I didn't mean a damn thing to her,* Nathan thought bitterly as he sipped his beer. He reached in his pocket and pulled out his cell phone. He dialed Caprice's number.

"Hello?"

He said nothing. His thoughts wouldn't turn into words.

"Hello?" she said again.

Nathan hung up the phone. *Now I'm acting like a stalker,* he thought as he waved for the bartender. "Another beer," he said.

"Are you sure?" the bartender asked. She leaned in and looked at Nathan. "You seem like you've had enough."

"Isn't it your job to serve drinks?"

"It's also my job not to send a person out there soaked."

Nathan stood up, a little wobbly on his feet. "I guess you're right."

"Do you need me to call a cab?" she asked.

"I'll walk." As Nathan headed out the door, Thom spotted him.

"Hey, Nathan," he called out. Nathan turned around and nodded at Thom, who walked over to him. "Man, you look bad. Do you need a ride home?"

"Nah. I need the fresh air."

"No, I'm driving you home. You might walk in front of a bus or something. How much did you have to drink?"

Nathan shrugged his shoulders.

"Should I call Caprice?"

"Hell no," Nathan exclaimed. "I don't need her pity."

Thom threw his hands up. "I just don't get it. I thought there were going to be wedding bells for you guys."

"So did I. I even proposed. She turned me down like a bed sheet. Can you believe that? She said she loved me, but when I asked her to marry me, she turned tail and ran. If she wants to go back to Chicago, good riddance."

"I don't believe that," Thom said. "You guys can work this out."

Nathan shook his head. "Caprice doesn't love me. If she did, she would've married me."

"You are seriously stupid."

"What?"

"Have you ever thought that the woman just isn't ready to be married? Marriage is a big step, and sometimes it takes more than love to make it work. That said, just because she said 'no' right now doesn't mean she doesn't love you. I see Caprice every day, and she's miserable. But, hey, if you want to throw that away, go ahead. Come on, let me take you home."

Nathan and Thom walked to his car in silence. Nathan didn't say anything while Thom drove. He thought about what he said in the bar. If Caprice wasn't ready to be married, who was he to force her? He was behaving just as Lisa did when she faked her pregnancy. As Thom pulled into Nathan's driveway, Nathan was determined not to let Caprice walk out of his life. Wife or not, he needed her.

"Hey, thanks for driving me home."

"No problem," Thom said.

"I need a favor, though."

"What's that?"

"Find out when Caprice is planning to leave for Chicago. I have to stop her."

Thom nodded. "I got your back. Glad you came to your senses."

"Thanks," Nathan said as he got out of the car.

Caprice woke up feeling stiff and tired. She spent most of the night tossing and turning. Her decision to move back to Chicago was weighing heavily on her mind. Was she running away again? Caprice stretched in the bed and yawned. She was glad she didn't have to work, but she couldn't sleep either. She decided to go to the gym to clear her head. She hopped out of bed and grabbed her gym clothes. She'd shower after her workout, she determined as she brushed her teeth.

When Caprice arrived at the gym, Nathan was there working out with some hand weights. Her breath caught in her chest when she saw him. Nathan's muscles rippled and glistened with sweat. She wanted to run into his arms, but she stopped herself. *I'm just here to work out. It's a public place, I can't help it that he's here,* she thought. *I only have a few more days before I leave.*

Caprice had talked to a realtor about putting her house on the market, but she hadn't yet finalized the plans. Doing so would make it too real that she was leaving, and despite all the machismo she tried to put in her thoughts of leaving, she didn't want to go back to Chicago.

She walked over to the treadmill and refused to look at Nathan. He dropped his weights and started in her direction. Caprice took a deep breath and kept her eyes straight ahead.

"Good morning," he said.

"Morning," she replied.

"It's been a while since we talked."

"I know."

"Can you look at me, please?" he asked.

Caprice turned to him, but continued jogging. "What?"

"You asked me if you had a reason not to go back to Chicago."

She slowed her pace to a brisk walk. "Yeah."

"I don't want you to go."

"It's not about what you want. I tried that, Nathan. And the moment you didn't get your way, you ended everything. You made me feel like a fool. You know I love you."

"How do I know that? Not many people show their love by turning down a marriage proposal."

Caprice quickened her pace on the treadmill. "This is pointless, okay? If you loved me as much as you say you do, then it shouldn't matter if we're married or not."

"It matters because I want to show you every day for the rest of my life that you are the most important thing in the world to me."

Caprice turned her head as water sprang to her eyes. She wanted to love Nathan. She wanted to be with him, but there was something stopping her. "Nathan, I'm scared. If you put an engagement ring on my finger, things are seriously going to change."

Nathan hit the stop button on the machine, bringing Caprice to a screeching halt. "Yes, for the better."

She stepped down. "I'm getting on a plane to Chicago in two days. I don't need this. You said you can't be with me if I don't marry you, and I haven't changed my mind."

Nathan shook his head. "I was wrong. I don't understand why you're afraid to be my wife, but I was wrong, Caprice. I don't want to lose you. The department doesn't want to lose you."

"What did you say?" she asked.

"I said I don't want to lose you."

"No, you said the department doesn't want to lose me. Is this some PR bullshit? Are your words supposed to keep me at CMPD? This isn't even about us, is it? The bosses are pressuring you to get me to stay, huh? I can't believe you."

"No, that's not what I'm doing—"

Caprice pushed past Nathan. "Goodbye," she said then stormed out of the gym.

Caprice seethed with anger as she started her car. *He has to hide behind the department to ask me to stay here! Who does Nathan think he is?* Caprice peeled out of the parking lot and sped down the street. She came to a four-way stop and sighed. *Why are we doing this to each other? If the love is real then we should just be together,* she thought. *Maybe it isn't as real as I thought it was.* She shot across the intersection and headed home.

When Caprice walked into the house, she headed straight for the bedroom and started packing. If she had been wavering in her decision to return to Chicago, her conversation with Nathan solidified her resolve. Caprice pulled a small suitcase from the top of the closet and began piling clothes into it. At first, she folded her slacks and shirts, then she started throwing them in haphazardly. She looked down at the mess she had made and took a deep breath. She knelt down and began folding the garments until she could easily zip her suitcase. She walked into the bathroom and began packing her toiletries. She dropped her perfumes, lotions, and face creams in an overnight bag. She took the bag and set it on top of the suitcase in her bedroom. She sat on the bed and looked around her bedroom.

She had grown so accustomed to her house. It felt like home, and now she was abandoning it. Abandoning all of the memories she'd made in North Carolina. She wasn't going to miss dealing with psychos like Donovan and his crew. But she knew she was going to miss Nathan like crazy. The last few weeks without him had been hell. She couldn't take seeing him every day and suffering the distance that had formed between them. Even catching a glimpse of him in the hallway was too much for her to bear. Just talking to him at the gym made her realize how much she loved him and how much she didn't want lose him. But she couldn't be what he wanted—his wife. She couldn't marry him, because the last time she was engaged, her hopes bottomed out with Damien's infidelity. She didn't want Nathan to break her heart, so she had to break his first.

Caprice picked up the phone and called Century 21.

After the confrontation Nathan and Caprice had in the gym, he redoubled his efforts to avoid her at all costs. The days ticked away steadily, and he knew she'd be leaving soon. *I can't let this happen,* he thought. He jumped up off the sofa and grabbed his keys and jacket. He drove by Caprice's house, but her car wasn't in the driveway. Nathan pulled in when he spotted the brown and gold "for sale" sign in the front yard. He hopped out of the car and grabbed the sign. Holding it in his hand made it real; Caprice was leaving. Was he too late?

Nathan pulled out his cell phone and called the realtor listed on the sign.

"Deana Parker's office," the receptionist said.

"I'm calling about a house I saw on the market. It's on Harris Boulevard."

"Let me get the address."

Nathan rattled off Caprice's address.

"That house just went on the market."

"It shouldn't have," Nathan muttered.

"Excuse me?"

"Nothing. I just want this house. I have to make sure no one else buys it."

"All right, sir," she said. "But, if someone wants to make an offer…"

"I'm willing to put down as much as I need to take this house off the market. I have ten thousand dollars right now." Nathan knew this would drain his savings, but if it meant bringing Caprice back, he didn't care.

"Well, that is a lot of money for this house. I just need to get a number so Deana can call you back."

Nathan gave the woman his cell and home numbers. "Please tell me this house won't be sold."

"I can't guarantee that, but with a down payment like that one, I'm sure Deana will hold it for you."

He turned his eyes upward, saying a silent prayer. His next thought was finding Caprice. *I wonder what time her flight leaves. Maybe there's something on her desk at work,* he thought as he returned to his car and headed for the station.

Nathan walked into the police department and headed straight for Caprice's desk. He went through the papers in search of anything with her flight information on it. He found a scrap of paper with what looked like a flight number and departure date scribbled on it. Nathan tucked the paper in his pocket. He had to make sure he was at that gate when Caprice got ready to leave. Because if there was any way to stop her, that's what he intended to do.

"Nate, what's going on?" Thom asked when he spotted his friend walking out of the vice unit's squad room.

"Not much, just gotta catch a plane to Chicago."

"You're going after her. I knew you would. Good luck, man," Thom said as he patted Nathan on the shoulder.

Nathan ran to his car and headed to a florist shop near the station. He bought two dozen red roses. After paying for the flowers, Nathan sped to the airport, ignoring all posted speed limits. He had about an hour to get to Caprice before her plane took off. If he were lucky, it would be late.

Caprice stood in line to pass through the enhanced security checkpoints at the airport. It was just her luck that she was the random person selected for the hand search. She rolled her eyes as the security officer peered inside the pockets of her carry-on bag.

"I'm sorry, but you can't take this on the plane, Miss," he said holding up a nail file.

"But it's not a weapon," she said incredulously.

"You still can't take it on the plane," he said as he dropped it in a pile of contraband. He opened her make-up kit then closed it. "Please take off your shoes," he instructed.

Caprice unzipped her boots and handed them to the officer. He inspected the inside of the boots then handed them back to Caprice. "I need to look in your handbag," he said.

Caprice gave him her purse. He opened it and saw her Charlotte-Mecklenburg Police badge. "Why didn't you tell me you were a police officer?"

She shrugged. "Because I have a plane to catch, okay?" She glanced down at her watch. She had thirty minutes before the plane was set to take off.

He motioned for Caprice to walk through the metal detector. She was thrilled that it didn't beep. Now she only had to walk quickly to make it to the boarding gate instead of impersonating O.J. Simpson in his Hertz commercial and making a mad dash.

"Caprice," she heard Nathan call out. She turned around and looked at him.

"What are you doing here?"

"Don't go. Please don't leave me. I don't care if we don't get married. Caprice, I love you so much. I can't live without you, and if you get on that plane, I'm coming after you on the next one."

"Nathan, don't do this. It's too late," she said as she turned and walked to the boarding gate. Nathan stood in the middle of the floor and dropped his head as he watched her walk away.

He ran over to the ticket counter. "When is the next flight to Chicago?" he asked the agent.

"That was the last one for today," the agent replied.

Nathan ran his hand over his head. "So what time is the first flight tomorrow?"

"The first one is at 6:50 a.m."

"I need a reservation now!"

"Sir, can you calm down? You need to call our reservation line," she said. "We don't do sales at the counter anymore."

Nathan exhaled loudly. "Look, I'm an officer with the Charlotte-Mecklenburg Police Department. I need a ticket—now!"

"I'm sorry, sir, but our policy clearly states that—"

"Fine." He stomped away. When he got to his car, he pulled out his cell phone and called the U.S. Airways reservation line. He booked a roundtrip ticket to Chicago. His next step was finding Caprice in Chi-Town.

When Caprice's flight landed at O'Hare, she didn't know if she should have felt relieved or sad. Seeing Nathan at the airport confused and upset her all at once. She thought he had stopped caring about her, but there he was begging her to stay. *Maybe I should have stayed,* she thought. *No, because it would only be a matter of time before he started with the talk about marriage again, and I just don't want to get back on that merry-go-round.*

Caprice stood at the baggage claim and grabbed her luggage. She told Serena not to meet her at the airport. She wanted some time to be alone before she was hit with a barrage of questions from her best friend.

She headed to the taxi stand and waved for a cab. When one stopped she got in the back seat.

"Where to?" the driver asked.

"North Wells Street."

"Going to Malnati's, huh?" he asked.

"I guess that's a good place to start," she said.

"First time in Chicago?"

"Can you just drive and cut the questions?"

"Sorry." He pressed down on the gas and sped away from the curb.

The nearly twenty-mile trip was going to cost Caprice a fortune, but she didn't care. Maybe a slice of deep-dish pizza would prepare her for what was waiting on Lawndale Avenue.

Caprice walked into Lou Malnati's, and it was crowded with tourists who read about the famed restaurant on the Internet. She remembered when the place was a haven for locals.

Change is so overrated, she thought. If things are going well, people should leave well enough alone. Caprice walked up to the counter and ordered a large sausage and beef deep-dish pizza. Maybe Serena's favorite meal would distract her from asking questions about Nathan. "Would you like a drink while you wait for your order?" the clerk asked.

"A diet cola," Caprice said.

"Do my eyes deceive me?" a man standing near the register boomed. "Officer Johnson!" Caprice looked at the man—it was Carlos DeGault, the manager of the restaurant.

Carlos DeGault used to run a hotdog stand in Garfield Park. The first time he saw Caprice walking the beat, he stopped her and asked where she bought her badge from. Caprice was ready to write him off as a sexist old curmudgeon, but his jovial laugh and sparkling personality made her give him a chance. They developed a friendship, and that was solidified when Caprice saved his life.

One day, a robber attacked Carlos with a lock-blade knife. Caprice ran over to the stand and dropped the masked robber to his knees. After that day, Carlos began calling Caprice *his* officer. Even when he took over at the pizza restaurant, he could call on Caprice when he had problems.

"Hi, Mr. DeGault," she said as she gave the older man a tight hug.

"I missed you. I knew you would be back."

"Well, where else could I get great pizza?"

"Nowhere, just imitation slices of the original. Welcome back to Chicago. Is this a visit or are you staying?"

Caprice shrugged her shoulders. *I don't know what I'm doing here,* she thought sadly.

"What's wrong?" Carlos asked.

"Nothing, I'm just tired," she lied. "It was a long flight."

"Come over here and sit down," he said, leading her to an empty table in the corner. "Tell me, where have you been?"

"I moved to Charlotte."

"Wow, the Carolinas, huh? You like it?"

"I did for a while, but I'm thinking of coming home. I like snow in my winters," she said with a tense smile.

"If you say so," he replied, noting the look on Caprice's face.

"Come on, you know Chicago is a helluva town. That's what the song says, right?"

"Well, I hope you find whatever you came back for."

I think I left it in Charlotte, she thought sadly.

"Number 1342," the clerk called out. Caprice headed for the counter.

"It was nice seeing you again," she said to Carlos.

He waved goodbye to her as she walked out of the restaurant. Caprice stood on the sidewalk and hailed a cab. She took a deep breath. It was time for her to face the music.

"Well it's about time you got here," Serena said when Caprice got out of the cab.

"And I came with food, so don't start," Caprice said as she handed the steaming pizza box to Serena.

"This smells great. I hope you don't think this pitiful pizza is going to stop me from finding out why you're really in Chicago without Nathan."

"Let's eat the freaking pizza before it gets cold."

Serena frowned then walked inside. She set the box on the kitchen table then turned to Caprice. "First let me say, I'm happy to see you. But what in the hell are you doing here, and what is the real deal with you and Nathan?"

"He asked me to marry him."

Serena looked at her friend with wide-eyed wonderment. "Let me see the ring."

"I turned him down."

"Are you out of your mind?" Serena shrieked. "Are you allergic to happiness? Nathan loves you, and you love him. What is the problem?"

Caprice sat at the table. "Serena, I really don't need this right now. I came here to put my life back together, without Nathan, without Damien's ghost, and without nosey friends second-guessing my choice. So let's eat and talk about something else. The Bears are horrible this year. Are they ever going back to the Super Bowl in our lifetime?"

Serena rolled her eyes at her friend. "I could give a damn about the Bears. I'm not going to stress you, because you did bring me my favorite pizza, but I'm not going to let this go."

Caprice smirked. "I didn't think you would." She grabbed a slice of pizza and bit into it.

Later that night, Caprice went to bed early, faking a headache to avoid any more of Serena's questions about Nathan. While Caprice slept, Serena grabbed her friend's cell phone. She flipped though the electronic directory until she found Nathan's number. She pressed the talk button when she found his number.

"Caprice?" he asked hopefully.

"No, it's Serena. I'm calling from her phone."

"What's going on? Is Caprice all right?"

"You tell me what's going on. Why did you let her leave?"

"I didn't. I tried my damnedest to stop her from getting on that plane today."

"Well, you should have been on the next one," she said trying to keep her voice low so she wouldn't wake Caprice. "Nathan, I know how much you love Caprice. That was evident when I saw you two together. You belong with each other."

"I know this. I'm flying to Chicago in the morning. There were no other flights today."

"Good, but we have to do this right," she said. "I want you to call me when you get to O'Hare. My number is 312-555-4481. Then we'll go from there."

"Serena, thank you for your help."

"I just hope Caprice doesn't kill me for doing this." She quickly hung up the phone and peered around the corner to see if Caprice had gotten up.

CHAPTER THIRTY-FOUR

The ringing of the telephone woke Caprice from her slumber. She rolled over and reached for the phone, and then she remembered she wasn't at home. She was in Serena's guest room. She looked at the alarm clock on the dresser; it was 10 a.m. *I guess I should get up,* she thought as she slowly kicked back the covers. Even though Caprice had about eight hours of sleep, she wasn't rested. Her night was racked by thoughts of Nathan. Memories of their relationship flooded her mind. The times they made love, the tender kisses they shared, and his face when she turned down his proposal. That image haunted her most. Caprice sighed as she walked into the bathroom.

"Caprice? Are you up?" Serena called out.

"Yeah."

"Wanna have lunch at Parrinello?"

"Not particularly," she replied. "I need to go to the police department and see about getting my job back."

"That can wait. I need to do some shopping, and since you're here, we can go together."

"Didn't you dress yourself while I was in Charlotte?" Caprice sighed as she looked in the mirror. *Well, I can't stay here sulking all day,* she thought. "Fine, I'll go."

"Can you show a little enthusiasm today?" Serena ribbed.

Caprice ignored her and stepped into the shower.

After both women were dressed, they headed downtown to the Atrium Mall. "Why are we going all the way downtown, then turning around to go back to Parrinello?" Caprice asked.

"Because I need to get something from the mall. By the time I'm finished, it will be time for lunch," she replied.

"Why don't we just eat downtown?"

"Because its too pricey and too crowded down here. Come on, quit acting like you have something better to do."

Caprice rolled her eyes. "You're right," she said. "Is this shopping trip related to your early-morning phone call?"

"There you go using your supercop senses to get all up in my business. In a way, it is. And you could use a new dress, and maybe while we're in the mall, you can pick up a new attitude."

"And what store are we going to?"

"Uh, the Dress Barn. I saw a blazer in there I want."

"The Dress Barn?"

"Yes."

"Uh-huh." Caprice eyed her friend suspiciously.

When the women got to the mall, Serena took her time looking through the polyester blend jackets in the store. She glanced at her watch. Nathan should be at Parrinello at 12:30. It was 11:45. Depending on traffic, if she and Caprice left at noon, they would make it to the restaurant on time.

"Serena, you can't seriously want one of these jackets," Caprice said. "This isn't your style. What's really going on?"

"You're too suspicious for your own good; you know that? But you're right. These jackets aren't me. The one I wanted is gone. Let's head to the restaurant."

Caprice nodded. "Fine."

At 12:35, Nathan walked into Parrinello with a dozen long-stemmed red roses under his arm. He didn't see Caprice or Serena. He had hoped they would have been there before he arrived.

"Sir, may I help you?" the hostess asked.

"I'm looking for someone," he said. "I'll just wait at the bar."

She nodded and pointed him in the direction of the bar. Nathan sat on the leather stool, sat the flowers on the bar, and watched the door. When he saw Serena and Caprice walk in, his heart dropped. Caprice didn't look happy. She had a forlorn frown on her face. Her eyes looked blank and hopeless. Nathan didn't know if he was the cause of her pain or not, but he hoped that today he could make things better. He hoped they could repair what went wrong. He prayed that his presence would prove that he loved her and would always be there for her.

Nathan watched as the hostess led Serena and Caprice to a table near the rear of the restaurant. It's now or never, he thought as he stood up. Slowly and deliberately, Nathan walked over to the table. Caprice had her back to him, but Serena faced him. She smiled slightly when she spotted Nathan, but didn't give it away to Caprice that she saw him.

"Excuse me," Nathan said.

Caprice turned around and stared at Nathan. She couldn't believe that he was in Chicago, standing in the restaurant. She'd been set up. A wave of emotions from happiness to anger washed over her. In the end, though, happiness won out. She smiled. Her eyes twinkled with delight.

"Nathan," she said in a near whisper. "What are you doing here?"

He handed her the flowers. "It's never too late when the love is real."

"What?" She furrowed her eyebrows.

"At the airport, you said it was too late, but it isn't. Caprice, I love you, and I'm not giving up on you."

She stood up and looked deep into his eyes. "Oh, Nathan, I don't want to give up on us either. I've been a fool, and I didn't know that until I came here."

Nathan pulled Caprice into his arms. "Come home with me. My life is empty without you."

She nodded and fought back the stinging tears in her eyes. "Nathan, I've never had happiness in my life that lasted. That's why I kept pushing you away, and I can't do that anymore. I thought about our memories all night. When I'm with you I want to melt. And when you touch me it's like fire. I crave you and your touch. I can't live without you, Nathan. But everything has changed. I don't have a home in Charlotte anymore. I put the house on the market."

"And I took it off. Caprice, I can't live without you either," he said. "But when I tell you that I love you, you always run away."

"You did that for me? Oh, Nathan, I'm not going to run anymore. I need to be with you. I want to be with you," she said, nearly pleading with him.

"Take each other back already," Serena said. Nathan and Caprice looked at her and smiled.

"We're getting there," Nathan said.

"I'll be at the bar," Serena said, excusing herself from the table.

Nathan and Caprice sat down. "This may sound corny, but while I was on the plane, I wrote a poem for you," he said.

Caprice blushed. "I didn't know you wrote poetry."

"Not well, so don't laugh," he said as he pulled a piece of paper out of his jacket pocket. Nathan cleared his throat.

What would you say if I told you I love you?
Would you hang up and walk away or do you feel the
   same way?
Thoughts of you dance in my mind
I remember all the times we kissed and how you felt
   in my arms
I remember the taste of your lips
I miss that, I miss your touch even after a day
I don't want you to ever go away
So what would you say if I told you I cared?
Would you reply so do I or would you turn and run,
   letting me know I was never the one
So just what will you say when I tell you I love you
   and want you in my life?

She grabbed his hand. "I say I love you, too, and I want to be in your life forever."

"I know the marriage thing—"

She placed her index finger to his lips. "When I said forever, I meant as your wife, if you'll still have me."

He grabbed her hand and kissed it. "Yes, Caprice."

She wrapped her arms around his neck and kissed him with a yearning passion. Her body melted against his like a burning candle. They parted and looked at each other. "How did you know where to find me?" Caprice asked, even though she had a good idea about the answer.

Nathan smiled at her. "Serena called me last night. I already had the plane ticket. I told you I was going to woo you, and there was nothing you could do about it."

She stroked his cheek. "And that you did, Inspector Wallace; that you did."

2008 Reprint Mass Market Titles

January

Cautious Heart
Cheris F. Hodges
ISBN-13: 978-1-58571-301-1
ISBN-10: 1-58571-301-5
$6.99

Suddenly You
Crystal Hubbard
ISBN-13: 978-1-58571-302-8
ISBN-10: 1-58571-302-3
$6.99

February

Passion
T. T. Henderson
ISBN-13: 978-1-58571-303-5
ISBN-10: 1-58571-303-1
$6.99

Whispers in the Sand
LaFlorya Gauthier
ISBN-13: 978-1-58571-304-2
ISBN-10: 1-58571-304-x
$6.99

March

Life Is Never As It Seems
J. J. Michael
ISBN-13: 978-1-58571-305-9
ISBN-10: 1-58571-305-8
$6.99

Beyond the Rapture
Beverly Clark
ISBN-13: 978-1-58571-306-6
ISBN-10: 1-58571-306-6
$6.99

April

A Heart's Awakening
Veronica Parker
ISBN-13: 978-1-58571-307-3
ISBN-10: 1-58571-307-4
$6.99

Breeze
Robin Lynette Hampton
ISBN-13: 978-1-58571-308-0
ISBN-10: 1-58571-308-2
$6.99

May

I'll Be Your Shelter
Giselle Carmichael
ISBN-13: 978-1-58571-309-7
ISBN-10: 1-58571-309-0
$6.99

Careless Whispers
Rochelle Alers
ISBN-13: 978-1-58571-310-3
ISBN-10: 1-58571-310-4
$6.99

June

Sin
Crystal Rhodes
ISBN-13: 978-1-58571-311-0
ISBN-10: 1-58571-311-2
$6.99

Dark Storm Rising
Chinelu Moore
ISBN-13: 978-1-58571-312-7
ISBN-10: 1-58571-312-0
$6.99

2008 Reprint Mass Market Titles (continued)

July

Object of His Desire
A.C. Arthur
ISBN-13: 978-1-58571-313-4
ISBN-10: 1-58571-313-9
$6.99

Angel's Paradise
Janice Angelique
ISBN-13: 978-1-58571-314-1
ISBN-10: 1-58571-314-7
$6.99

August

Unbreak My Heart
Dar Tomlinson
ISBN-13: 978-1-58571-315-8
ISBN-10: 1-58571-315-5
$6.99

All I Ask
Barbara Keaton
ISBN-13: 978-1-58571-316-5
ISBN-10: 1-58571-316-3
$6.99

September

Icie
Pamela Leigh Starr
ISBN-13: 978-1-58571-275-5
ISBN-10: 1-58571-275-2
$6.99

At Last
Lisa Riley
ISBN-13: 978-1-58571-276-2
ISBN-10: 1-58571-276-0
$6.99

October

Everlastin' Love
Gay G. Gunn
ISBN-13: 978-1-58571-277-9
ISBN-10: 1-58571-277-9
$6.99

Three Wishes
Seressia Glass
ISBN-13: 978-1-58571-278-6
ISBN-10: 1-58571-278-7
$6.99

November

Yesterday Is Gone
Beverly Clark
ISBN-13: 978-1-58571-279-3
ISBN-10: 1-58571-279-5
$6.99

Again My Love
Kayla Perrin
ISBN-13: 978-1-58571-280-9
ISBN-10: 1-58571-280-9
$6.99

December

Office Policy
A.C. Arthur
ISBN-13: 978-1-58571-281-6
ISBN-10: 1-58571-281-7
$6.99

Rendezvous With Fate
Jeanne Sumerix
ISBN-13: 978-1-58571-283-3
ISBN-10: 1-58571-283-3
$6.99

2008 New Mass Market Titles

January

Where I Want To Be
Maryam Diaab
ISBN-13: 978-1-58571-268-7
ISBN-10: 1-58571-268-X
$6.99

Never Say Never
Michele Cameron
ISBN-13: 978-1-58571-269-4
ISBN-10: 1-58571-269-8
$6.99

February

Stolen Memories
Michele Sudler
ISBN-13: 978-1-58571-270-0
ISBN-10: 1-58571-270-1
$6.99

Dawn's Harbor
Kymberly Hunt
ISBN-13: 978-1-58571-271-7
ISBN-10: 1-58571-271-X
$6.99

March

Undying Love
Renee Alexis
ISBN-13: 978-1-58571-272-4
ISBN-10: 1-58571-272-8
$6.99

Blame It On Paradise
Crystal Hubbard
ISBN-13: 978-1-58571-273-1
ISBN-10: 1-58571-273-6
$6.99

April

When A Man Loves A Woman
La Connie Taylor-Jones
ISBN-13: 978-1-58571-274-8
ISBN-10: 1-58571-274-4
$6.99

Choices
Tammy Williams
ISBN-13: 978-1-58571-300-4
ISBN-10: 1-58571-300-7
$6.99

May

Dream Runner
Gail McFarland
ISBN-13: 978-1-58571-317-2
ISBN-10: 1-58571-317-1
$6.99

Southern Fried Standards
S.R. Maddox
ISBN-13: 978-1-58571-318-9
ISBN-10: 1-58571-318-X
$6.99

June

Looking for Lily
Africa Fine
ISBN-13: 978-1-58571-319-6
ISBN-10: 1-58571-319-8
$6.99

Bliss, Inc.
Chamein Canton
ISBN-13: 978-1-58571-325-7
ISBN-10: 1-58571-325-2
$6.99

2008 New Mass Market Titles (continued)

July

Love's Secrets
Yolanda McVey
ISBN-13: 978-1-58571-321-9
ISBN-10: 1-58571-321-X
$6.99

Things Forbidden
Maryam Diaab
ISBN-13: 978-1-58571-327-1
ISBN-10: 1-58571-327-9
$6.99

August

Storm
Pamela Leigh Starr
ISBN-13: 978-1-58571-323-3
ISBN-10: 1-58571-323-6
$6.99

Passion's Furies
AlTonya Washington
ISBN-13: 978-1-58571-324-0
ISBN-10: 1-58571-324-4
$6.99

September

Three Doors Down
Michele Sudler
ISBN-13: 978-1-58571-332-5
ISBN-10: 1-58571-332-5
$6.99

Mr Fix-It
Crystal Hubbard
ISBN-13: 978-1-58571-326-4
ISBN-10: 1-58571-326-0
$6.99

October

Moments of Clarity
Michele Cameron
ISBN-13: 978-1-58571-330-1
ISBN-10: 1-58571-330-9
$6.99

Lady Preacher
K.T. Richey
ISBN-13: 978-1-58571-333-2
ISBN-10: 1-58571-333-3
$6.99

November

This Life Isn't Perfect Holla
Sandra Foy
ISBN: 978-1-58571-331-8
ISBN-10: 1-58571-331-7
$6.99

Promises Made
Bernice Layton
ISBN-13: 978-1-58571-334-9
ISBN-10: 1-58571-334-1
$6.99

December

A Voice Behind Thunder
Carrie Elizabeth Greene
ISBN-13: 978-1-58571-329-5
ISBN-10: 1-58571-329-5
$6.99

The More Things Change
Chamein Canton
ISBN-13: 978-1-58571-328-8
ISBN-10: 1-58571-328-7
$6.99

Other Genesis Press, Inc. Titles

A Dangerous Deception	J.M. Jeffries	$8.95
A Dangerous Love	J.M. Jeffries	$8.95
A Dangerous Obsession	J.M. Jeffries	$8.95
A Drummer's Beat to Mend	Kei Swanson	$9.95
A Happy Life	Charlotte Harris	$9.95
A Heart's Awakening	Veronica Parker	$9.95
A Lark on the Wing	Phyliss Hamilton	$9.95
A Love of Her Own	Cheris F. Hodges	$9.95
A Love to Cherish	Beverly Clark	$8.95
A Risk of Rain	Dar Tomlinson	$8.95
A Taste of Temptation	Reneé Alexis	$9.95
A Twist of Fate	Beverly Clark	$8.95
A Will to Love	Angie Daniels	$9.95
Acquisitions	Kimberley White	$8.95
Across	Carol Payne	$12.95
After the Vows	Leslie Esdaile	$10.95
(Summer Anthology)	T.T. Henderson	
	Jacqueline Thomas	
Again My Love	Kayla Perrin	$10.95
Against the Wind	Gwynne Forster	$8.95
All I Ask	Barbara Keaton	$8.95
Always You	Crystal Hubbard	$6.99
Ambrosia	T.T. Henderson	$8.95
An Unfinished Love Affair	Barbara Keaton	$8.95
And Then Came You	Dorothy Elizabeth Love	$8.95
Angel's Paradise	Janice Angelique	$9.95
At Last	Lisa G. Riley	$8.95
Best of Friends	Natalie Dunbar	$8.95
Beyond the Rapture	Beverly Clark	$9.95

Other Genesis Press, Inc. Titles (continued)

Blaze	Barbara Keaton	$9.95
Blood Lust	J. M. Jeffries	$9.95
Blood Seduction	J.M. Jeffries	$9.95
Bodyguard	Andrea Jackson	$9.95
Boss of Me	Diana Nyad	$8.95
Bound by Love	Beverly Clark	$8.95
Breeze	Robin Hampton Allen	$10.95
Broken	Dar Tomlinson	$24.95
By Design	Barbara Keaton	$8.95
Cajun Heat	Charlene Berry	$8.95
Careless Whispers	Rochelle Alers	$8.95
Cats & Other Tales	Marilyn Wagner	$8.95
Caught in a Trap	Andre Michelle	$8.95
Caught Up In the Rapture	Lisa G. Riley	$9.95
Cautious Heart	Cheris F Hodges	$8.95
Chances	Pamela Leigh Starr	$8.95
Cherish the Flame	Beverly Clark	$8.95
Class Reunion	Irma Jenkins/ John Brown	$12.95
Code Name: Diva	J.M. Jeffries	$9.95
Conquering Dr. Wexler's Heart	Kimberley White	$9.95
Corporate Seduction	A.C. Arthur	$9.95
Crossing Paths, Tempting Memories	Dorothy Elizabeth Love	$9.95
Crush	Crystal Hubbard	$9.95
Cypress Whisperings	Phyllis Hamilton	$8.95
Dark Embrace	Crystal Wilson Harris	$8.95
Dark Storm Rising	Chinelu Moore	$10.95

Other Genesis Press, Inc. Titles (continued)

Other Genesis Press, Inc. Titles (continued)

Other Genesis Press, Inc. Titles (continued)

Last Train to Memphis	Elsa Cook	$12.95
Lasting Valor	Ken Olsen	$24.95
Let Us Prey	Hunter Lundy	$25.95
Lies Too Long	Pamela Ridley	$13.95
Life Is Never As It Seems	J.J. Michael	$12.95
Lighter Shade of Brown	Vicki Andrews	$8.95
Love Always	Mildred E. Riley	$10.95
Love Doesn't Come Easy	Charlyne Dickerson	$8.95
Love Unveiled	Gloria Greene	$10.95
Love's Deception	Charlene Berry	$10.95
Love's Destiny	M. Loui Quezada	$8.95
Mae's Promise	Melody Walcott	$8.95
Magnolia Sunset	Giselle Carmichael	$8.95
Many Shades of Gray	Dyanne Davis	$6.99
Matters of Life and Death	Lesego Malepe, Ph.D.	$15.95
Meant to Be	Jeanne Sumerix	$8.95
Midnight Clear (Anthology)	Leslie Esdaile Gwynne Forster Carmen Green Monica Jackson	$10.95
Midnight Magic	Gwynne Forster	$8.95
Midnight Peril	Vicki Andrews	$10.95
Misconceptions	Pamela Leigh Starr	$9.95
Montgomery's Children	Richard Perry	$14.95
My Buffalo Soldier	Barbara B. K. Reeves	$8.95
Naked Soul	Gwynne Forster	$8.95
Next to Last Chance	Louisa Dixon	$24.95
No Apologies	Seressia Glass	$8.95
No Commitment Required	Seressia Glass	$8.95

Other Genesis Press, Inc. Titles (continued)

Other Genesis Press, Inc. Titles (continued)

Revelations	Cheris F. Hodges	$8.95
Rivers of the Soul	Leslie Esdaile	$8.95
Rocky Mountain Romance	Kathleen Suzanne	$8.95
Rooms of the Heart	Donna Hill	$8.95
Rough on Rats and Tough on Cats	Chris Parker	$12.95
Secret Library Vol. 1	Nina Sheridan	$18.95
Secret Library Vol. 2	Cassandra Colt	$8.95
Secret Thunder	Annetta P. Lee	$9.95
Shades of Brown	Denise Becker	$8.95
Shades of Desire	Monica White	$8.95
Shadows in the Moonlight	Jeanne Sumerix	$8.95
Sin	Crystal Rhodes	$8.95
Small Whispers	Annetta P. Lee	$6.99
So Amazing	Sinclair LeBeau	$8.95
Somebody's Someone	Sinclair LeBeau	$8.95
Someone to Love	Alicia Wiggins	$8.95
Song in the Park	Martin Brant	$15.95
Soul Eyes	Wayne L. Wilson	$12.95
Soul to Soul	Donna Hill	$8.95
Southern Comfort	J.M. Jeffries	$8.95
Still the Storm	Sharon Robinson	$8.95
Still Waters Run Deep	Leslie Esdaile	$8.95
Stolen Kisses	Dominiqua Douglas	$9.95
Stories to Excite You	Anna Forrest/Divine	$14.95
Subtle Secrets	Wanda Y. Thomas	$8.95
Suddenly You	Crystal Hubbard	$9.95
Sweet Repercussions	Kimberley White	$9.95
Sweet Sensations	Gwendolyn Bolton	$9.95

Other Genesis Press, Inc. Titles (continued)

Sweet Tomorrows	Kimberly White	$8.95
Taken by You	Dorothy Elizabeth Love	$9.95
Tattooed Tears	T. T. Henderson	$8.95
The Color Line	Lizzette Grayson Carter	$9.95
The Color of Trouble	Dyanne Davis	$8.95
The Disappearance of Allison Jones	Kayla Perrin	$5.95
The Fires Within	Beverly Clark	$9.95
The Foursome	Celya Bowers	$6.99
The Honey Dipper's Legacy	Pannell-Allen	$14.95
The Joker's Love Tune	Sidney Rickman	$15.95
The Little Pretender	Barbara Cartland	$10.95
The Love We Had	Natalie Dunbar	$8.95
The Man Who Could Fly	Bob & Milana Beamon	$18.95
The Missing Link	Charlyne Dickerson	$8.95
The Mission	Pamela Leigh Starr	$6.99
The Perfect Frame	Beverly Clark	$9.95
The Price of Love	Sinclair LeBeau	$8.95
The Smoking Life	Ilene Barth	$29.95
The Words of the Pitcher	Kei Swanson	$8.95
Three Wishes	Seressia Glass	$8.95
Ties That Bind	Kathleen Suzanne	$8.95
Tiger Woods	Libby Hughes	$5.95
Time is of the Essence	Angie Daniels	$9.95
Timeless Devotion	Bella McFarland	$9.95
Tomorrow's Promise	Leslie Esdaile	$8.95
Truly Inseparable	Wanda Y. Thomas	$8.95
Two Sides to Every Story	Dyanne Davis	$9.95
Unbreak My Heart	Dar Tomlinson	$8.95

Other Genesis Press, Inc. Titles (continued)

Order Form

Mail to: Genesis Press, Inc.
P.O. Box 101
Columbus, MS 39703

Name _____
Address _____
City/State _____ Zip _____
Telephone _____

Ship to (if different from above)
Name _____
Address _____
City/State _____ Zip _____
Telephone _____

Credit Card Information
Credit Card # _____ ☐ Visa ☐ Mastercard
Expiration Date (mm/yy) _____ ☐ AmEx ☐ Discover

Qty.	Author	Title	Price	Total

Use this order

form, or call

1-888-INDIGO-1

Total for books	_____
Shipping and handling:	
$5 first two books,	
$1 each additional book	_____
Total S & H	_____
Total amount enclosed	_____

Mississippi residents add 7% sales tax